The Year of the Short Corn
and other stories

The
Year of the Short Corn

AND OTHER STORIES

Fred Urquhart

with an introduction by
Isobel Murray

Kennedy & Boyd

Kennedy & Boyd
an imprint of
Zeticula Ltd
The Roan
Kilkerran
KA19 8LS
Scotland.

http://www.kennedyandboyd.co.uk
admin@kennedyandboyd.co.uk

First published in 1949 in London by Methuen.
Text Copyright © Estate of Fred Urquhart 2013
Introduction Copyright © Isobel Murray 2013

Front cover photograph © Patryk Moriak, 2013
www.fotoprofeo.com

Back cover photograph from Fred Urquhart's own collection
Copyright © Colin Affleck 2013

ISBN-13 978-1-84921-125-3

A number of these stories have appeared in *At Close of Eve* (edited by Jeremy Scott), *Harper's Bazaar* (U.S.A.), *Illustrated, Life and Letters To-day, New Short Stories of 1944 and 1946* (edited by John Singer), *The Scots Magazine, Scottish Art and Letters, Seven, Story* (U.S.A.), *Voices* and *Writing To-day*, and I wish to thank the editors for permission to reprint. *The Pool* and *He Called Me Girlie* have been broadcast, and I make the usual acknowledgements to the B.B.C.

Introduction

In 1949, when *The Year of the Short Corn* was published, novelist and short-story-writer Fred Urquhart, aged 37, was at a personal and professional peak. I do not at all mean that he was successful or making a lot of money: he was admired by perceptive critics, but he never became rich. But he *had* finished the various farm jobs he was assigned as a conscientious objector during the war; he had gone south to London. He found London a congenial place, and met a liberal, Bohemian society that he felt relaxed in. He was picking up a book-related living from reviewing and other jobs, and in 1947 he had met Peter Wyndham Allen, with whom he was to have 'a happy homosexual marriage' until Wyndham Allen's death in 1990. In the late forties he had no trouble placing his short stories in a wealth of little magazines of the time.

Before the war he had worked for years in an Edinburgh bookshop, which he called his university. After the outbreak of war in September 1939, he went to stay with a friend in Cupar, while waiting to register as a conscientious objector. After two tribunals, in July and December 1940, he was refused exemption from military service, and was ordered to undertake agricultural work as a conscientious objector. He worked on a farm near Laurencekirk in the Mearns, where he picked up the dialect and observed the folk with loving detail. After this, though, he did not return to live in Scotland until after his partner died: but he told me when he was eighty that he still thought in Scots.

By this time, he had a wide variety of places and people to write about that he knew well: Edinburgh, parts of London, the Mearns among them, and the Second World War in civilian life as a major topic, and he gradually began to look at conscientious objection as a topic, and homosexuality as story material. Critics praised him most often for his wonderful dialogue, or for his portrayal of women characters, and these will be found abundantly in the following pages; but his subject matter was steadily expanding. George Orwell wrote:

> Fred Urquhart is a short story writer with vastly more life in him than the majority of the tribe. A striking thing about his stories is their great variation in subject matter.

He also went back to his first love, the novel. His first published novel had been pre-war. *Time Will Knit* (1938) was loosely based on his working-class grandparents' lives, and his conscientious objection may have its roots there, in the portrayal of a strongly political and anti-war grandfather. In 1948 he finished the first of the pair of novels already republished in this series, *The Ferret was Abraham's Daughter* (1949). *Jezebel's Dust* (1951) was not finished until 1950. And in 1949 he also published this collection of short stories, *The Year of the Short Corn*, which included a few items written before 1942, and a majority written by 1946. So the war recurs in many of these stories, and the North-East of Scotland farming background he knew from his conscientious objector's war work.

The return of peace, and returning servicemen, are also recurrent, although the angle may be unexpected, as in 'Quiet Sunday', where a woman has returned home from the WAAF. The whole small town is anxious severally to 'drop in' and see her. It is extraordinary how many emotions and implications are hinted at in so short a space. Her mother is glad of the visitors, because the house has been so quiet in her absence. But the girl is back, she says, for a rest, and resents the villagers, whom she sees as intruders. It appears she has become resistant to home and home town. She has mentally moved on. She only wants to write to her fiancé, or to sit quiet in an easy chair, after the helter-skelter of life in barracks. In the end she puts on her outdoor coat to face the rigours of a wartime bedroom, and flees the visitors to write to Harold in peace. A gentle undercurrent in the story is that she has not heard from Harold, a faint worry that distance has cooled his ardour, and that she is now in the wrong place at a crucial time.

The volume thus has a certain unity of background in period and general subject matter, while at the same time exhibiting a great variety of situations and characters. The title story, 'The Year of the Short Corn', almost uniquely spells out a constant dilemma for the Scots writer. Since the heyday of the 'Kailyard' novel from the mid-1890s, the larger Scottish reading public, here and in the diaspora overseas, had developed a taste for nostalgic country tales, set in small towns or farms, 'in touch' with the land and the simplicities of life. It was a literature of misty escape from unpleasant realities, where sacrifice was rewarded, and even death was surrounded with a pious, rosy glow; nothing too violent, or unfair or over-exploitative was allowed to disturb the comforting sense of security it induced.

Grassic Gibbon had fought the Kailyard in the Thirties, with his *Sunset Song*. That country love story contained suicide and murder, fire and attempted incest and unpleasant illness. Readers of the time were famously shocked. Jessie Kesson, with her background of illegitimacy and the Elgin slums, had found the same thing, with the 'editress' of a magazine constantly urging her to 'keep it cosy'. Hard-up, as always, she had begun to produce what was asked for, but she early rethought her path, to the great advantage of her writing. In Urquhart's story, a young countryman has written a true story of farm life, and had some small success in critical approval, but sales are low and earnings negligible. He too is approached by what turns out to be a female editor for contributions.

> I'd like you to consider writing a series for us
> – a series along the lines of *The Year of the Short Corn*, but without – what my managing director calls its coarseness! (58)

What she means becomes clear when she goes on asking for Kailyard. She details her demands. No fine writing: clichés are much better understood by the readership. 'Good' characters: no faults for them, no virtues for bad ones. The central figure she imagines is 'a sympathetic character, somebody who's always helping lame dogs over stiles. A nice cheery girl with a heart of gold.' (59) Like the girl in the novel, almost, but of course, no sex.

But it becomes very clear that Kitty's own standards are very different. She accepts a whisky or two, although she claims to be teetotal. She has 'sea-green, sex-greedy eyes', which she turns repeatedly on Charlie's brother. Hypocritically, she enjoys what she condemns for her readers:

> It's very funny in places. I thought the scene in the lavatory, for instance, was *screamingly* funny. I was reading it in a bus and I laughed so much I'm sure the other passengers thought I was cracked. (61)

Charles' mother and brother join in on Kitty's side, mother liking the sound of what's wanted, both liking the sound of the money involved. Kitty goes on:

> Keep off politics. There must be no trouble between master and man. No religious differences. No trade union disputes. You mustn't even mention any of these things. (63)

Charles is appalled, but neither agrees nor disagrees, even when Kitty goes off, shaking her finger, 'and remember – no lavatory stuff!'

Urquhart was all too aware of such seductions for the aspiring and poverty-stricken writer, but opposed them fiercely in stories like 'The Red Stot', which positively revels in the muck, smells and physical labour of the farm loon's life. This young castrated ox is greedy and violent, choking on food in his haste, fighting others away. He is unpleasantly physical:

> It was standing, head held high, front legs braced among the straw- and dung-littered muck, and its hind legs shoved forward under it. Thick ropes of white saliva were hanging from its mouth. And it heaved its sides and stretched its neck as if it were in a death-throes. . . The loon held his face away from their slobbering, fawn coloured muzzles, slimy with saliva, and their great, walloping tongues. (45-6)

The stot himself almost becomes a metaphor for a literature emasculated, like the stot. His kind were bred to impregnate many cows, but all he can do, in the end, is empty his bowels in an old woman's hallway.

This is a society riven with division, where classes and subdivisions of classes do not communicate. 'Glamour Boy Among the Neeps' illustrates the discomfort of a town electrician trapped by snowdrifts on a working farm, and the desperation of his hosts, who are soon sick of his distant ways:

> He was a big, flabby, young man – what the cattleman scornfully called a 'townser'. He had a sallow, unhealthy-looking skin and blank-looking pale grey eyes, and he always looked half-shaven. (83)

But it is not the lack of glamour that gets his hosts. He has no conversation, will not play cards; 'he just sat and yawned', and despite many suggestions will not help efforts to clear the snow and free his car. The effect on the farmer is powerful:

> 'I'm nae looking forward any more than you are to another night or two of him sitting in the sitting-room so that I canna even let off wind!' (84)

But the land girls take over, and in response to his advances do their successful best to injure his dignity and his car.

A number of the shorter stories are slight, and the aim is clear. In 'Atrocity Story', Edinburgh wifies with blind faith in what they read in the paper discuss the war news. In 'Two Ladies' a shopkeeper attends to two female customers who want new curtains: he suits his service to what he knows of their circumstances, the newness of their money, and willingness to spend – and no comment is necessary. In 'Sailors, Beware of Witches', a colourful assortment of pantomime performers, staying in character, is called up for war work, and the fantastic story will appeal more the more the reader knows of the world of pantomime. But 'You Kill Me' is a deeper tale, though brief. It is told through the experience of a self-absorbed central character with a diagnostic appointment at a medical clinic. He considers himself a genius, and therefore thinks that his health is more important than that of anyone else. He meets an old man with kidney trouble, and a shabby and flippant young man, who insists on singing and chatting; he addresses the nurse, with whom he flirts, 'You kill me, sister!' Ravelston resents the flippancy:

> Didn't he realise that he was in the presence of a genius whose sphere of activity would be cut off before it had a proper chance to flower? (120)

The lump in Ravelston's side turns out to be an easily curable cyst, especially for one who like him can pay for the private ward. The sting, for once, is in the tail:

> When he was dressed, he said: 'That fellow was a bit of a fool, wasn't he? There couldn't be very much wrong with him.'
> The nurse looked up from the sink where she was washing some bandages. Her mouth flickered queerly.
> 'We never discuss patients with other patients,' she said. (124)

The war or its after effects almost always form at least a background to the longer, richer stories. All of these repay careful rereading. 'Hunting Buffalo' was written early in the war, before December 1942 at least. It takes place in Edinburgh during the war, in a boarding-house full of young people. It is a chaotic place that awaits Kathe, a refugee from Vienna, who is to perform domestic work. She finds it bewildering:

> A number of silk stockings hung on a pulley on top of sheets of *The Daily Worker* and *The Scottish Daily Express*. The newspapers were sodden beneath the stockings, and a pool of water lay under them on the dirty linoleum. A red jumper was drying on the back of a chair in front of the grey ash-strewn fireplace. Some newspapers were sticking from beneath the rug at the fireside. Later Kathe discovered that another jumper was laid between these sheets; it was Skipper's favourite method of pressing her clothes. Improvised book-cases were in odd corners, filled with ex-library copies and Penguins. An empty bottle of South African sherry stood on top of the Singer's sewing-machine. Clippings of white silk had been pushed beneath the treadle; some of them were lying in the dog's dish beside the machine. Kathe looked at her neat typist's hands, then she looked at the tableful of dirty dishes and sighed. She would have to begin those horrid 'domestic duties' some time. . . (153)

Kathe's foreignness helps the reader to look carefully at what she sees. It is like a typical student flat – a society formed by strangers thrust into intimacy by chance. The young man Abby, who is studying French, helps Kathe to comprehend somewhat, as the flatmates shout, bicker and tease, while the amorous bulldog plagues the women. Gradually she sees them more as individuals. Esther is a committed movie devotee, tired of Doris's Communist preaching, while Doris, unhappily yearning after the married 'love of her life', makes an assumption about Kathe that puzzles her – that she is a refugee because of Communist Party activities. But Doris is as strange to Kathe as the others are: Kathe is a refugee because she is Jewish. Urquhart hardly needs to explore this, writing in the Forties. Here it is just another way of isolating her from the others. But Kathe's vulnerability is underlined by her immediate response to the entrance of final year medical student Julian, whose stunning good looks affect her at once and henceforth. She becomes habituated to the boarding-house, even surviving the grotesque episode where the bulldog consumes a human brain Julian has brought home to dissect, and she yearns after Julian perpetually. She misses hints many times: Julian is waiting to be called up, and is keen on some refugees. When he is late, Esther says, 'Probably he's seen somebody he just had to follow.' (56) And when Abby has met a male friend Julian's response is quick, and a baffling joke passes Kathe by. She remains in a state of desperate, solitary yearning, but even two rather accidental dates with her provoke no response from Julian, and he disappears the next day.

Only after this does she begin to understand the mysterious phrase 'hunting buffalo'. A dictionary of slang shows that the meaning of the phrase moves quickly in the twentieth century, but it certainly means looking for sex, and probably a man looking for sex with another man. At last we learn that a year ago Julian married a refugee so that she would get British nationality. Poet W H Auden's marriage to Erika Mann in 1935 is only the best known instance of this occasional quixotic practice by British homosexual men.

I would argue that a woman is also the central character in 'The Prisoners', one of the longest stories, which Urquhart spent some time writing. He was engaged on it September-November 1942, and revised or finished it in July 1944. It is another story to which the war is central, and yet it has wider implications than simply being a story about prisoners of war. As in 'Hunting Buffalo', the central female character is a relatively isolated one. Mary, the farmer's wife, who is separated by her status and education from most of the farm servants, and by a much wider distance from the Italian prisoners of war who are sent to work on the farm – and from her patriarchal husband by a conflict of emotions, sometimes including fear. In the course of the story we learn that Mary and Will have been married for two years, and that although she loves him, she is troubled about him in many ways. He is secretive; he doesn't tell her things, much less discuss them:

> He kept her guessing about things; she never knew where she was with him. She could not imagine what he was thinking. He never told her anything. . . she wanted him to confide in her, to ask her opinion about things. But he never did that. He never spoke about his business. (129)

Her thoughts about husband and mother-in-law are often bitter, and she can see how many of Will's faults have been planted and nurtured by his mother:

> Often Mary felt that next to throttling Will she would have liked to throttle his mother. Indeed she would have preferred to throttle his mother. For, after all, his mother had none of Will's endearing points. She was a small, thin woman with an eager face. She was always rushing about after Will – rushing after him as she had rushed

for the last twenty-five years. She was so eager
to please him. She had spoiled him so much, ran
after him and waited on him hand and foot, that
she had quite spoiled him for any other woman.
Even yet when he had a wife who was in her way
as eager to please, to make a footstool of herself,
Mrs Murray could not refrain from rushing about,
jumping at his slightest command. (130-1)

Mary, still childless, is manoeuvred into competing
with Will's vivaciously servile mother for his
satisfaction. This is an extreme form of a recurrent
problem some Scottish men have with relationships,
here blamed on the mother. Urquhart handles Mary's
thoughts and feelings very well. But it is all dramatised
by the arrival of the Italian prisoners of war. There is
an obvious comparison to be made with Jessie Kesson's
novella, *Another Time, Another Place*. The situations
are fairly similar, and both wives are impressed by the
arrival of the foreigners. Kesson's young woman, much
more sheltered from the world than exteacher Mary, is
thrilled:

Prisoners-of-war, heroic men from far-flung
places: the young woman felt a small surge of
anticipation rising up within her at the prospect
of the widening of her narrow insular world as
a farm-worker's wife, almost untouched by the
world war that raged around her. She always felt
she was missing out on some tremendous event,
never more so than when she caught a glimpse
of girls of her own age, resplendent in uniform,
setting out for places she would never set eyes on.
(ATAP 3)

The two women are different in that the young woman's husband is more taciturn than Will – she sometimes thinks he has forgotten how to speak; and that his lovemaking has made no impression on her: she remains unawakened, and thus possible prey for the Italians.

But Mary is more objective about them, even if 'sentimental':

> Even in their captivity there was something romantic about them. They sang, and when they spoke or shouted to each other, their voices had a lilt. They brought an exotic note into the drab life of the farm. You felt that they should be going about with gold rings in their ears, that there should be bright sunshine and laughter and a full ripe moon and love. . . . She felt a fellow-feeling with them, she told herself. For, after all, she was as much a prisoner as they were. A prisoner bound by her love and fear of Will. (132)

The focus never really shifts from Mary, though we share her interest in and pity for the unhappy young Italian she talks with, who hates Mussolini, was made to go to war, is anti Fascist, will never go back to Italy. She wants to help him, but Will finds him a poor worker, and sends him back to the camp. Then he does go so far as to wonder about it overnight, but does not change his mind:

> 'It's a pity, but . . . Well, I suppose war's war and work's work, and that's an end of it.' (143)

There is enough material here for a novel, even without the prisoners of war.

The other two stories I want to draw particular attention to are both set in families, and so convincingly that I keep feeling they have some relation to Urquhart's own family. The first, 'A Sailor Comes Home', is at first reading more straightforward than another reading begins to reveal. On the face of it, it only tells, in the first person, of a sailor going home after the war, and taking as many luxury goods as he can find home to the women of his family, who fight greedily over them. But there is more to it. Andrew is a real home-bird, hating the sun in the East, where he has been mine-sweeping, and longing for the rain and dirt of Glasgow, and his parents at home. His love of and anxiety for his mother, who is to undergo a hysterectomy, is evident throughout, and clouds his happiest moments. He delays his demob so as to get immediate leave.

The gifts he gathers to take home, known as 'rabbits', are of great interest to his civilian family, who have been deprived of all luxury during the war. Silk stockings feature as a kind of metaphor for all the shortages in the war years. When he is home, his bossy sister-in-law Nancy sends him up town every day, to try to buy them the scarce rationed stockings sometimes available – presumably rayon? She says that will let the family save the silk ones he brought for very best. The women almost seem to worship the 'rabbits'.

Andrew rarely mentions his war experience, but one strategically placed story near the beginning is enough; he'd met a big commando, who'd been a rugger International, on his way to the beach-head. He gave Andrew a bottle of whisky to keep for him. He comes back:

> shot through the spine and all about the middle. He just lay on that stretcher, and he

couldn't speak. He lay and looked up at me, and his eyes sort of flickered, and his mouth twisted a bit as if he was trying to smile. (19)

The simplicity of the language and the avoidance of blood-and-guts language only adds to the impact.

Much of the story is taken up with Andrew's resentment of his bossy sister-in-law, who has taken over his mother's role in the house during her absence in hospital. But as the story goes on, he thinks more about her and her situation, that of so many young wives:

> But I had more than a bellyful of her this leave. If only she'd left me alone and hadn't nagged Sooner [his younger brother] so much. Mind you, I'm sorry for Nancy. It's not right that young married wives like her should have to stay with their in-laws. I'll see that it doesn't happen to me if I ever get spliced. It's too cramped. Everybody gets on everybody's else's top like fellows huddled together on a ship. It's not natural, see. Nancy has all my sympathy. (25)

When we look closely at the presentation of the story, we realise that this mellowing is partly due to the fact that the story is told in sections, and that Andrew is confiding in someone else in a pub, during his final wait for demobilisation. He is drinking as he tells the story, and this accounts for the marvellously speaking voice we hear throughout.

The other story that reflects a vital, happy home life is 'Allow the Lodger', when all of a couple's four sons manage to get leave for Christmas 1942. Urquhart's gift for rendering dialogue is at its sustained best here, as two parents, four sons, and two wives celebrate together with 'their vivacity, their coarse animalness, their charm and their good looks'. (182) The unity of the family is undiminished, although they all react to the war in different ways:

> Robin joined the RAF, Arthur went into the Navy, Bill was in the Merchant Navy, and Charlie was a Conscientious Objector and had to do land work. 'All shades of opinion!' Mrs Wright said. 'There's nothing like it!' (177)

There is no disunity over this: neighbours may carp and criticise, but the family sticks together in Charlie's defence:

> 'That was right, lady!' Bill grinned. 'Give her the good old frozen mitt!'
> Tell her to mind her own bloody business,' Robin said. 'Tell her to go and fight herself if she's so bloody keen about it.' (184)

[Urquhart was one of three brothers, and the others were in the Navy and the Merchant Navy, and this caused no trouble in the family.] Their lively conversation is persuasively littered with old jokes, like the family saying that forms the title of the piece, 'Allow the Lodger'. It is what would be said if anyone took more than his share – only a paying guest would get the best of everything.

But this time there *is* a lodger, and he has a dampening effect on the whole family, as he sits silently, listening to all the banter, rather like the 'glamour boy' on the snowbound farm. Mr Bertram gives Mrs Wright the creeps; he looks and behaves oddly, 'aye slippin' aboot in his stockin' feet'. Like Charlie, he is single, but there is something much odder about his nature. Charlie may be a disguised author figure, homosexual as well as Conscientious Objector, but Mr Bertram gives no indication of any sexuality. 'Almost bald', with 'a smooth round face', he listens silently and rarely speaks. His interests are said to include nudism and Spiritualism: a text on his wall reads *Service, not Self*, and the brothers have fun with one of his books, *Guide to Self-knowledge through Space and Time*. To the Wrights he is definitely peculiar, and although Charlie's mum says he's not to grow a beard – 'Ye're queer enough, Charlie Wright, wi'oot growin' a beard' – we are liable to find the lodger odd, rather than the sociable Charlie.

Mr Bertram does succeed a bit in dampening the five precious days they have together, and Mrs Wright resolves again to give him notice. But it is true that she needs his rent money, and true that people with more space than they need are having strangers billeted on them willy nilly. The reader suspects that Mr Bertram will still be there when silence descends on the family home again.

CONTENTS

A SAILOR COMES HOME

ALL the time I was in the East I thought about nothing else but getting home. Calcutta, Bombay, Colombo, the seas around Borneo, none of them meant anything to me. I hated the sun, see. I thought about a damp, foggy, wet night in Glasgow, and wished I was home, sitting in an easy-chair beside a big fire with my shoes off and my sleeves rolled up. With the old man sitting on the other side of the fire, reading his paper. And the old lady bustling around with her fag in her mouth, stopping every now and then to tell me what Mrs. So-and-So had said to Mrs. Somebody-Else that day in the grocer's. And Anne Shelton and Vera Lynn singing on the wireless. And Sooner and me joining in the songs, singing *September in the Rain* and *Room Five Hundred and Four* and things like that, see. Maybe they're a bit out of date now, but they were the songs Sooner and me used to know best before I went East.

Sooner is my youngest brother. His real name is Gilbert, but if you saw him you'd know why we never call him that. He used to be called just 'Sonny'. But we've called him 'Sooner' ever since he was thirteen or fourteen. How it happened, see, was that he said one day he'd sooner be dead than married. And so the name's stuck.

Sooner went into the R.A.F., and all through the war he's written me regular. Before I left Singapore he wrote he'd be demobbed pretty soon and he hoped he'd be home before me. He was stationed near London, so he got home fairly often and kept me posted with news. It was him that told me the old lady didn't look too good. He thought the war had told on her.

We were in port at a small place in Batavia when I heard I'd get demobbed as soon as my relief arrived. I wasn't long in getting all my gear packed, I can tell you. And I had a lot of gear, see. I'd been doing a bit of trading, buying all sorts of things for the old lady and the girls. The other P.O.s laughed their heads off, and little Finlayson said : ' What's all your rush, Mackinnon? Going home to get spliced or what? You should be able to start a harem with all those rabbits! '

But it was nothing like that, see. I was just fed up with the glamorous East and the Navy and mine-sweeping and being cramped on a ship amongst a lot of fellows, some of them the kind that got me brassed off. I wanted to get back home and go with Sooner and the old man to see a good game between Celtic and the Rangers. I'd had two or three games of football in the East, but they were few and far between.

When my relief arrived it was well past the official demob date of my Group, and I said good-bye to the old Byms without regret. I was real browned-off. But I got more browned-off when we were disembarking at Colombo. One of the coolies working the crane was puggled on hooch, and he let a lot of gear fall in the oggin. My kit-bag was amongst this stuff. Christ, was I mad! I thought this was a nice send-off after six years in the Navy. But I was friendly with one of the W.R.N.S. there, and I got this young lady to wash the sea-water out of the silk underwear. The stockings hadn't suffered much because they were wrapped in cellophane paper, see. I gave this W.R.N. three pairs of silk stockings and a silk night-gown for doing it. No, nothing else. I wasn't feeling that way just then.

I'd got a letter from Nancy and it said the old lady was going into hospital for the Big Operation. From its date I guessed that the old lady would be just about due to go in right then, so I didn't feel too good. I worried about her all the time I was in Colombo. We were adrift there for three weeks, waiting on a trooper. Most of the boys didn't mind; they were having a good time in the bag-shanties. But I wanted to get home. The sooner I got out of Ceylon and home the better.

The morning we left Colombo I got an air-mail from Sooner saying he'd be demobbed within the next week. He said Nancy was going to keep house while the old lady was away, and he made a crack about wondering how he and Nancy would get on together while they were holding the fort.

Nancy is my sister-in-law, and she likes everything to be just so. She's a bossy piece of goods, and she and Sooner have always been at loggerheads. She's married to my brother, George, who's in Palestine. He won't be home for a while yet; he's got a high Group Number. Sooner says pity help the poor bloke when he does, he'll have a handful. But I don't know about that. Nancy's all right, I guess, and she and George get along pretty good. But she certainly is some handful! I reckon she's as heavy as me. Must be going on for fourteen stone, and she's only twenty-eight, see. I can't imagine what she'll be like by the time she's forty.

All the way through the Meddy I kept worrying about the old lady and wondering how Sooner and Nancy were getting on. Nancy's a pretty good manager—but she's just a bit too managing at times. I remember at George's wedding she had everything planned out to the last detail. She's the oldest of six sisters, and she's bossed them all her life, so she can't get out of the bossing habit. I was Best Man at the wedding, and I'll never forget it. She gave me a list of instructions the length of my arm. I had a hell of a busy forenoon, seeing about this, that and the other, and finally I had to get a taxi and collect different guests and take them to the church. For an hour before the ceremony I was dashing all over Hillhead in that taxi, going to strange houses where friends of Nancy's stayed, and saying: 'I'm the Best Man. I've come to take you to the wedding.' My last port of call was at Nancy's house to collect her three youngest sisters who were brides-maids. Nancy was bumming around in her wedding-dress, superintending everything, telling one sister she hadn't enough lipstick on, and sorting her father's tie, and telling her mother her petticoat was hanging down. All the time she kept complaining because her father hadn't taken the steel tips off her dancing-shoes. You see she was wearing a pair of gold sandals she'd worn at tap-dancing competitions, but the poor old bloke had been in such a dither that he'd forgotten. And so Nancy was raging about, wondering if the steel tips would show when she knelt down during the ceremony. I said what did it matter. 'Your long frock 'll cover them,' I said. But when Nancy and George were kneeling at the altar a good bit in front of where the bridesmaids and me were kneeling—it was in an English church, see—Nancy is awful religious—I noticed the steel tips sticking up in the air like nothing on earth. However, I never said anything either then or since; I've just kept it in mind so that some day when me and Nancy fall out I'll cast it up to her. I've always wanted to pay her out for all that assing around she made me do at the altar.

I kept thinking about all this, see, while the trooper ambled through the Meddy, and I was worried stiff about the old lady. And as soon as we docked at Southampton, I was all set to take the first train to Glasgow. But there was nothing doing. A bunch of us were told to report to our depot at Plymouth. I didn't half curse this. I'd already sent a telegram to say I'd be home on Thursday. When we got to Plymouth we were told it would take a week to take us through the demobbing barracks. So I kicked up hell. 'Look here,' I said. ' I want to get home because my old lady's in hospital. She might be dead by this time for all I know.'

'Or for all you care,' I said.

' All right, Jock,' they said. ' Keep your hair on. You can have ten days' leave, but you'll have to report back on the 11th February. It just puts your demob off a bit longer that's all.'

Well, I didn't stop to argue with them. I was desperate to get home, see. I'd thought maybe there would be a letter waiting when I docked, but there was nothing. Of course, neither Sooner nor Nancy could have known the day or the place I'd land.

To kill the time waiting for the night train I thought I'd go up to Mutley Plain to see a girl I'd knocked around with when I was doing my training. I hadn't been in Plymouth since then. I'd heard it had been blitzed, but I certainly got a shock when I got off the bus at the Theatre. I looked over in the direction of King Street, and when I saw the great wide space filled with rubble I began to think maybe I'd better not go and see Edna after all. I didn't like the idea of going there and finding . . . Well, you know, six years is a long time. So I walked up Athenaeum Street where I once had a billet, trying to figure out what I'd do. And when I saw that the house where my billet had been was just a gap and there were kids playing amongst the stones it made me think a bit harder. I walked along the Hoe, but it didn't make me feel any better. So I went back down Lochyer and into a pub and had a few. Then I walked over to the Theatre and got on a bus for Mutley. I thought I'd risk it.

Funny, I thought as the bus wove its way through the great space that had only kerb-stones now to show that it had once been covered with streets, funny that almost the only building left should be the huge red Insurance Building.

Edna's mother met me at the door. It took her a bit to remember who I was, but she asked me in for some tea, and then she said she supposed I knew Edna was married now and lived in Birmingham. ' She's got a little boy,' she said. ' Three 'Arry must be now. Lumme, ducks, 'ow the time do fly ! '

I said it did, and I left three pairs of silk stockings for her to give Edna as a wedding present. I gave the old girl a pair for herself, too. She'd always been awful nice to me, though she talked an awful lot like lots of English mothers.

Long before 11.25 I was at North Road Station waiting for the London train. I paced up and down platform seven, thinking about the old lady and wishing I was home. Plymouth depressed me terrible. Some of the lads who were travelling with me wanted me to go into the Buffet, but I couldn't face it. I walked up and down until the train came in. But even on the journey I couldn't find peace because one of the boys kept saying: 'I wonder what's happening on the old Byms now?' I could have socked him.

II

It was after ten the following night when I got home. Dad and Sooner and Nancy and the kid sister, Mabel, were at supper. They were all over me, of course. 'Home is the sailor, home from the sea!' Sooner cried, and I thought he was going to kiss me, he looked so pleased.

'And the hunter home from the hill!' Mabel said not to be outdone and to show she hadn't forgotten what she'd swotted up at school. 'What have you brought me, big boy?'

I'd often imagined coming home. Often and often I'd thought about it when I was lying sweltering on the deck with nothing on but a pair of pants—and often without even them. I'd thought about the old lady rushing to the door as soon as the taxi drove up and putting her arms round my neck and saying: 'Well, son, how are ye? Are ye ready for a feed?'

Christ, I must have had too many drinks. I'm beginning to get sentimental.

You see, somehow or other it wasn't like what I'd imagined. The old lady wasn't there. They said she'd been in hospital a week now and the operation had been successful. 'But I doubt she won't be home for a few weeks yet, lad,' Dad said. 'She's had a tough time.'

The place looked the same. All the old photos, and some new ones. And everything clean and tidy just like the old lady would have had it. But somehow there was something lacking. I noticed it first when we finished supper and Nancy sprung up and began to clear away the dirty dishes. Now the old lady wouldn't have bothered clearing away the dishes like that at once; the old lady is a great believer in sitting with her elbows on the table, smoking a fag and letting her meals digest. Not that she doesn't look after things or let anything slide, mind you. She's a damn good housewife. But Nancy doesn't smoke, and she doesn't hold with this sitting after you've eaten. She's all for getting the dishes washed as quick as possible. She began to bang around, and when I saw Sooner and Mabel were going to help her I thought I'd better get on my pins, too. But she chased me out of the scullery. 'Go and speak to Father,' she said. 'Tell him all your news. After all, you haven't seen him for nearly three years. You must have a lot to tell him. Sooner can easy dry the dishes. He's done nothing all day, anyway, except dot around in my way.'

Sooner winked and said: 'That's right, sailor, you go and tell the old man about the monkeys and the bears, the elephants and the hares you didn't manage to shoot in the jungle!'

Two or three times when I was talking to Dad I heard Nancy's voice raised rather loud, getting on Sooner's top about something. One time he wasn't putting the plates in the right place in the cupboard, and another time he was dropping cigarette-ash on the linoleum. I didn't think much about it at the time, but I've remembered it since, see.

I'd brought only one case with me, and Mabel was gasping for me to open it. 'C'mon, hurry up, big boy,' she kept saying. 'Put Nancy and me out of our misery.'

'I've hardly anything in that,' I said. 'Most of the stuff's with the rest of my gear. I have a kit-bag and a big case coming up Advance Luggage. Most of the rabbits is in it. I hope to God it doesn't get lost on the railway.'

But after we'd all got sitting down and Nancy and Sooner had finished the dishes I opened the case. It was mostly dirty clothes. Mabel was pretty cut up about that. Practically the only rabbits in it were two or three little ivory ornaments I'd bought in a bazaar in Calcutta. 'These are for Ma,' I said, putting them on the mantelpiece.

'More stuff for me to dust!' Nancy said. 'And all those

dirty clothes! I thought sailors always washed their own
things. As if I hadn't had enough to wash already for Sooner!
I think he'd been saving his stuff for weeks before he came
home. Did you ever send anything to the laundry at all?'

'Of course, I did,' he said. 'Anyway, I offered to wash
them myself, and you wouldn't let me.'

'I wasn't wanting my scullery turning into a swimming-
pool,' Nancy said. 'It was quicker to do them myself.'

'It'd help to take some of the beef offen you,' I said, laughing. 'Eh, Mrs. Mac? You've put on a lot of weight since I
saw you.'

'Once round the gas tank!' Sooner said.

'None of your lip,' she said. 'You could do with a bit of
my weight, Sooner Mackinnon. You're like a wee shrimp!'

'I've lost a lot of weight myself,' I said. 'The heat fairly
goes for you. I'm down to thirteen stone three.'

'Listen to him,' Nancy said. 'You aren't half sorry for
yourself, aren't you? I don't see any signs of night-starvation!
Do you, Dad?'

'No,' the old man said. 'He's looking well.'

Have another drink?

III

The next afternoon Sooner and me went to the hospital to
see the old lady. It wasn't a visiting-day, but we reckoned
we'd get in as I'd just come home from the East. 'Put on
your uniform,' Nancy said. 'That'll impress them.' But it
didn't. We had an awful struggle to get in. I had to talk
love to an awful sour nurse and promise her a pair of silk
stockings before we did. And even then she said: 'If the
Sister comes into the ward, scram as quickly as you can.'

I was pretty shaken when I saw the old lady in a bed at the
far end of the ward. I never remember seeing her in bed
before. She was a lot thinner and terrible pale. But she
brightened up no end when she saw us. 'I just thought you
might arrive to-day, laddie,' she said, keeping her arms round

my neck after she'd kissed me. 'I dreamt about ye last night.'

Well, I had a lot of things to say to her, but I just couldn't say them. Not then anyway, with all these women in the other beds watching us. We just sort of sat, and I twiddled my hat in my hands. Sooner and the old lady gave each other some bright back chat, and I remember the old lady saying: 'How're you and your sparring-partner getting on, son? Is she aye feeding ye all right?'

I told her a few things about the ship and about Colombo and the stuff I'd brought home, but somehow I had no heart to talk much. And then suddenly the old lady whispered: 'Here's the Sister comin'. I think you boys had better go.'

And so we went home for another bout between Sooner and Nancy. As soon as I got in I asked if my kit-bag had come, but Nancy said: 'No, do you think the Railway Company has nothing better to do than deliver your stuff? It'll likely be a day or two before it arrives.'

'There'll be one pair less of silk stockings for you to fight over, anyway,' Sooner said, grinning. 'The big boy here has promised a pair to one of the nurses.'

'Really, Andrew Mackinnon, you're daft,' Nancy said quite snappy-like. 'Wasting a pair of stockings on a nurse! What good 'll they be to her?'

'Can we do anything to help you?' I said to change the subject.

But she said there was nothing. 'Just sit there by the fire and keep out of my road,' she said, bustling about from the scullery to the living-room, setting the tea. 'And watch that cigarette-ash, Sooner! Use an ash-tray and not spatter it all over my clean fireside.'

Christ, I must say Nancy did get on Sooner's top a lot. It wasn't just once; it was all the time. I'd always known she hadn't liked Sooner much, but it had never struck me how strong the feeling was until then. I can't imagine why she didn't like Sooner. Even though he is my own brother he's a nice enough guy. He wanted to be an artist, and because he

YSC—B

was the youngest son and the rest of us were working the old lady and Dad had thought maybe they'd send him to the Art College. But the War came along just then and Sooner had to go into the R.A.F., and so now here he was with six years of his life wasted, demobbed and not very sure of what he was going to do. He'd only been out about a month, and he was still looking around for something. Nancy kept telling him to go after jobs and reading advertisements for him, but Sooner kept saying: 'Ach to hell, there's plenty of time. My demob leave isn't up. There's time enough to think about a job when it's finished. I'm here for a rest, lady, and I'm going to have one!'

I could see his point all right, but Nancy couldn't. 'Sitting around in my road letting good chances go past,' she kept saying.

That morning I'd given Nancy the Emergency Food Card I'd got at Plymouth. 'What do I do about this?' I said.

'You'll have to go and see Glasgow's Forgotten Women, sailor!' Sooner said with a grin.

'He will not,' Nancy said. 'You don't need to go there with an Emergency Card.'

'I had to go,' he said.

'He means the Food Office,' Nancy said to me. 'You didn't have to go there with your Emergency Card at all, Sooner Mackinnon. It was after you got demobbed that you had to go about your ration book.'

'So it was,' he said, and he pretended to faint on the sofa. 'You never saw such dames, big boy! I was in the place for an hour, so I had time to study them! I had a hell of a time to wait. Even the man at the door said: "You've been a long, long time!"'

'It's worth your while going to see them,' he said.

'They're not forgotten women at all,' Nancy said. 'You've a right cheek to say that, Sooner. They're all married women. You just look at their hands and you'll see their rings.'

'Ach, they'll buy them out of Woolworth's for show!' he said.

'Nothing of the kind,' Nancy said, and I remembered then that she'd worked in a branch of the Food Office at the beginning of the war. 'You won't need to go, Andrew,' she said. 'It's after you're demobbed that you'll have to go.'

'I'll go with you, son,' Sooner said. 'To see that none of them pinch you!'

'I wish one of them would pinch *you*,' Nancy said. 'Poor soul, she'd be made up with you! But I'd be damned glad to get you married and off my hands. It's high time you were thinking about it. Remember you won't always have your mother running at your beck and call.'

Another drink?

IV

I'd been home three days before my kit-bag arrived, and I was beginning to get windy in case it'd got lost. It came before tea one night. Mabel had just come in, and she was all for opening it then and there. But I said: 'No, you'll get your claws on the stuff soon enough, young lady. God knows they're long enough and painted enough!'

And so she and Nancy had to content themselves until after tea and we'd cleared away the dishes and washed them. By that time Dad had sat down in his easy-chair by the fire and he'd dropped off to sleep over the *Evening Citizen*.

They all crowded round as I opened the bag. The wireless was on, and Sooner joined in singing a song Betty Driver was singing. 'In a blue serge suit,' he sang, 'and a bright new. necktie . . .'

'Just like mine!' he said. 'Have you seen me in my demob suit yet, sailor? Gosh, I'm a smasher—and I don't bloody well think!'

'There's nothing wrong with it,' Nancy said. 'It's a very nice suit. Very smart.'

'Ooooo, what's this?' Mabel cried as I hauled out the swag at the top of the kit-bag.

'That's two pairs of stays I bought for Ma in a shop at Trinco,' I said. 'I hope they'll fit her.'

'You should have got roll-ons,' Nancy said, holding them up. 'These'll be far too big for her now that she's got so much thinner since her operation.'

'Ach, she'll fatten up again,' I said.

'That's what you think,' Nancy said, and there was such a funny note about her tone that I bent down and pulled out more stuff.

'Oh, nighties!' Mabel cried, grabbing them like a vulture. 'What lovely stuff! Feel the silk, Nancy! Oh, I haven't felt silk like this since before the war!'

'Pyjamas,' I said, throwing them at Sooner. 'They're a bit high-coloured, but I thought they'd suit you.'

In two or three minutes the living-room was like a draper's that had been blitzed. Silk pyjamas, nighties, cami-knickers, brassières, silk stockings were spread all over the place.

'Where am I going to put this?' Sooner said, pretending to stagger under a load of gash I'd shoved into his arms.

'Put it on the deck,' I said. 'Don't ask questions.'

'*Don't ask him questions, for he's not talking,*' Sooner sang, putting the stuff on the floor. '*All that he wants is to go out walking in a blue serge suit and a peaceful mind—and the girl he left BE-hind!*'

'Though I don't think the last bit's right,' he said. 'That's just been put in to keep a lot of dames' minds easy. There's not many blokes coming back to the girls they've left behind. They've all had a few girls through their hands when they were away, and they're not so keen on the old ones.'

'You're a right cynic, Sooner Mackinnon,' Nancy said.

'I'm not a cynic at all,' he said. 'It's the truth. A lot of the girls have been having high-jinks anyway with Poles and what-nots when their blokes were away, so you can't blame the fellows.'

I folded the empty kit-bag. 'That's that,' I said, going into the lobby and bringing in my case. 'I think there's some more rabbits in here.'

When the old man woke up he stared about in amazement.

'Good God, what's all this?' he cried. 'The place looks like a bloody bazaar!'

By the time the old man had got properly woken up the girls were arguing about the silk stockings, trying to sort them out, see, so that each of them would get the right size and the right shade. 'I don't want those,' Mabel cried, throwing two or three pairs on the deck. 'I don't like that shade at all.'

'You'll like what you get, young lady,' I said. 'You've got to remember that these stockings have to be divided out amongst more people than you and Nancy. There's Ma and there's Penny and there's Auntie Nell . . .'

'Auntie Nell!'

Mabel and Nancy let out shrieks and looked at each other.

'You're not going to give Auntie Nell any of these, sailor,' Nancy cried. 'Over my dead body you're not. You know fine that she never wears anything but lisle thread. Real silk stockings would just be wasted on Auntie Nell.'

'Nevertheless, Auntie Nell's to get a couple of pair,' I said.

'Here, how many pairs did you say you had?' Mabel said, beginning to count them. 'I thought you said you had forty pairs?'

'I had when I left the Byms,' I said. 'But there's not forty pairs now. I gave three to that W.R.N. in Colombo, and I gave a couple of pairs to a bloke on the trooper who did me a favour, and I gave two pairs to young Graham who was coming home to get married, and——'

'You promised a pair to the nurse in the hospital,' Sooner put in.

'Oh, there'll be none left for us!' Mabel cried.

'No, no, you can't give Auntie Nell a pair,' Nancy said. 'There would be no sense in giving Auntie Nell a pair.'

'Nevertheless,' I said, 'Auntie Nell's getting two pairs.'

'I think this is your Auntie Nell at the door now,' Dad said. 'I heard the bell ring, but, of course, you're all making so much damned row.'

The bell rang again. 'It's Auntie Nell all right,' Nancy

cried. 'Nobody ever rings our bell like that except her! You'd think we were all as deaf as she is!'

Yes, thanks, I'll have another. God, I need a drink when I think about that night.

v

Nancy didn't half put on the flannel with Auntie Nell. It was Auntie Nell this and Auntie Nell the next thing. Sooner kept winking at me, and when Nancy shoved a couple of pairs of stockings at Auntie Nell and said: 'We kept a darker shade for you, Auntie Nell, because we knew you liked dark things,' Sooner near had hysterics and he went away to the Heads to let himself rip.

By this time Nancy and Mabel had put on stockings to see what they looked like. Dad sat, looking at his paper, and then looking at them and grinning. 'By God, you'll both have to go staving up town to-morrow,' he said. 'There'll be no holding you back now! You'll be wanting folk to admire your legs!'

Auntie Nell kept raking amongst the gear, crying: 'Oh, isn't that gorgeous! Oh, my goodness, isn't this simply glorious! They're unique. I must say I like things that nobody else has. I like uncommon things. I like thae *abroad* things.' And she kept holding up her stockings and saying: 'Just wait till I put these on! My goodness, won't folk stare!'

'But I won't dare to wear them,' she said. 'They're far too fine to wear. I'd be terrified I'd ladder them. No, I doubt I'll have to keep them in a box and just look at them occasionally.'

'Oh, Auntie Nell, you surely wouldn't do that!' Nancy cried, sitting on the sofa with her legs stretched out. 'I'd never dream of keeping mine in a box. No, no, wear them and give folk a treat! I can't keep from admiring my own legs.'

I thought it was a good job she admired them herself, for nobody else would. Nancy's legs are like miniature tree-trunks. I was glad Sooner was out of the room just then, or I bet he'd have winked and made me laugh.

'What's Sooner doing all this time in the lavatory?' Nancy said.

'I think he's a bit fed up with silk stockings,' I said.

'He'd be more fed up if he had to make a round of the shops to try to buy them,' Auntie Nell said. 'My goodness, the trouble you have going from shop to shop looking for fully-fashioneds!'

'Farquharson and Conklin had some the other day,' Nancy said. 'I got a pair. I just happened to be lucky. I wasn't really in for stockings at all. I've seen me going in day after day, week after week, and there's never been any. The card's always been up. You know that card: No RAYON STOCKINGS ON SALE. But when I was in on Monday I nearly had a fit when I saw the card was down. So I got a pair. Really, I was terribly lucky!'

'Well, I managed to get two pairs yesterday,' Auntie Nell said.

If Auntie Nell had dropped a bomb on the living-room deck she couldn't have caused a greater sensation. Mabel and Nancy stared at her the way I've seen some of the boys stare at women in the streets after they've been afloat for a longish spell.

'*Two pairs!*' Nancy cried. 'But *nobody* ever manages to get two pairs.'

'Well, I did,' Auntie Nell said. 'I got up early yesterday morning because Farquharson and Conklin's were selling remnants. I wanted to see if I could get a bit tweed to make a skirt. I did, too, a lovely bit stuff. I wish I'd brought it to show you. Pale green with a brown check—it's glorious. Well, as you can imagine, I was in a terrible rush to get to the remnants counter in time, but as I was going upstairs I saw that the card was down at the stockings counter. I just stood: I didn't know what to do. I wondered if I should risk it, or if I should head straight for the remnants. But I thought: Och to hang, it's not every day you get a chance of fully-fashioneds. So I took my place in the queue, and I got a pair. Aristoc, too!'

'Aristoc!' Mabel cried. 'Oh, you were lucky, Auntie Nell! I haven't seen a pair of Aristocs for years. They were the best stockings you could get before the war.'

'It takes an auld wife like me, doesn't it, to take the trick!' Auntie Nell laughed. 'I just shoved them in my bag and hared for the remnants counter. I must say I was lucky! There was still a lot of stuff left, but there was a terrible crowd. But I just barged my way through, and the first thing I set my eyes on was this piece of green and brown tweed. Just the thing I want, I says to myself, and I got my fists on it and held tight. There was an awful bitch of a woman standing beside me and she had her eye on it, too, but I kept a right good grip and I kept shouting to the assistant: "I'll have this, miss," until she was *forced* to attend to me.'

'To get peace, I suppose,' Sooner muttered, sitting on the arm of my chair. 'And to get rid of her!'

'What's that, Mr. Cheeky!' Auntie Nell said, grinning. Auntie Nell isn't as deaf sometimes as she makes out.

'So I got it,' she said. 'Then when I was going back past the stockings counter I saw that the card was still down and there was still a lot of women standing. I stood and wondered if I dared risk it. Then I said to myself, Ach, I might as well be hanged for a sheep as a lamb! After all, I had the coupons, and I didn't see why they shouldn't sell me two pairs if I wanted them. So I stood again, but while I was waiting I began to get awful nervous. Heavens, I thought, what if the girl says you've been here already, you can't have two pairs. So I edged up the counter so that a different girl would serve me, and I tried to coory down as far as I could inside my fur coat—to camouflage myself you might say! Oh, but I was fairly getting the wind up! I thought what an affront it'll be if they won't let you have them. Then I glanced at the woman next me—and here she was the woman who'd been standing next me when I bought the first pair! I looked at her and she looked at me. Then we both dropped our eyes.'

'My word,' Auntie Nell said, 'I fairly scurried out of Farquharson and Conklin's as if I was expecting a policeman to put his hand on my shoulder at any minute!'

'You were lucky,' Nancy said. 'Fancy getting two pairs! You should be all right for stockings for a long time now with those two that Andrew's brought you.'

'I don't know,' Auntie Nell said. 'I was thinking I'd take a trip to Farquharson and Conklin's to-morrow to see if they hadn't any more.'

'You're lucky that has the coupons,' Nancy said.

She rose, looking down at her legs. 'Still,' she said, 'these are far, far nicer stockings than anything Farquharson and Conklin's could ever have. Farquharson and Conklin's are bullet-proof in comparison.'

'They're really too fine,' Penny said. 'They fairly show up the marks on your legs. Is that varicose veins you're starting?'

By this time, see, my oldest brother, Dan, and his wife had come in. Penny must have smelled the stockings and other gash a mile away. Penny and Nancy don't get on very well. They used to be chums all bubbly, but after Nancy was head bummer at Penny's wedding—matron of honour or something, they call it, don't they?—they haven't been quite so pally. Penny didn't arrange her wedding quite to suit Nancy's idea of the proper etiquette, so Nancy took in hand to manage things. She said it wouldn't do to let the family down and a lot of muck like that. I've often thought since that Dan and Penny should have got married quietly at a registry office the way Dan wanted—but, of course, Nancy wouldn't hear of that, and so everything was done in style. Too much style for my taste. If I ever get spliced I won't tell Nancy anything about it until after the deed's done.

Yeah, I think we both need another drink.

VI

'Varicose veins nothing!' Nancy said. 'That's where I

bumped my leg getting off a tram the other day. I was right mad, I can tell you. A stupid fool of a man pushed against me. I looked at once to see if my stockings had got torn. But they were all right.'

'It didn't matter if her leg got all black and blue as long as her stockings didn't ladder!' Sooner said.

'No, I was that relieved that I forgot to tell the man where he got off!' Nancy said. 'I was wearing those ones you brought me once from Algiers, Andrew. They're the only decent pair I had left. Gee, am I glad that you've brought these!'

'I wish you'd brought more size tens, though,' she said. 'You know perfectly well that tens are my size. There are an awful lot of nines and a halfs here.'

'All the more for us!' Penny said.

'You'll just get your share like the rest of us,' Nancy said. 'Do you know that he started off with forty pairs and there's only twenty-nine left?'

'You're not to give that nurse a pair,' she said.

'Do you mean to say that he gave away eleven pairs?' Penny cried.

'You *are* a fool,' she said to me.

Of course, Penny had to go through all the rabbits, so they were kept busy for the next half-hour, holding things up and letting them fall as soon as they saw something they liked better. I kept wishing the old lady had been there to keep them all in order. Dad and Dan and me talked about some of the things I'd seen out East, and Sooner tried to divide his attention between us and the women. I looked at them every now and then, too, while I told Dad and Dan about the things I'd seen on the Burma beach-head.

And I'd seen a lot. Christ, it gives me the horrors to think of it far less to speak about it. One time we were running commandos up, see, and waiting to take back the wounded. I remember one bloke—a big, handsome bloke, he'd been an International rugger player—well, he laughed and joked all the way to the beach-head, and he gave me a bottle of whisky

when he landed. 'Keep that for me until I come back, Mac,'
he said. 'And if I don't come back—well, you can drink my
health!'

But he came back. The next night we drew in to collect the
wounded, and he was one of the first they brought aboard.
He'd been shot through the spine and all about the middle.
He just lay on that stretcher, and he couldn't speak. He lay
and looked up at me, and his eyes sort of flickered, and his
mouth twisted a bit as if he was trying to smile.

I was thinking about him when I heard Auntie Nell say:
'Isn't that a lovely nightie! My goodness, it's gorgeous. It
would do for a first night!'

Sooner nudged me and giggled. He said afterwards: 'I
was going to say it was too good for a first night, that what
did you need a nightie for on a first night, anyway! But I
thought I'd shock the old dear too much.'

'I have a lovely nightie, too,' Auntie Nell said, folding it
carefully. 'But I keep it in a box. It's far too good to wear.
My goodness, I'd be feared. I just open the box occasionally
and take a bit keek to see that it's still there.'

VII

Sure, I'll have another. But this has got to be the last, see.
I'm beginning to see things. Things I want to forget—like
some of those bodies we found in the jungle. Christ, chum,
have you ever seen a body that's been half-buried for weeks
and then's been dug up?

Cheers!

The next morning Nancy was buzzing around like a hen on
a hot girdle. She was polishing the linoleum round the corners
of the living-room when Sooner and me went in. 'So you've
got up at last?' she said. 'I was beginning to think you intended to lie in your beds until we got the undertaker for
you.'

'What's for the breakfast, toots?' Sooner cried, rushing and
crouching on his hunkers in front of the fire. 'Jees, it's cold

this morning! What're you doing with that back door open?
You'd think it was the height of summer!'

'You should get up in time and do some work and then
you'd feel warmer,' Nancy said, rubbing furiously with her
duster. 'I've been up since before seven this morning and
I'm as hot as a pie.'

'What's for the breakfast, toots?' Sooner said.

'Wait till I'm ready,' she said. 'Or make it yourself.'

We tried to jolly her, but Nancy wasn't to be hurried. 'I'm
going to finish my dusting before I cook anything,' she said.
'If you want your breakfast on time you'll have to get up
earlier after this and not come staving in here at ten o'clock
in the morning.'

'One more crack like that, young lady,' I said, 'and I'll
have to stick you on the rattle! If you're not careful you'll
get your hat!'

'That's right, sailor,' Sooner said. 'Stick her on! Don't
argue the toss with her!'

'Number Eleven for her straight away,' I said.

'No, we'll give her the sack!' he said.

'It'd be a sad day for you,' Nancy said without looking up.

'Well, what do you want?' she said after a bit more catter-
battering. 'Although, it's not what you want—it's what
you'll get! Will some dried eggs and fried potatoes suit
Your Majesties?'

'Wonderful,' I said.

Still, I thought when I was eating them, they didn't taste
as wonderful as they'd have done had the old lady been at
home and on her pins.

Afterwards me and Sooner washed the dishes for Nancy.
She kept buzzing around behind us in the scullery, sweeping
under our feet and saying: 'I wish you boys would hurry up!
You're a couple of pests!'

'Quit it, sister!' I said. 'You're like a Jimmy the One that's
just been made, feeling his feet aboard a ship. "We'll mix
red lead with paint, coxswain!"'

But Nancy wasn't taking any chaff. 'You shouldn't wash

the dishes with a cigarette in your mouth,' she said to Sooner. 'See! You're dropping cigarette-ash into the water. Take it out of your mouth.'

'Ach to hell!' Sooner said.

'You and your cigarettes,' Nancy said. 'I wish they'd put them up to five bob for twenty. You wouldn't be able to smoke so many then. I'm fed up tidying cigarette-ash. It's all over the place!'

'All over the place!' Sooner sang. 'Tra ra ti da da! From the East and the West—all over the place!'

'Hurry up and get yourselves cleaned and get out of here,' Nancy said. 'Away up town and leave me in peace until I get the dinner made.'

'Ach, we've nothing to go up town for,' I said. 'I want to sit here and—well, just sit.'

'You're not going to sit here in my road,' she said. 'Get out of this. I'll soon give you a job to do up-town.'

'You can go to Farquharson and Conklin's and see if you can't get me two pairs of fully-fashioned silk stockings,' she said.

'Well, for Pete's sake!' I said. 'Haven't you got enough silk stockings already?'

'I can't wear the ones you brought me,' she said. 'They're too good to wear. Besides, Farquharson and Conklin's have got them, and I might as well have them as anybody else.'

'I thought you didn't have any coupons,' Sooner said.

'Neither I have. But you have your demob ones,' she said. 'I'll pay you back when the next period starts.'

Well, we argued the toss with her again, but it was no go. 'You'll have to hurry up,' she said. 'They just have a limited supply, and this is the best time to get them. If you're much after eleven o'clock they'll be all sold out.'

'Why don't you go yourself and leave us here in peace?' Sooner said.

'Yes, we'll make the dinner for you,' I said.

'It'd be some dinner,' she said. 'I don't fancy your Nelson's Body or whatever it's called.'

'You'll have a better chance of getting them than me,' she said. 'The assistants 'll do anything for a man.'

So we went. I'd rather have stayed at home, but I knew it wouldn't be comfortable with Nancy bumming around in a bad temper. There was a crowd of women round the stockings counter in Farquharson and Conklin's and there was no ticket up, so we knew that silk stockings were on. We stood and waited, and by and by our turn came. The assistant was an old dame about forty with a hell of a lot of lipstick on.

'I'm sorry I've just got two shades,' she said, holding a couple of boxes in front of us.

We told Nancy this when we went home. 'Just got two shades!' she cried. 'Gosh, you were highly honoured. They never say that to us! They just ask you the size, then they put a bit string round them and shove them at you.'

'It's easy seen you were men,' she said. 'You'll have to go back to-morrow.'

And so we went to Farquharson and Conklin's again the next morning. Both of us were glad to get out. Even two more pairs of silk stockings hadn't put Nancy in any too good a humour. We got the same assistant, and she beamed all over and said: 'Good morning, I'm sorry I've got only one shade to-day.'

'I've never seen her smile at anybody yet,' Nancy said when we told her. 'She's an old sour-puss. She's seen a few bon-fires, I can tell you!'

'So have I!' Sooner said. 'I've not only seen some—I've lit a few!'

Well, every morning that week we went to Farquharson and Conklin's and we were lucky enough to get silk stockings every day. 'It's easy seen that folk's coupons are all finished,' Nancy said.

'So will mine at the rate we're running through them,' Sooner said.

'I'll give you them all back,' Nancy said. 'You can go up again to-morrow and get another two pairs.'

We got to the stage where we were stringing this assistant

along, and almost every day I chaffed her to see if she wouldn't give us two pairs each. But there was nothing doing. 'One to each customer only,' she said. 'My word, you boys are fairly going your dinger!'

'Your girl-friends have surely got awful big feet,' she said. 'They've got a good grip of Scotland!'

'I haven't got a girl-friend,' I said, grinning. 'I'm looking for one. I'm just buying size tens in case I get one with big feet.'

'Another day,' Sooner said to me as we were leaving the shop, 'and you'll be asking that dame to meet you for a drink. I see you've got that look in your eye, sailor!'

'What do you think she gives us the stockings for?' I said. 'She's living in hope!'

'Do you think I should ask her out for a night?' I asked Nancy.

She was horrified. 'Not even though she gave you three pairs at a time!' she cried. 'No, you just keep stringing her along. You'll get on better that way.'

VIII

Home is the sailor, home from the sea. . . . Yeah, I'm beginning to see things all right. C'mon, let's get out of here. The fresh air 'll do us both good. Might make me forget Nancy and the old lady for a bit.

Mind you, I'm sorry for Nancy. There she is with her man in Palestine and him not likely to be home for a long time. And she's never had a home of her own, see. She's always lived either with her own people or with us. It's pretty tough on a girl, and mind you, there must be hundreds of thousands of girls like Nancy. And I guess none of them know when they'll get a house and get settled down to a proper married life. No wonder they get discontented and a bit snappy.

But Nancy was all smiles that day she went to Hillhead to show off her stockings and other gear to her sisters. She came back all excited and as happy as a rating who's just changed from temperance to grog.

'Well, what did the girls think of your stockings?' I said.

'They were green with envy,' she said. 'Our Betty couldn't eat her tea for looking at them.'

'As for our Ella!' she said. 'Though she says she'll soon be upsides with me. She says Will Grierson's in Turkey and he'll try to bring her stockings from there. "But where will he manage to get stockings in the jungle?" she says. I told her there wasn't a jungle in Turkey. But she said: "He says his boat's gey far up the river, so there must be a jungle."'

'There's not a jungle in Turkey, is there?' Nancy said.

'Of course not, you galoot!' Sooner said. 'There's nothing but delight in Turkey!'

'That's because you're not there!' she said.

'Don't be daft,' he said. 'That's all you know. I'd be the delight of any harem I got into.'

'You'd have to put on some beef first,' I said. 'Young ladies like fellows to have a bit of flesh about them.'

'How do you know?' Nancy said.

'I've seen a few bonfires, too!' I said.

Nancy was all right at times like that, see. She was all right when she was in the mood for a bit of chaff and some snappy cross-talk. But these times were too few and far between for my liking. As soon as she thought you were trying to take a rise out of her she went all haywire and hey-nonny-nonny. Like the times in the forenoons when Sooner and me tried to jolly her into giving us a stand-easy.

'You and your cups of tea!' she'd say. 'You've just had your breakfast. Do you think I've nothing else to do but make cups of tea for you two lazy so-and-sos?'

Sooner took it pretty good, I must say. He just winked at me and said: 'It's a great life, sailor, if you don't weaken!'

But I was weakening by the end of my leave, see. Another two days of it and I've been telling Nancy about those steel tips showing at her wedding. Maybe I'll tell her yet. There's no knowing what reception I'll get when I go home the day after to-morrow. Nancy couldn't very well stick me on the rattle when I was on leave, but there's no knowing what her attitude will be when I go home for good. I'll be in the same position as Sooner then : looking for a job and just a damned nuisance about the house. It wouldn't be so bad if the old lady was at home to keep the peace, but the old lady's still in hospital.

All the time I was home I went to see her every day—and mind you, I had to do a lot of bribery to get in—even took one of the nurses to the pictures—and every day she said it wouldn't be long before she got out. She said the Sister had told her she'd get out three days before I was due to come back here. But the day after that the doctor said she couldn't; that if she went out he wouldn't be responsible for the consequences. She'd have to stay in another week, he said. So the poor old lady just had to smile and say rather. 'I might as well get right better, laddie,' she said to me. 'Never mind,' she said, 'I'll be home by the time you come back from your demob.'

I sure hope she will. I was expecting a letter to-day to say she was out, but it hasn't come yet. I hope it'll come to-morrow. Otherwise I don't know how I'm going to stand Nancy.

Mind you, I think you'd like Nancy, chum. She's all right as dames go. She's pretty, and she's got a good enough figure if she could stop putting on the beef. But I had more than a bellyful of her this leave. If only she'd left me alone and hadn't nagged Sooner so much. Mind you, I'm sorry for Nancy. It's not right that young married wives like her should have to stay with their in-laws. I'll see that it doesn't happen to me if I ever get spliced. It's too cramped. Everybody gets on everybody else's top like fellows huddled together on a ship. It's not natural, see. Nancy has all my sympathy. But there was no call for her to keep telling Sooner and me we were just lolling about while she was doing all the work. She should have *smiled* when she said that. We knew she was doing the work, and we appreciated it. But after all we were on leave. We'd had six years of being bossed around by all sorts of guys, some good and some bad, and some you wouldn't wipe your feet on. We hadn't gone through all that to come home and be bossed around still more by her. Can you wonder that I was proper browned-off by the time my leave was up? All I wanted was to have a quiet time, see. I told them that. I said: 'I just want to sit in an easy-chair and have a quiet time.'

'Better join the Oxford Group, sailor,' Sooner said to that.

But I don't want to join any Oxford Group. I'm like the bloke in the song: All I want is a blue serge suit and a bright new necktie: All I want is peace of mind and quietness. That's what we've been fighting for, isn't it?

The song says so.

I'm feeling a bit better now I've got that off my chest. It's been worrying me for the last ten days. How're you feeling now yourself, chum? The fresh air does you good. Blows the cobwebs out of your brain. Makes you see things a bit clearer like.

Well, will we get on back to the billet? Just another day now and then I say good-bye to the Navy and bell-bottom trousers and all the bull-shit. Good-bye to rum, bum and gramophone! Hail to wine, women and song!

Though I hope all the women aren't like Nancy. I keep wondering how she and Sooner are getting on. Poor Sooner, I hope he's got fixed up in a job by this time. Maybe that 'll keep Nancy's trap shut.

But still it won't be so bad when I go back. The old lady 'll be home and on her pins again. At least, I hope she will.

EVERYBODY HAS SOMEBODY ELSE

SHE got into an empty third-class Pullman and took the seat nearest the door. This was partly from habit; she was so used these days to sitting down on the first available seat. But it was partly because she wanted to see everybody who came in, hoping if it had not happened before the other corner seats were filled that somebody attractive would sit beside her.

She took off her Land Army hat and put it on the rack on top of her small case. She glanced out at the dimly lit platform to see that nobody was coming in, then she started to make up her face. She took off her glasses, but after a few seconds' thought put them on again. It was essential that she should see clearly, and she couldn't see well enough without them. She was rubbing the lipstick into her lips with her little finger as Elsie had shown her when a soldier came into the carriage. She looked up expectantly at him, but he passed on and took a seat about the middle. She watched him sling his gas-mask and great-coat on to the rack, then when he sat down she could see nothing more of him beyond the top of his forage cap above the back of the seat. She gave a mental shrug. He had been no great catch, anyway.

Settling herself comfortably in her corner, she opened her book. But she held it on her lap and peered out of the window. She could not make up her mind whether it was a good idea coming half an hour early and getting an advantageous seat, or whether it was better to arrive at the last gasp and then pick a seat beside somebody who attracted her. The trouble with the last method was that usually all the seats beside attractive

men were filled and she invariably found herself sitting beside
a fat middle-aged man who over-lapped her or some irritating
woman who talked about the difficulties of travelling these
days. Let's hope she would fare better to-night.

She needed something exciting and wonderful to make up
for her week-end. It had been sheer hell staying with Dora
and Harry. They were so devoted to each other, so wrapped
up in each other that you couldn't help feeling an outsider.
Really, the way they kept pawing each other and kissing whenever they came into contact. Even when they were washing
the dishes, Harry hadn't been able to pass Dora on his way to
the coal-cellar without kissing the back of her neck. It was
most annoying. She had felt quite out of it and embarrassed.
She must have been in a constant state of blushing, for Harry
had said at lunch-time : 'It's easily seen that Jean isn't used
to staying with young newly married couples.'

He had a cheek! After all, he and Dora had been married
for five years. You'd have thought they would have got past
the silly loverish stage by this time. She had been infuriated,
feeling out of it all the time.

A sailor pushed his kit-bag through the door and dumped
it on the passage. She caught a glimpse of glittering fair
curls dangling over a brown brow, and then he turned and
spoke to somebody outside the carriage. 'Empty compartment
in 'ere,' he said. 'I shall be all right. Don't bother to wait,
Alf. I want to get settled comfortably before the train fills up.
S'long.'

She looked at him as he came through the door. He glanced
at her, then he bent down and began to knee his kit-bag up
the passage in front of him. 'Anybody got this seat, mate?'
he said, nodding to the seat opposite the soldier.

'No, plenty of room, chum.'

The sailor swung his bag on the rack beside the soldier's
gas-mask, then he flung his hat on top of it. Jean watched
him over the top of the intervening seats. He had a strong,
thick neck which began to whiten towards the edge of his
sailor's collar. He looked all right. She sighed and looked

down at her book. After all, if he wanted to sit opposite somebody, why couldn't he have sat opposite her? Still, it was
early yet. There were plenty of good fish left in the sea . . .
she hoped.

She had read three lines when a small crowd of people
bustled in. It was evidently a few friends seeing off a newly
married couple. Jean glanced at them, thinking really it was
terrible the people who managed to get married these days.
How did they do it? She was relieved when they went up to
the far end of the carriage; she did not want them spooning
and looking coyly at each other anywhere near her. They
giggled and chattered a great deal and stowed their luggage
first at one side of the carriage and then at the other because
the young woman who was travelling thought there was a
draught coming through one of the windows. 'It's coming
through like a knife!' she cried, and they all laughed as if
she had said something wildly funny.

Jean drew her coat-collar up behind her neck and tried to
look over the backs of the seats to see if she could catch the
sailor's eye. But she could see nothing but a few blond curls.
She heard the deep murmur of his and the soldier's voices, but
couldn't make out one word they were saying. She edged herself out of the corner towards the aisle and craned her neck a
little to the side to see if she could see them any better.

'Excuse me.'

She shrank back as a soldier pushed a large case past her
ear. 'Sorry,' he mumbled, squeezing past her. He stood for
a second; he looked at her and she smiled; then he swung his
case on to the rack opposite and sat down in the corner across
the aisle from her.

She looked down at her book and read a couple of lines that
meant nothing to her, then she looked across at him. He had
taken off his forage cap and laid it on the seat beside him. His
head was tilted back a little. She gazed for a second at his
profile, then looked down at her book again. Oh, Christ, why
had he not sat down beside her or on the seat opposite! He
really looked marvellous. She was sure that nothing that came

into this carriage to-night would be half as handsome. She sidled back into her corner, turning her shoulders and head round so that whenever she looked up she was looking straight at him. The sailor and the soldier farther up the carriage had got into conversation with two of the young couple's friends. They were talking in quite loud voices, but Jean was no longer interested in anything the sailor might say.

Now, if this bloke, who was a Corporal in the R.A.S.C., had just sat down opposite her instead of putting the passage between them. . . . He had spoken, mind you, and he had looked sort of interested. . . . She looked up from her book and saw that he was looking at her. She lowered her eyes, feeling herself blush.

After a few seconds she laid aside her book and fished in her pocket for a packet of twenty Gold Flake. She put one in her mouth. She had matches in her other pocket, but she was careful not to rattle them when she put in her hand. She made a pretence of going through her pockets, never looking in the direction of the soldier.

She made a clicking noise of annoyance with her tongue and then looked at him. He was staring at the seat opposite him, frowning a little. She leaned across the aisle and said:

'Excuse me, I wonder if you'd give me a light? I seem to have lost my matches.'

He looked blankly at her, then he said, 'Oh!' and brought out a lighter. She jabbed the end of her cigarette so violently into it that the flame went out. The corporal flicked it again. This time Jean put up her hand to cup the flame, her fingers touching the back of his hand. 'Thank you,' she said, inhaling.

'Excuse me.'

A large woman in a light grey coat shoved a case and a parcel between them. Jean was forced to edge back into her seat. The large woman stood for a moment, then she put her luggage down on the seat opposite Jean. 'Nobody sitting here?' she said.

Jean shook her head. She felt too annoyed to answer. The

large woman began to place her belongings on the rack. She stuck her behind almost into the land girl's face as she poked her umbrella securely along the back of the rack. She was such a large woman and she took up so much room that Jean was forced to tuck in her legs and feet. It was no easy matter, since she was almost as large as the woman. She got as far into her corner as she could, then she looked across at the corporal.

He was peering out of the window at the other side.

The carriage was beginning to fill up rapidly. Jean looked expectantly at everybody who came in, but either they had somebody with them or they sat down elsewhere. It would just be like some other damned old woman to plank herself down here. Why did old women always feel they were so much safer sitting beside other women?

The large woman had settled herself with many rustlings and sighings opposite her, and she had taken off her hat and placed it possessively on top of her hand-bag on the seat beside her. Jean kept looking at them. Every time somebody came in and glanced at the hat and the bag and then passed on up the aisle, she felt like screaming. It's not fair! Why should old fuffs like this who've had their life spoil things for young ones like me. . . .

Fuffs? She turned round and looked at her reflection in the window. It wasn't a bad face; it was quite a decent shape. Of course, maybe it did look a bit more glamorous in the dimness; you couldn't see how red and weather-beaten it was, and her nose didn't look so hooked. She drew her forefinger down the bridge. Surely it wasn't as curved as all that. . . .

Why in God's name had this old dame chosen this seat? There were plenty of seats farther up the carriage. The interfering old bitch—had she never been young herself? Jean could have screamed with temper. For a few moments she considered the idea of changing her seat. There was still quite a lot of room. She might go up and sit down opposite the sailor with the flaxen curls. But even as she flexed her muscles to rise and do this, she thought that if she did she would make herself noticeable. The trouble was that she could never do anything like that without blushing. And she was so big and awkward. . . .

Well, what if she was? She had a right to change her seat if she liked. She'd be a fool to allow herself to be baulked by public criticism—if there was any, for likely enough nobody would notice her. She was half-rising from her seat when a couple of soldiers burst in from the door at the other end and sat down on the seat she had contemplated.

At the same time a girl and an American soldier sat down opposite the corporal in the R.A.S.C. *You missed your chance, that's the way of romance.* . . . The girl was very small, and either her head was very large or her neck was too short, for she gave the impression of being top-heavy. She wore a black dress and a short scarlet swagger coat. A round black hat was stuck on the back of her head, with a veil falling forward half over her face. As soon as she sat down she threw this back. Her nails were the same colour as her coat.

She oughtn't to wear such bright colours and make herself so conspicuous, Jean thought disapprovingly. With a figure like that, anyway. If it was mine I'd be trying to hide it (though deep in herself she knew that she could never have dared to wear those kind of clothes). If Elsie had been here she'd have called it a certain case of ' duckitis '. She saw now that that was what was wrong. The girl's body was too long and her legs too short. Jean wondered what the American could possibly see in her. And if her talk at the moment was a sample of her usual talk, well . . .

Well, the American deserved all he got, that was all she could say. She lifted her book firmly in front of her face, resolving to read it and not to look about again. She knew already that this journey was going to be a frost. After all, what did she need to pick up anybody for? What good would it do her? Get into conversation with somebody on a train and then at the very first station—even though Oxbridge was an hour's journey—she would have to get off, and likely enough he would be going straight on and she would never

see him again. What was the good of that? All this hoping
and scheming and imagining. . . . She just made herself unhappy. No, better to read her book. And anyway, Ron was
going to meet her with the car at Griffins Edgeworth.

Or was he? He'd said he wouldn't promise. If he could
manage he would. It all depended on how he was situated.
'I might 've to mend a tractor or attend to a calving—Lucky
Star's about due—I don't need to tell you what it is on a farm,
girl! But I'll come if I can manage and save you walking
that three miles.' She sighed. He'd promised that several
times before and never come. Though to give him his due,
there had been occasions when he had met her. It was funny
about Ron. Funny why she should be so crazy about him—
when he was there, anyway. For she wasn't so crazy when
he wasn't. When there were men like this R.A.S.C. corporal
in the offing for instance. . . . After all, Ron never really gave
her any encouragement. He treated all the other land girls in
exactly the same way. And, of course . . . well, as Elsie said:
'He isn't much to look at and he thinks more of his cows than
he does of any of us.'

She lit a second cigarette off the end of the first one. She
would likely have to chain-smoke all the journey now. She
couldn't very well use her matches in case the corporal noticed.
Of course, she could always ask him for another light. That
would be an excuse to get into conversation with him, wouldn't
it?

Don't be a fool! Determined to read her book, she found
that she couldn't. But she kept looking at it, and to prevent
herself from becoming irritated by the giggling of the girl in
the scarlet coat she started to count to herself. She could hear
the deep murmur of the sailor's and the soldier's voices accom-
panying the giggling of the girl and her American, but she
was determined not to look up. She was especially determined
not to look across at the corporal in the R.A.S.C.

But this determination lasted only a few seconds. In spite
of herself she was forced to look across the aisle. He was sitting with his arms folded and his eyes shut; he looked remote

and far away from the American and the girl who were flirting excitedly with each other.

Jean made no further pretence of reading; she looked almost anxiously at everybody who came into the carriage, and she kept looking at the hat and bag beside the large woman. She glared frozenly at any woman who looked as if she might sit down, but she tried to put on what she thought was a seductive look for the men—except for a portly elderly man who had commercial traveller written all over him. She glared at him, too. But he looked from her to the large woman and then passed up the carriage.

Two or three minutes before the train started an A.T.S. sergeant sat down beside her. She was a little slip of a thing with very fair hair done in an enormous roll round the nape of her neck. Jean was sure that no loose strands would ever be allowed to escape from that glittering sausage. She tried to shrink into her corner, for beside the A.T.S.'s fragility she felt enormous, conscious of her huge shoulders and massive thighs.

She glanced down at her book, aware of the A.T.S. bringing out a silver cigarette-case. Then she felt the other girl's elbows brushing against her as she searched through her pockets.

'Excuse me, I wonder if you could give me a light? I seem to have lost my matches.'

Jean looked up.

But the A.T.S. was leaning across the passage, and the corporal already had his lighter out and was flicking it.

'Thank you.' The A.T.S. leaned back and inhaled. The corporal smiled at her and brought out his own packet of Capstan. 'Funny thing, isn't it?' he said. 'Whenever you see anybody else light a fag you think you should have one yourself, although you might not really be wanting one.'

'It is funny, isn't it?' the A.T.S. said. 'I've seen men doing it in the pictures.'

'Sort of auto-suggestion,' the corporal said.

'Yes, isn't it?' The sergeant leaned her chin on the elbow nearest him and leaned slightly across the passage, turning her back on Jean. 'Terrific crowd in this train, isn't there?'

'Terrific,' he said.

Jean looked out of the window. The train gave a preliminary jolt. Some people at the door of the carriage began to shout 'Good-bye.'

She still kept looking out of the window as the train began to gather speed. She was aware vaguely of a woman's high-pitched voice approaching from the next carriage, but it was not until the woman had passed her crying, 'All blinds down, please!' that she understood what was happening. The next minute the large woman in grey had seized the blind and tugged it down. The glamour of her own reflection was blotted out in an instant.

She sighed and lifted her book. The large woman leaned forward and said : 'Would you mind fastening this blind at your end, please?'

Her fingers seemed to be all thumbs, and she blushed as she fastened it, feeling that everybody was looking at her. But at last she managed it. 'Thank you,' the large woman said. 'Big crowd on this train to-night, isn't there?'

Jean nodded, then she looked down hastily at her book before the woman could say anything else.

It isn't fair, it isn't fair. . . . The wheels of the train began to say the same thing over and over again. It isn't fair. . . .

Oh, for heaven's sake, change it to something else. Something else . . . somebody else. . . . Everybody has somebody else. Everybody has somebody. . . . Oh shuttup! Haven't you got Ron? Ron who'll be waiting for you at Griffins Edgeworth . . . and anyway, there was still the bus-journey from Oxbridge to Griffins Edgeworth. Maybe there would be somebody in the bus. . . .

She did hope Ron would come for her. It would be no joke to walk three miles through this snow. But then, of course, the snow might be the very reason why he mightn't come for her. Several times she drew aside the blind cautiously, careful not to look at the large woman, and every time she looked the

countryside seemed to get whiter and whiter. And it was getting colder. Probably the snow would be worse than it had
been in town.

· She hunched her shoulders and snuggled her head down
into the collar of her coat. For a second she rashly allowed
herself to look at the woman in grey.

The woman smiled and said : ' It's no joke travelling on a
Sunday night these days, is it? '

' No,' Jean said.

She leaned her head in her corner and closed her eyes.
Above the noise of the train she heard every word the A.T.S.
sergeant and the corporal were saying to each other. They
were getting along nicely. The corporal had already told her
that he was a radio salesman in civvy street. She ground her
teeth in her cold and misery and wished that it was time to
reach her station.

As they got nearer and nearer Oxbridge, she lifted the corner
of the blind more and more often. But she could not make
out any familiar land-marks. There was a bright moon, but
the countryside was so shrouded with snow that nothing was
distinguishable. A silvery sheen swum over everything. It's
beautiful, she told herself, beautiful, beautiful . . . but what's
the good of its being beautiful when you can't point it out to
anybody else?

She was relieved when the guard came through the carriage
calling, ' Passengers for Oxbridge move forward, please.' And
she lifted her case and stumbled awkwardly past the corporal
and the A.T.S., and she was still blushing uncomfortably as
she paced with the queue through the guard's van and the other
carriages.

There were several inches of snow on the station platform.
She clumped her heavy W.L.A. boots through it, hurrying to
get to the bus in the station square before it would fill up. But
when she got inside she saw that all the corner seats were
taken. There were a number of couples, some of whom she
knew by sight from other Sunday nights. She hesitated, looking for someone interesting to sit beside. A young man at

the far end caught her fancy. She was a bit surprised to see that he was sitting at the outer edge of the seat, and for a moment she thought he was keeping the seat vacant for somebody. But she determined to chance it.

She pushed her way along to him and said: 'Is this seat engaged?'

'No.' He rose and let her pass him.

She was putting her case on the rack when she noticed that there was a mess of sickness on the floor and that some of it had got smeared on the seat and down the panelling under the window. For a second she hesitated. Then she sat down.

She looked at the young man, but he was looking away from her. She pulled her coat as tightly around her legs as she could, and sat with her heels in the air, the toes of her boots just touching the vomit. After all, her coat would clean if she got any marks on it. But it really was a scandal the bus-conductress not cleaning it up after whoever had done it. It looked as if it had been done several journeys back; it had dried in streaks on the wooden side of the bus.

Sitting in her cramped position, she leaned as heavily against the young man as she dared, but he was sitting on the edge of the seat, and just after the bus started he got into conversation with the man opposite him.

Why had she been such a fool as to sit down beside him? Why hadn't she shifted as soon as she saw the sickness? Anybody else would have done. No wonder the bloke had turned his back on her. He must have thought she was daft. She should have sat down across the passage from him where the man he was talking to now was sitting. Then now he would have been speaking to her. They could have started a conversation about the sickness. . . .

Or why hadn't she sat down beside somebody else? There was that old fat woman getting off. If she had sat down beside her she would have been able now to slip into her corner seat. And then maybe at the next stop a good-looking boy might have got in and sat down beside her. . . .

She tried to be philosophical, thinking that a bus or a train journey was a bit like life. You never knew who you were going to sit beside or who was going to choose to sit beside you. It was just a chance if you took the right seat. And like a bus ride people got off and on at different stops, and although you had been terribly interested in them for the short time you were sitting opposite or beside them you soon forgot them when somebody else took their places. You jogged along beside some people for years and you never noticed them much —or if you did notice them they were sitting at the other end of the bus and you could never get a chance to get near enough to talk to them; or they were with somebody else and never noticed you. Others again came on for only short journeys, and you quickly forgot them. . . . Or did you? You couldn't help noticing some people, and a few minutes of them did more for you than years spent beside other people. That corporal in the R.A.S.C. and the girl in the scarlet swagger coat. . . . Now, she would remember them all her life!

She was still musing and still trying to be cynical when the bus reached Griffins Edgeworth. She slipped in the snow as she stepped down, and she was still trying to regain her balance when the bus moved on.

She looked around. The place was deserted. A few lights shone from behind faulty blackouts, but on the whole the short street of houses looked like a row of tombstones nestling under snowy shrouds. There was no sign of Ron or the car.

She looked at her watch. The bus was late, so there was no excuse for him. Of course, this snow. . . . She looked at the road that turned right towards the farm. The moon was shining on the smooth centre which had been polished by car wheels. So it wasn't as bad as all that. No, something must have delayed him. She would start walking, and maybe she would meet him on the road.

She set off walking briskly, clutching her case so tightly that in a very short time her fingers in their heavy gloves were frozen into a cramp and she was forced to shift the case to her other hand. It's a lovely night for a walk, she said to herself. It would do her good after sitting in that cold train.

The sky was clear and frosty, and there were innumerable stars. She strode along, looking up at them for a few minutes, then she looked anxiously at the road ahead. No sign of him coming. She looked back. If a car came along she'd thumb it. You never knew who might be in it. There were quite a lot of Americans driving jeeps around this district just now.

She strode on hopefully, the snow crunching under her heavy Land Army boots.

TWO LADIES

MR. BENTLEY bowed stiffly as the stout, over-dressed woman with the large pearl studs came into the department.

'Good afternoon, madam,' he said.

'Good afternoon.' She smiled and sank with a sigh of relief into the chair on the other side of the counter. 'Hot, isn't it?'

'Very hot,' he said.

He leaned his hands on the counter and waited with an impassive face for her order. But she was in no hurry to give it. She wiped her hot face with a small handkerchief, and chatted pleasantly about the weather. Then when he was beginning to lose patience, she said:

'I want to see some stuff for curtains for my drawing-room. Good stuff, y'know. None of your trashy dirt at five and elevenpence-halfpenny. Something real classy. Y'understand?'

'Yes, Mrs. Little,' he said.

He brought out three bales of their most expensive material, the first that came to his hands, and spread them out before her. He looked moodily at his nails and said nothing as she examined the cloth.

'Um, they're nice,' she said. 'Wonder what I should take now? That pale blue and gold would go nice with the furniture, but I like that red and green myself. I like something cheerful, don't you?'

Mr. Bentley nodded frigidly.

'Ummmm.' Mrs. Little pursed her thick lips. 'I suppose

I'd better take the blue and gold. Jeannette would kick up rough if I took the other stuff. She's always on about bein' classy.' She sighed. ' Well, you can send along that blue and gold. You know the measurements? '

' Yes, madam.'

She got up, giving her hat a tweak to the side. ' Oh, my poor feet! I think I'll go right home and stick them in a tub of cold water! '

She glanced regretfully at the garish red and green brocade and was starting out of the department when she stopped. ' By the way, how much is that blue stuff? '

'Twenty-six and six the yard, madam.'

' Okay,' she said. ' Send it along.' And with a gay wave and a ' Cheerio! ' she waddled out of the department.

Disdainfully the young man gathered up the bale of blue and gold cloth and carried it along to the other counter. ' Cut out curtains for Mrs. Little,' he said. ' You have the measurements of her drawing-room windows somewhere, Mr. Grierson.'

' All right, Mr. Bentley,' the other young assistant said.

He started to measure the cloth. ' Didn't take her long to make up her mind, did it? ' he said.

' No, the fat old cow would take whatever you pawned off on her! ' Mr. Bentley laughed sneeringly. ' She's going home to shove her feet in a tub of cold water! '

' She should shove her head in when she's at it,' Mr. Grierson said.

' What a common piece of goods,' Mr. Bentley said. ' You only need to look at her to see that she's no lady.'

' She can't get rid of the fact that her old man was a publican,' Mr. Grierson said. ' It sticks out all over her. All her money can't hide it.'

The phone rang. The buyer for the department answered it. ' For you, Mr. Bentley,' he called.

' Hello,' Mr. Bentley spoke into the mouthpiece with his carefully-rounded Oxford vowels, and when he heard who was at the other end, his face broke into obsequious smiles. He

YSC—D

half-bowed as he said: 'Oh, yes, Lady Chrysler. Certainly, Lady Chrysler. I'll bring them right round, Lady Chrysler. Good-bye. Gooood-bye.'

'That was Lady Chrysler,' he cried excitedly. 'She wants patterns of cloth for her drawing-room curtains.'

Quickly the buyer and the two young men and the apprentice rushed here and there, collecting pattern-books. 'Do you think that will be enough, Mr. Bentley?' asked Mr. Grierson.

'No, I think we'd better have some more, Mr. Grierson,' said Mr. Bentley.

With a pile of pattern-books under each arm, Mr. Bentley presented himself at the Hotel Imperial and asked for Lady Chrysler. He held his head very high as he stalked after the small page-boy, and going up in the lift, he examined himself in the mirror. He took out a small comb and passed it through his smooth black hair.

The page knocked at a door, and when a high voice cried 'Come in,' he opened it, and motioned Mr. Bentley in.

A tall, angular lady with a peevish face was writing at a desk. She glanced up, but when she saw who it was she went on writing. A tall, flabby young man with a small moustache that he kept caressing was lounging in a chair.

Mr. Bentley stood inside the door, holding himself as stiffly as a soldier on parade, a bundle of pattern-books under each arm. Nobody spoke. The lady went on writing, and after glancing at the shop-assistant in a bored way, the flabby young man went on caressing his moustache.

Five minutes passed, then the flabby young man rose and lounged towards the door. Immediately Mr. Bentley sprang out of his way. He dropped the pattern-books on a chair and opened the door.

The flabby young man nodded slightly as he went out.

'Good afternoon, sir,' Mr. Bentley said, bowing.

He stood stiffly to attention again. Lady Chrysler went on writing for another ten minutes, then she threw down her pen and said: 'Now.'

At once the perfect salesman, Mr. Bentley glided forward

and unfolded the pattern-books. Lady Chrysler gazed frigidly through her lorgnette at them.

'This is very nice, your ladyship,' Mr. Bentley murmured obsequiously. 'And this would look charming . . . or this. It's the very latest from our warehouse.'

But Lady Chrysler discarded pattern after pattern with cold insolence. 'Terrible,' she kept saying. 'Simply atrocious.'

'Now this would be lovely in your drawing-room, Lady Chrysler,' said Mr. Bentley, displaying a pattern of the blue and gold brocade that Mrs. Little had bought earlier in the day.

'Horrible,' said Lady Chrysler. 'Atrocious taste.'

'This is very nice,' Mr. Bentley said.

'Well '—Lady Chrysler looked appraisingly at the red and green brocade that Mrs. Little had rejected. 'That might do. How much is it?'

'Twenty-five and sixpence the yard,' he said.

Lady Chrysler snorted. 'Oh, it's far too dear,' she exclaimed. 'You know perfectly well not to bring me anything as expensive as all that. You know perfectly well that I don't want anything over twelve and elevenpence.'

'Certainly, Lady Chrysler,' murmured Mr. Bentley.

Lady Chrysler dismissed him with a haughty gesture. 'No, I'm afraid you have nothing there to suit me. You must bring me more patterns.'

'Certainly, Lady Chrysler,' Mr. Bentley said. 'It'll be a pleasure, Lady Chrysler.'

He bowed himself out.

He returned to the shop, glowing with pleasure. 'She's a perfect lady, Mr. Grierson,' he said, describing the entire interview in detail to his admiring and envious fellow-assistant. 'You should have seen the way she looked at me through her lorgnette.'

THE RED STOT

ONE of the stots was choking. The loon heard it as he was
wheeling the heavy barrow-load of turnips out of the neep
shed, across the muddy ruts in the snow. He sniffed up the
drip at the end of his snub nose. It was just after eight o'clock
on a February morning and it was still so dark that when he
went into it he could not see the rear of the large cattle-shed.
He put down the barrow, sighing from the effort of pushing it
up the short slope that led on to the path beside the troughs. A
few feet below him the cattle were snorting and slobbering at
the turnips in the first two troughs. Their heads were shoved
under the wooden rails. 'Goutyebrute!' the loon cried as a
turnip was sent hurtling in front of the barrow. He heaved it
back into the trough, then he hurled the barrow along to the
third trough. He put it down with another sigh of exhaustion,
pushing back the imitation airman's helmet that he wore, showing his closely-cropped, blind-fair hair. Beads of sweat were
trickling down his brow. He could feel it running coldly down
his chest and back, aggravating the tickliness of his woollen
semmit. He scratched himself.

He made a tremendous effort and tilted over the barrow,
shooting the turnips with a squelching rumble into the trough.
There was a scamper, and heads were shoved under the railing. The cattle dunched each other, their mouths groping
greedily for the turnips. The loon staggered another few yards
and emptied the other half of the load into the fourth trough.
'Another four barryfu',' he muttered.

This was the sort of work that made you wish you were back

44

at the school. Auld Stormont was the coarsest dominie in the
Howe o' the Mearns, but you'd rather get strappit twice a day
than attend til thae store cattle. You were right fed up with
them and you'd be glad when you saw their hint ends on the
way to the Mart.

He was picking up the empty barrow when he heard the
wheezing and hoasting again above the crunching of the other
cattle. He peered over one of the straw-racks. 'It's that reid
ane,' he muttered. 'Chokit again!'

A red stot with a white diamond-shaped mark on its forehead had backed out of the struggling mass and retreated into
the centre of the shed. It was standing, head held high, front
legs braced among the straw- and dung-littered muck, and its
hind legs shoved forward under it. Thick ropes of white
saliva were hanging from its mouth. And it heaved its sides
and stretched its neck as if it were in a death-throes. 'Goutye-
bastard!' the loon cried. 'That's what ye get for gutsin'.
See!'

The stot opened its mouth wide and lowered its head, stretching and retching. But still it could not get the piece of turnip
out of its thrapple. It heaved for a few more seconds, then it
charged again into the crowd around the troughs, butting its
way into the centre of one; where it shoved away the others,
not bothering about the turnips until the other stots had gone
to the neighbouring troughs. Then it grabbed a huge turnip
in its mouth, shaking it vigorously. The loon swore and
wheeled the barrow back to the neep shed.

By the time he had given the cattle four barrow-loads of
turnips and two of potatoes the loon was completely exhausted.
He was wheeling away the barrow when he noticed a brindled
stot with a gentle face standing in the centre of the shed. It
had been shoved away from the troughs. 'Ye stupid hoor!'
he called. 'If ye dinna push yer way in ye'll never get onythin' in this world!'

What a difference it was from that red one! The red stot
was more bother than the rest of them put together. It was
aye choking. Just now it was trying to keep the others away

from the seventh trough which was still almost full of neeps and tatties. It was butting those on one side and lashing out with its hind legs at those on the other.

The loon shook his head, wondering why they did not join together and give it a dunt out of the way. There was plenty of meat for them all. He began to hash the biggest neeps that were left in the first trough. Hearing the clatter of the iron on the stone the cattle rushed away from the turnips they were gnawing in order to get the slices that fell whitely from the hasher. They crowded in so that the loon could not get room to lift the hasher up and down, so he moved to the next trough. But the cattle rushed to it, grunting and paiching in their anxiety to get the best slices. They swallowed greedily, throwing up their heads and stretching their necks to the full. The loon held his face away from their slobbering, fawn-coloured muzzles, slimy with saliva, and their great walloping tongues. 'Keep yer stinkin' breaths oot o' ma face, damn ye!' he cried.

The red stot had been choking again in the middle of the shed. But, although the froth was still clogging its mouth, it came charging in again, sending the other stots hurtling away from the troughs. It seized the huge turnip the loon was try-ing to hash and pulled it away from him. The loon was so angry that he struck the stot across the muzzle with the hasher. 'Take that, ye hoor o' hell!'

Thankfully he flung the hasher back into the neep shed and went into the barn. As he pushed open the large sliding-doors he noticed suddenly that it was light. The sun hadn't risen yet over the snow-covered Mearns hills, but its first rays were shining behind a thin mass of cloud. The rest of the sky was a pale heliotrope. Only this peculiarly shaped mass of cloud was vividly coloured. It was like one of yon birds in the book the dominie had. Flamingoes they were called. Queer-like birds that bed in Egypt or one of those places. . . .

He was dragging bunches of straw and putting them in the racks when he heard somebody say: 'Ay, ay, loon, ye're sortin' them again!'

A tall, bandy-legged man, wearing dirty khaki breeches, was slouching along the narrow path. He had a high-coloured face, and he hadn't shaved for several days. A shapeless cap was stuck jauntily on the side of his head. He stood on the edge of one of the troughs, shoving back the cattle's heads while he looked over the railing at them. 'Ane o' yer stots is chokit, man,' he said.

'Ay,' the loon said.

'Dae ye hash yer neeps?'

'Ay,' the loon said.

'I widna if I were you, boy. That's what makes them choke. Thae three-cornered edges that the hasher makes stick in their guzzles.'

'But the grieve tellt me to hash them,' the loon said.

'Thae cattle ha'e got teeth, boy! What's their teeth for? Dinna you bother aboot the gaffer. I ken mair aboot cattle-beasts than he kens or's ever likely to ken.'

He was repeating this with greater emphasis when the farmer came into the shed and cried: 'Are ye there, cattler?'

The cattler shambled quickly towards him. The loon hurried back into the barn for more straw. He worked so quickly that soon he was almost breathless with exhaustion. He stopped only when the farmer cried: 'Here, loon, seek the grieve if he can gi'e ye a stick. And tell him I want to see him.'

When the loon came back with the grieve, the farmer said: 'Thae beasts 'll ha'e to go to the Mart this mornin'.'

'But I thocht they werena to ging for three weeks yet,' the grieve said.

'Ay, but I got a Ministry o' Food order wi' this mornin's post. It seems the Army needs food.'

'Ye can take the loon wi' ye,' the farmer said to the cattle-man. 'Ging ower there, loon, and dinna let them into the steading.'

The loon stood at the opening between the barn and the potato-shed, holding his stick in readiness, while the grieve opened the gate of the cattle-shed. The cattler went inside. The cattle came out slowly. They blinked and mooed, lowering

their heads and sniffing at the tractor-ruts in the snow. One
or two of them leaped skittishly, but most of them seemed dis-
inclined to leave the shed. But as the cattler prodded some,
they forced the others out. 'Come on, man, come on!' the
cattler shouted irritably to the last beast inside. The loon heard
the whacks of the stick, then the red stot galloped out. Immediately it sent the others into a flurry of activity. They ran
here and there, butting each other and leaping on each other's
backs, mooing and tossing their heels in the air. The loon had
to keep on the alert, waving his stick frantically at those that
tried to get past him. Beside him the cattleman's dog yapped,
rushing at the most forward stots and snapping at them.

'A' richt, gaffer!' the farmer cried.

The grieve stood away from the end of the loan and let the
beasts get past him. Then he scrambled over a fence and ran
across a field, ploughing his way through the snow. 'Awa'
wi' the grieve, loon!' the farmer cried.

The loon followed the grieve. He could see the cattle running down the road, followed by the cattler and his dog. The
grieve was making for an open gate, but before he could reach
it, the foremost cattle had come into the field. They waved
their sticks and shouted, and after some skirmishing the beasts
went back on to the road. 'Now, loon,' said the grieve.
'Awa' doon the field and get oot in front o' them. Just ging
at a walkin' pace.'

The loon scampered down the field, the snow sucking at his
Wellingtons as if it would drag them off his feet. Just ging
at a walking pace! He was running as fast as he could, but
he saw the cattle getting farther and farther away from him.
The cattler was shouting on the road behind him, but except
for an oath here and there he could not make out what the
man was crying. He tried to run faster, but the more he tried
the more the snow sucked at his boots, making him stumble
and slither. He almost cried with relief when he saw the
cattle stopping at a straw-soo about a quarter of a mile down
the loan. And so he stopped running. And when he had
recovered his breath a little he climbed the fence. He wiped

the sweat off his face with his checked scarf while waiting for
the cattler.

'Ay, loon,' the cattler said. 'They're awa' at a richt rate.
They're het wi' bein' in sae long, but they'll soon cool doon.'

'I hope so,' the loon said. 'They're nae the only anes that's
het.'

The cattler began to fill his pipe, rubbing and squeezing the
Irish Roll between his large dirt-engrained palms.

'Will we nae better hurry up?' the loon asked tentatively.
'They'll ha'e a' that stray eaten.'

'Ach, what's a' yer chase?' The cattler laughed. 'They'll
nae dae muckle damage.'

And right enough the cattle had done no damage. One or
two had pulled a few strands of straw out of the soo, but most
of them were too busy galloping round and round it to bother
about anything else. A few shouts from the cattler, some waving of sticks and some yapping from the dog, and soon they
were back on the road. Their gallop had cooled them down a
bit, and they walked quietly. The cattler went in front of
them. The loon walked behind, one hand in the pocket of his
blue dungarees, the other swinging his stick. Now that he'd
got his breath back he'd rather be doing this than spreading
dung or pulling neeps. It was even better than dressing tatties,
and dressing tatties wasn't so bad sometimes; it was warm in
the potato-shed, and there was aye a lot of speak among the
tattie-dressers, and a lot of laughing and chaff.

Most of the snow had disappeared off the road, but there had
been frost earlier in the morning and that made it slippery.
They had safely passed all the open gates, so the cattler came
back to walk beside the loon. Sometimes one of the cattle
would slither on its haunches, but it aye got up quickly when
the cattler yelled at it or prodded it under the tail. The sun
was shining brightly now and it glittered on the snow-laden
branches of some fir-trees. The loon thought they looked like
yon tinsel-covered trees you saw on cards at Christmas.

'There's mair cattle comin' doon that road,' the cattler said.
'We'd better get a move on and get in in front o' them.'

The loon heard men shouting and a dog yapping behind the snow-covered hedges, and when they were passing the end of the road he saw them. The cattler waved his stick and shouted a greeting. 'They're a gey mangy bunch o' stots, thae,' he said.

As they approached Auchencairn several other herds came on to the main road and there was some difficulty in keeping them separated. The cattler walked in front of the lot from Dallow, and the loon and the dog followed them. The loon felt that the herd behind was pressing in on him, and he was relieved when they came to the Auction Mart.

Soon the stots were penned in a large shed. It was full of local farmers and cattlemen, and the atmosphere was thick with tobacco-smoke and the breath of the cattle. The farmers walked about, greeting each other and looking at the cattle. The loon heard one man say when he stopped before the Dallow lot: 'This is a fine bunch. They surely havena been rationed.' His companion said: 'Ay, but ha'e ye seen mine? They're ootside in the pens. A' Silage fed. Come on oot and see them.'

'Silage!' The cattler snorted contemptuously. 'I dinna haud wi' that stuff at a'. It's nae fit for beasts.'

The loon did not listen. He was wondering when the cattler intended to start back for Dallow; he was beginning to feel hungry. It must now be about eleven, he judged. It would take him and the cattler all their time if they were to get back to Dallow before lousing-time at half-past eleven.

But the cattler walked about, looking critically at the other cattle and speaking to cattlemen from neighbouring farms. The loon leaned against a pen, making patterns with his stick on the sawdust-covered floor. The air was getting thicker and thicker. You couldn't see much farther than three yards. Beyond that the men and the beasts were indistinct and then lost.

The loon yawned, wishing he was eating his dinner. His mother had promised to make bannocks this forenoon. They

would go fine with the tattie-soup left over from yesterday.
He looked up when somebody said : ' Hello, John ! '

He had noticed a girl going about among all the men, a
sheaf of papers in her hand, taking note of all the cattle that
came in. He saw now that it was Elspeth Dickson, who had
been in his class at school. He hadn't recognized her in her
swanky pale blue pixie-cap and brown coat with the fur collar.

' Ay, ay,' he said, giving his head a slight jerk to the side.

She leaned against the railing beside him. ' I hear you're
fee-ed at Dallow,' she said.

' Ay,' he said.

' Like it? ' she said.

' Ay, it's a' richt,' he said. ' D'you like this job? '

' Ay, it's all right,' she said.

She twirled her pencil in a strand of dark hair that fell across
her cheek. The loon had never noticed before how pretty she
was. It must be that pixie-cap and that coat. She looked
right grown-up like. He wished he hadn't been dressed the
way he was. Although he was usually very proud of his
working-clothes, he wished that he was wearing his new long-
trousered blue serge Sunday suit.

' It's always a job,' Elspeth said.

' Ay,' he said.

He wondered what he could say to her. They had never
got on very well at school; they had aye been fighting. He
drew some more patterns with his stick.

Elspeth flattened herself against the pen when a man pushing a trolley stopped in front of them. ' Thae anes next,' the
man said, taking some iron-lettered brands from the trolley
and dipping them in yellow paint. He opened the gate and
began to stamp the cattle's haunches with the iron. ' Twenty-
eight to fifty-two, that's Dallow, isn't it? ' he asked Elspeth.

' Yes,' she said, looking at her bunch of papers. ' Poor
things,' she said to the loon. ' They dinna ken what's comin'
to them. You know I'm fair scunnert wi' beef now. I canna
eat it for thinkin' about thae cattle and where the beef comes
from.'

' Ach, dinna be daft,' the loon said, grinning.

But he looked at the gentle-faced brindled stot hemmed in the corner. And he turned away quickly. ' Dinna be soft,' he said to Elspeth. ' That's what beasts are for, aren't they? '

She looked at them pityingly. The loon leaned his elbows on the top rail and tried to look at them in the professional way the cattler looked at them. The red stot was bucking about in the middle of the pen, clearing a place for itself with heels and lowered head. It charged into the corner where the brindled stot cowered and leaped upon it.

The loon did not look at Elspeth; he drew some more patterns in the sawdust. He was glad when he saw the cattler approaching. He readjusted the strap of his helmet under his chin.

' This beats a',' the cattler said, pushing back his cap with disgust. ' That reid ane's been rejected, loon. We'll ha'e to take him back.'

' God! ' the loon said.

' Well, cheerio! ' Elspeth said, moving off. ' I'll be seein' you.'

' Ay ay,' the loon said, glancing at her, then watching the cattler go amongst the cattle to drive out the red stot. The loon hit it a crack on the rump. ' Get on, ye beast! ' he cried.

' What's a' yer chase, loon? ' the cattler said when they had driven the stot into the street. ' Just bide here a meenit till I ging intil this shoppie for fags.'

The stot was snuffling at the gate of old Mrs. Morrison's house. The loon yawned and leaned against the railings, wishing the cattler would hurry up. He was hungry, even if the cattler wasn't. And he was wondering what would happen about this troublesome beast. Would he still have to sort it? Or would it be put in the cattler's charge?

' Hoy! '

The cattler had come out of the shop. He rushed past the loon, waving his stick. His bandy legs curveted on the slippery pavement. But he was too late. The red stot had pushed open Mrs. Morrison's gate and was already half-way up the path. Hearing the cattler's yell, it lurched forward and lumbered into the porch.

'Hell, what are we to dae noo?'

The stot was nuzzling the inner multi-coloured glass door. 'If ye dinna watch it'll ging richt through the glass,' said the cattler. 'What way did ye nae keep an eye on it, loon?'

'Here, man!' he called softly. 'Here, man! Guid lad!'

But the stot stood still, its hindquarters sticking out of the porch with massive disdain. The loon felt like giving them a crack with his stick, but he remembered old Mrs. Morrison's face and what he had heard about her nippy tongue. 'If it moves at a', it'll break that glass and then there'll be hell to pay,' the cattler muttered anxiously. 'What way did ye nae keep an eye on it, loon?'

He chirruped and smacked his lips enticingly, but the beast did not move. He put out his hand and touched it cautiously, but the stot gave such a lurch that the cattler jumped back. 'Christ!' he muttered. 'Ye've been a nuisance ever sin' we got ye. Are ye goin' on to be a worse nuisance, ye ill-gettit hoor?'

Suddenly the loon had an inspiration. He sidled past the stot and pulled the bell. Surely to God the sight of Mrs. Morrison's face would make the stot step back!

But when Mrs. Morrison opened the door it was she who started back. And the stot, as if hypnotized, advanced a few feet into the hall. Then, its bowels contracting with fear at the women's yell, it raised its tail.

.   .   .   .

'God knows what the boss'll say when he hears,' the cattler kept saying as they drove the stot homewards. 'Mrs. Morrison kicked up a hell o' a fuss, but she'll be sure to kick up an even bigger ane wi' him. As if we could help it. . . .'

The loon said nothing. He pushed his hands farther into his trousers-pockets, completely miserable. He wondered what his mother would say if he got the sack. She had been so pleased when he got fee-ed at Dallow. His wage meant so much to them. . . .

'Dammit, snaw again!' the cattler exclaimed suddenly. 'There was ower reid a sky this mornin' for ma taste.'

What had looked like a thin mist creeping down from the hills, flattening out the land so that soon you thought you were walking on a wee bit plateau and that soon you'd come to the edge and fall over into the mist, now turned out to be a small fine snow. You only knew it was snow because the drops stung your face like blunt needles. And already you saw that the bits of reddish clay showing beneath the last fall were growing paler and paler pink as the drops fell on them like icing sugar.

The red stot lumbered from side to side, its head bent against the stinging flakes. Its back and rump were soon covered with the fine white powder, but before the covering got time to thicken the steam from the stot's heaving sides condensed it.

The cattler began to sing an old bothy song, *Macfarlane o' the Sprots o' Burniebosie*. 'Oh, I dinna like Macfarlane,' he roared, hitting the stot a hard smack, making it scamper for a few yards. 'It's awfa, but it's true. . . . His lugs would cast a shadow ower a sax-foot gate. . . .'

'His legs like guttapercha, ilka step his knees gang ki—nack!' the loon joined in, swinging his stick and walloping blindly in the direction of the dark shape in front. 'Macfarlane o' the Sprots o' Burniebosie!'

The snow fell faster and faster, and the flakes grew bigger. Soon they could see only a few yards in front of them. The going got more and more difficult. But on they struggled into the whiteness leading to Dallow, following the dark shape of the lumbering red stot.

THE YEAR OF THE SHORT CORN

ALL forenoon Mrs. Fraser dusted and polished in preparation
for the visitor. She electroluxed every corner of the
living-room, then she started on the stairs and the upstairs
landing. By this time Charles was losing patience. 'Good
God, Ma!' he cried. 'He'll not be going upstairs. It's me
he's coming to see, not the house.'

'Anybody can see that,' Mrs. Fraser said. 'Ye've dug-
danced about in front o' that mirror ever since ye got up this
mornin'. That's the third time ye've changed yer tie! But
it'll do no harm to have the house spotless. He may be interested in houses for all you know. What if he says: "This is
a nice house you've got. I'd like to see over it." What would
ye do then, my man? Ye'd be right ashamed o' me if it
was dirty.'

'Och, yer Granny!' Charles said.

'Dinnie speak disrespectful o' the dead,' Mrs. Fraser said.
'Ma Granny was a decent auld body that wouldnie ha'e
harmed a fly if folk had just left her alone—only they didnie
aye leave her alone, so they just got what was comin' to them!'

'Like her granddaughter!' Charles said. 'She's never backward in coming forward to say her little piece!'

'There's nothin' wrong wi' her granddaughter,' Mrs. Fraser
said. 'Except lack o' money! And a daft galoot o' a son!'

'The daft galoot of a son will be famous yet!' Charles
laughed.

'Famous!' Mrs. Fraser sniffed. 'I've got another word for
it, my man! Ye'll be landin' in the nick if ye write another

book like *The Year of the Short Corn*. My goodness, I get fair black affronted whenever folk speak to me about it. I just hope they dinnie think that the mother in it is me. I wouldnie like them to think I was a woman like that wi' all thae dirty sayings.'

'I don't see what's wrong with the mother in it,' Charles said. 'She's a very good human being. She's got life and vitality and guts.'

'Guts!' Mrs. Fraser laughed. 'Ay, she's got them all right. Her belly seemed to rumble on every second page. If I'd been her I'd ha'e taken a damned good dose o' Maclean's Stomach Powder.'

'All the same, Charlie,' she said, giving the Electrolux another push, 'I dinnie see why ye cannie write a nice book without any swearin' in it. All that swearin's not necessary.'

'Mr. Kerr seemed to enjoy it,' Charles said. 'What does he say in his letter again?'

He read the letter for the tenth time: 'Dear Mr. Fraser, May I say how much I have enjoyed reading your novel *The Year of the Short Corn*? It is one of the best books that have come out of Scotland for many years. You have put the essential bawdiness and raciness of the Scottish character on to paper in a way which few writers have done. Every character is alive and vital, and the entire picture of the rife unemployment and poverty in the industrial areas during the lean years is superb. I wonder if you would care to write anything for us?'

'See!' he cried. 'He likes what I write all right.'

'What time's this Kerr man comin', anyway?' Tom said. 'Give me good warnin', will you, so that I can get out.'

'Oh, don't worry, you'll get good warning,' Charles said. 'We don't want you to be sitting here, reading cowboy magazines, when he comes.'

'Ach, he may be interested in cowboy magazines,' Mrs. Fraser said. 'Maybe he reads them, too.'

'He'd get more fun out of them than he'd get out of the novels of Charles Barnton Fraser, anyway!' Tom grinned.

'Maybe,' Charles said. 'But it's the work of Charles Barnton Fraser he's coming to discuss. So make yourself scarce, big boy! He's coming at three o'clock.'

'Okay, toots!' his brother said. 'I'll scram when the going's good!'

But at ten to three when Charles was hovering nervously from the fire to the window and then from the window to the mirror to touch his hair, Tom picked up a couple of magazines and said: 'I don't think I'll go out after all. I'll away upstairs and read. Shout for me when the tea's ready, Ma. I might as well see some of the fun!'

'I wonder if he'll take a drink, Charlie?' Mrs. Fraser called from the scullery. 'Ye'd maybe better open this bottle o' whisky in case.'

'Here, that's my whisky!' Tom cried. 'I brought it home specially for Dad's birthday.'

'Och, ye can easy get another,' his mother said. 'I must say there's some advantage in havin' a son that works in a pub and gets whisky at cost price. Though ye're a damned nuisance when ye've got a half-day like this, gettin' in ma road. I could plant ye sometimes!'

'Shout for me when the whisky's doled out then,' Tom said. 'I've got to be in on it.'

Charles was struggling with the corkscrew when the bell rang. 'Oh, damn!' he cried.

'I'll answer it,' Mrs. Fraser said.

Charles pulled out the cork quickly, then he smoothed his hair before the mirror above the sink. He was going into the living-room when his mother brought in the visitor from the hall. It took Charles all his time to put out his hand and say: 'How d'you do?'

'How d'you do, Mr. Fraser?' said the girl in the tight-fitting grey costume. She shook back her shoulder-length fair hair, smiling at him. 'You know—you're quite different from what I'd expected! I was looking for a great big hulking tough!'

'Everybody does,' Charles grinned.

YSC—E

'It's that book of his,' Mrs. Fraser said. 'My goodness, I whiles say to myself: Did *he* write it!'

'But you're different from what we thought, too,' she said.

'Yes, we were expecting a sort of middle-aged man,' Charles said. 'I dunno—a sort of old-maidish kind of gent—you know!'

Miss Kerr laughed and sat on the settee with her brief-case on her knee. 'Thank you.' She took the cigarette Charles offered. 'I was amused when you kept calling me "Mr. Kerr" in your letters. I suppose I should have told you, but—well, it was amusing! It's the initials that did it, I s'pose.'

'K.L.P.,' Charles said. 'Yes, there was nothing to guide me.'

'No light in the window for my son!' she said, grinning.

'Katherine Louisa Pauline,' she said. 'But keep it dark.'

'Call me Kitty,' she said.

Mrs. Fraser disappeared into the scullery. Charles sat down on the other side of the fireplace, watching Miss Kerr as she put on a pair of horn-rimmed glasses.

'I liked your book,' she said, opening her brief-case. 'I told you that already, of course, when I asked you if you'd care to write anything for us. I've brought along some more of our publications for you to study.'

She handed Charles a bundle of weekly twopenny papers. 'They're not exactly in your style, of course!' She laughed.

'Hardly!' He grinned.

'But there's money in it,' she said.

Miss Kerr leaned back, her hands hitched inside the top of her skirt. 'I'd like you to consider writing a series for us— a series along the lines of *The Year of the Short Corn*, but without—well, without what my managing director calls its coarseness!'

'Well, I dunno,' Charles said.

'Have you read those papers I sent you at all?' she asked.

'Oh, yes, I looked through them. I know the kind of stuff that's in them, anyway. Most homes in Scotland get one or other of these papers every week.'

'Go on, say it!' she said. 'I read your bit in *The Year of the Short Corn* about the opium of the masses!'

'Will you take a drink, Miss Kerr?' Mrs. Fraser popped her head around the scullery door.

'We-ell!' Miss Kerr smiled. 'If you don't tell my managing director! I'm supposed to be T.T.—but I guess a little snifter wouldn't do me any harm!'

Mrs. Fraser went to the foot of the stairs and shouted: 'Tom!'

Tom stared when he saw Miss Kerr. And Miss Kerr stared back with sea-green, sex-greedy eyes. 'Hello,' she said.

'Now if you'd been Charles Barnton Fraser,' she said. 'You're more like what I expected.'

'Cheers!' she said, taking her drink almost at one gulp.

'Here's mud in your eye!' Tom grinned at her. 'Don't strain your tonsils, Miss Kerr.'

'I never strain anything,' she said. 'And the name's Kitty.'

'Nice easy name to remember,' he said. 'It's right up my street.'

'What I had in mind,' she said to Charles, 'was a series of stories—a different adventure every week—about a character rather like the young girl in your novel. You could make her a shop-assistant, the same as your heroine. Make her young and pretty and, of course, poor. Our readers prefer stories about poor girls who make good in the long run. Make her a sympathetic character, somebody who's always helping lame dogs over stiles. A nice cheery girl with a heart of gold. In one story you could make her help a grumpy old lady. Make her do this old dame a good turn of some kind. And then in the last story of the series the old lady could die and leave her some money. Not a fortune, of course. Say, five hundred or a thousand pounds. Our readers would understand that. It'd be a fortune to them, and they like virtue to be rewarded. I think you should find it easy enough to build this girl up—though, of course, you'd have to leave out a few of your *Short Corn* heroine's less pleasant characteristics, such as—well, sleeping with every Dick, Harry and Tom who asked her!'

'For our papers your heroine would have to be pure,' she said, looking at Tom's broad shoulders.

'Yes, thanks, I don't mind another,' she said to Mrs. Fraser, holding out her glass.

Charles leaned back, sipping his whisky, listening to Miss Kerr's sales-talk and watching the silent overtures she and Tom were making to each other. Apparently what she wanted him to do was to re-write *The Year of the Short Corn*; to emasculate it, tidy it up, give it a happy ending and make it saleable from the Dickson and Gutteridge angle. He realized now that when he got that first letter from her he should have written to say he wasn't interested. He had wanted to do that, but Tom and his mother had kicked up such a fuss. 'Here's your chance to make money,' they'd said. 'You'd be a fool to let the chance slip. Imagine! Folk *asking* for stories —yet you want to refuse them! You're daft!' And his mother had said : 'I aye knew there was somethin' daft about ye, Charlie Fraser, but I never thought ye'd be as daft as refuse *money* when it's offered.' 'I'll be true to my art,' Charles had said grandly. 'True to yer ass!' Mrs. Fraser had retorted. 'What guid's yer art goin' to be to ye if ye're starvin'? No, no, my man, dinnie refuse money when ye get the chance. Money's yer best friend in the long run.'

'A series like this would give you plenty of scope for your comic abilities,' Miss Kerr said. 'Though you'd have to soft-pedal a bit. I see one reviewer said your " humour was of the earth earthy ". Well, we couldn't have that. But you could have one comic character—say the heroine's mother—or no, maybe it would be better for her to be an orphan and live with her auntie. An orphan heroine always goes down well. Yes, she lives with her auntie, who's always getting into a pickle and has a lot of comic sayings.'

'I dunno,' Charles said.

'Of course, *The Year of the Short Corn* is primarily a serious book,' Miss Kerr said. 'I realize that. I realize that it's a dreadfully serious book—a very true-to-life account of work-ing-class life—but it's very funny in places. I thought the scene in the lavatory, for instance, was *screamingly* funny. I was reading it in a bus and I laughed so much I'm sure the other passengers thought I was cracked.'

'Och, it was funny enough,' Mrs. Fraser said, beginning to lay the table for tea. 'But I'm sure there was no need to *print* things like that. I'm sure I don't know where he gets them. He doesn't hear things like that at home.'

'Which of your papers did you want this series for?' Charles asked.

Miss Kerr said *The Women's Circle,* and Mrs. Fraser and she began to discuss this paper which Mrs. Fraser got every week. 'I'm awful fond of the "Doings of Dora",' Mrs. Fraser said. 'My goodness, what a case she is! I'll never forget yon story where she helped the two little bairns to find their father after their stepmother had deserted them. My goodness, she was a right bad lot, wasn't she? But Dora was the boy for her! I'm awful fond of Dora. I look forward to her every week.'

'There you are!' Miss Kerr cried. 'Your mother 'll help you. She knows *exactly* what we want. I'm sure you could get a lot of inspiration from her!'

Charles grinned. He did, but not in the way Miss Kerr was suggesting.

'And I bet you could get a lot of inspiration from Tom!' Miss Kerr winked. 'If you haven't had a lot already! I'll lay a pound to a penny that he was the original of one of the young men who went for a pub-crawl after the football match in the *Short Corn.* Am I right, Tom?'

Tom grinned and looked to see that his mother wasn't listening. 'Yeah, I've been around,' he said. 'You and I must get together some time, Kitty!'

'What's this you've been reading?' she said, picking up one of Tom's cowboy magazines as they sat down to tea. 'D'you ever read these?' she asked Charles. 'But no, of course you wouldn't!'

'Too low-brow for him!' Tom grinned.

'I'm a bit low-brow myself,' Miss Kerr said. 'Though I'm not so keen on the brow part!'

'Still, you should read these, Mr. Fraser,' she said. 'You might get some useful tips out of them. We could use a series of stories like these for some of our boys' papers.'

'I dunno,' Charles said.

'I'm sure you could do it,' she said. 'Why don't you try to write something on these lines between you? Tom could write a bit. Then he could pass it on to you. That's the way lots of our writers work. One thinks the hero into a difficult situation and then his collaborator has to think him out of it into an even more difficult one. They keep passing the buck to each other.'

'I'm sure you could do that, Charlie,' Mrs. Fraser said. 'My goodness, I just wish I could write—but it takes me all my time to write a letter!'

'It's really very simple,' Miss Kerr said.

'And mind you,' she said, 'for our publications you don't need any *fine* writing. You can use as many cliches as you like. In fact we prefer you to use cliches. Our readers understand them much better.'

'I dunno,' Charles said.

Listening to her and mentally noting the flirtation between her and Tom for future use, Charles wondered about Miss Kerr. Did she honestly believe in this muck she was touting? One minute he thought she did; then the next she would make some remark that made him think her tongue was in her cheek.

'I wrote a novel once,' she said. 'It was something like yours—well, not *exactly,* but a little bit. It was about a poor girl trying to make good—a minister's daughter . . .'

'But she kept her virtue!' She laughed. 'Not like *your* heroine.'

'Mind you, we pay well,' Miss Kerr said. 'We could give you thirty bob a thousand to start with—and then if we like the stuff we'll go up to thirty-five bob and so on. I'm sure you could write at least ten thousand words a week.'

'Ten thirty bobs. . . .' Tom began to count.

'I dunno,' Charles said.

He thought of the twenty-five pounds he'd got for *The Year of the Short Corn*. Despite the good reviews in the literary papers, his publishers said the book wasn't selling at all. I suppose it's only what they call a literary success, he thought ruefully.

'The money's all right,' Miss Kerr said.

'Yes, the money's all right,' he said.

But he wondered. . . . He knew these papers. He knew what a bad moral effect they had on the women and girls who read them. And on the men—for there were lots of men who read that love-tripe, too, and lapped it up. He didn't want to help in any way to propagate such insidious anti-social nonsense. It was dishonest, what he was fighting against in *The Year of the Short Corn*. But, as far as he was concerned, it was the year of the short corn all right! Money wasn't coming in as he'd expected. His short stories came back with great regularity: even from the most highbrow magazines, which didn't pay much anyway when they *did* take one.

'I don't see why you shouldn't try it, Charlie,' Mrs. Fraser said. 'My goodness, I'd jump at the chance like a shot if I could only write.'

'He'd be a fool if he didn't,' Tom said.

'You've spilled a mouthful, brother,' Miss Kerr said.

'One thing,' she said. 'Keep off politics. There must be no trouble between master and man. No religious differences. No trade union disputes. You mustn't even mention any of these things. We want something that can be read in the family circle.'

'The good people must always come out on top,' she said, taking a cigarette from Tom. 'And you must clearly differentiate your characters. They must be either black or white. You mustn't allow any sympathy to creep in for the unpleasant types. In fact you should keep off them as much as possible. If you do have them, you must see that they get their just deserts at the end of the story. Your heroine can always forgive them, of course. Our readers like a bit of sentimental forgiveness worked in.'

'Heavens!' she cried, rising quickly from the table. 'Look at the time. I'll have to fly to catch my train back to the Fantasy Factory.'

She giggled. 'That slipped out. Sorry! It's what a very earnest friend of mine calls it when he lectures me about being a bad little girl!'

'Well, what about it, Mr. Fraser?' she said, picking up her brief-case. 'Twenty stories, four thousand words each. You could rake in quite a tidy little sum for that. I'll have a talk with my managing director and see if we can't give you thirty-five bob a thousand to start.'

'I dunno,' Charles said.

'Of course you will!' She laughed. 'You see what you can do about it, Mrs. Fraser! Good-bye, thank you so much for the tea—and the whisky! Good-bye, Tom!'

'I'll see you to the bus-stop, Kitty,' Tom said. 'You might lose your way before you got there!'

'You mean somebody might run away with me!'

'Good-bye, Miss Kerr,' Charles said.

'What did I tell you!' she cried. 'Call me Kitty!'

'Well, you'll think it over, won't you?' she said, shaking hands and following Tom out. 'In fact, you'll do more than think it over, won't you! You'll let me have a couple of sample stories pretty soon.'

Charles felt the trap closing round him. 'I'll see,' he said.

'Of course you will!' She smiled gaily. 'Now, remember all the things I've told you. And remember——' She turned half-way down the garden path and shook her finger—'no lavatory stuff!'

BETTY PATERNOSTER AND THE
OLD TABBIES

IT was early yet for the regular locals, and the four soldiers were trying to relieve their boredom by playing darts. But they brightened when the door opened suddenly and a tiny, black-coated woman rushed in.

'Give us a pint, 'Arry, for God's sake!' she cried, leaning against the bar and sighing with relief in much the same way as a shipwrecked sailor clutching dry land. 'Oh, I 'ave 'ad such a scare!'

Sergeant Wells winked at Private Spottiswoode. They had seen the old woman before in the Black Bull, but she had never behaved in such a dramatic way. Usually she sat quietly in a corner and drank beer with several other old women. They knew that she lived in the almshouses and that her name was Betty Paternoster. They always called her 'The Ventriloquist's Doll'. Her head was too big for her tiny body, and it lolled on her shoulders. She wore an enormous black toque shaped like a flower-pot. A large jet buckle on the front still secured the ends of a bunch of broken-off ospreys.

The sergeant had been preparing to throw another dart, but he balanced it in his hand and moved over to the bar, reaching out for his half-finished pint. 'Now for some fun!' he whispered to Spottiswoode.

'Ta, 'Arry!' Betty Paternoster grabbed her drink and took a deep gulp before she raked in her purse. 'Lordame, but I needed that! I needed it bad!'

'Wot's the matter with you, gal?' the landlord said. 'You been seeing 'obgoblins?'

'No, worse nor that.' She took another gulp. 'I been seeing mice!'

She carried her beer to the settee beside the fire and hoisted herself on to it, perching on the edge like a comical little crow. Her little feet dangled two or three inches from the ground so that she looked more like a ventriloquist's dummy than ever. 'It's them old tabbies in the alms'ouses,' she said. 'They knows 'ow I hate mice. They knows I hate mice worse nor anything.'

She put her drink down beside her and took a white paper bag from her pocket. She unrolled the paper and was putting in her finger, but she drew it back and shuddered. 'This is wot done it,' she said. 'This snuff. I sent little Florrie 'Empseed to the shop for it, and it was then they played the trick on me.'

'They knows 'ow I can't live without me snuff,' she said. 'And they knows 'ow I 'ates mice. Ooooo, they are 'orrible old women!'

'What happened, ma?' the sergeant asked, winking again to the others.

'I saw Florrie going past with 'er auntie in the pram,' she said, pushing up her hat from her forehead. 'Ooooo, she is a one, Florrie is! She's only fourteen, but she'll come to a bad end, that she will. The way she wags 'er little tail and eyes all the men! Ooooo, it is wicked! I just wondered wot the Good Lord was thinking about it as I watched 'er sailing along there with 'er auntie in the pram.'

'Is the old lady a cripple?' one of the soldiers said politely.

Old Bet took a pinch of snuff, then she rubbed the point of her sharp little nose with her rheumaticky knuckles. 'Wot old lidy?' she said. Then she cackled. 'Ooooo, you mean Florrie's auntie! Lordame, boy, no! Florrie's auntie's only three! Florrie's mother's one of sixteen children and she 'ad Florrie before 'er own mother 'ad finished with 'ers. She was nothing but a kid 'erself. Ooooo, yes, it's in the blood. Bad blood, that's wot Florrie's got.'

She took another drink. 'Bad blood!' she said, placing her

hands together as if she were praying and putting them between her knees. 'Oh, it is terrible to think of a young gal like Florrie coming to a bad end!' She rocked backwards and forwards, kicking her little feet together with excitement. 'Ooooo, I am glad that I ain't 'er. Little does she know wot lies before 'er.'

She finished her drink and said broodingly: 'Serve 'er right, too, for putting a mouse in a pore old lidy's bag of snuff.'

'Even if it were a dead mouse,' she said. 'But it was them old tabbies wot put 'er up to it. Ooooo, I 'ates them, nasty old cats that they are. Why shouldn't I come 'ere for me beer, and why shouldn't I take snuff? I ain't doing them any 'arm, am I?'

'That's right, ma,' the sergeant said. 'Have another drink?'

'I don't mind if I do,' old Bet said. 'Well, 'ere's another five 'undred a year!' she said, raising her glass. 'May we spend it as quick as we spent the last lot!'

'What would you do if you had five hundred, ma?' Private Spottiswoode said.

Bet giggled and resettled her hat. She leaned forward, her lashless eyes wide open and her bloodless lips curved in over her gums. The soldier in the corner saw her face only as a large white circle with three black holes in it.

'Know wot I would do?' she said. 'Well, I'll tell yer.'

She took another gulp of beer and leaned back. 'I'd give them old tabbies in the alms'ouses a jolly good drink—just to see if it'd liven 'em up a bit. Oooooo!' she giggled. 'Shouldn't I love to see old Kitty 'Obson three sheets in the wind! Wouldn't it be fun if she started to jig around the backyard in 'er nightie!'

She took another drink and shook her head mournfully. 'But I shall never see that,' she said. 'Old Kitty wouldn't dare touch a drop. She's too scared. She's a Philistine, that's wot she is. A Philistine!'

'She won't never know wot she's missing,' she said, draining her glass. 'A drop of beer does yer good. It mikes yer forget, don't it?'

'That's right, ma!' the sergeant said. 'Have another?'

'No, it's my turn,' the private in the corner said. 'I'm in on this, too!'

By this time the pub was beginning to fill up. Old Bet nodded and called greetings to her acquaintances. Some of them seemed surprised to see her companions. ''Aving a night out, Bet?' one man said. 'You better watch yourself, gal!'

The soldiers crowded around her as if trying to shut her away from the other locals. They made no move to contact their usual pub-pals. The sergeant sat on one side and Spottiswoode on the other. Wells looked over the old woman's head, raising his eyebrows and holding up four fingers as she accepted another drink from Private Phipps.

'I do 'ope the beer don't go done to-night,' Bet said. 'Oh, I was annoyed when they was all sold out one night a week ago—last Tuesday it was. Oh, I did miss me glass!'

She held up her drink and nodded benignly before taking a gulp. 'I 'ear there's Americans coming to Pomfret Pond,' she said conversationally, wiping her lips. 'Ooooo, won't the gals be pleased! Pore young men, they won't never get no peace. All the gals 'll be after them. Clingin' round them. They're fine figures of men and they've got plenty money.'

'I reckon they'll have to put that kid whatdoyoucaller—Florrie!—under lock and key!' the sergeant said, grinning.

'They'll 'ave to put more than Florrie under lock and key,' Bet said, putting down her empty glass. 'Ooooo, all them gals won't 'alf be 'aving a time! They'll be chasing after them like stink! Women *are* wicked. They'll do anything for money.' She nodded graciously as the sergeant handed her another pint. 'Thank you! Well, 'ere's good luck to the Yanks!' She raised her glass. 'Pore lads, they'll be 'ounded like anything. Them gals 'll be waiting for 'em at all the corners and follerin' them into the pubs. Oooo, it is wicked!' She shook her head so violently with indignation that her hat slipped over her forehead. She jerked it back and said : ' Now, I wouldn't dare interfere with 'em. I'd be too scared.'

' Oh, ma! ' The sergeant nudged the soldier next him.

' No, I wouldn't drag on to any man,' old Betty said.

' No, but he might drag on to you! ' The private in the corner giggled.

' That he wouldn't,' Bet said vehemently. ' I shouldn't give 'im the chance. I'd run away. I'd knock daylight out of 'im! '

' If the Yanks are such fine figures of men,' Spottiswoode said, picking up the empty glasses and moving towards the counter, ' they might knock daylight out of you, ma! '

' That they shouldn't,' Bet said, opening her coat and clearing her throat as she expanded her shrunken bosom. ' I shall be fit for 'em! What's a fine figure, anyway? It's the 'eart that counts. Lots of men with fine figures are just blackguards.' She took a drink and leaned back with satisfaction. ' Anyway, lots of them Americans ain't got such fine figures, anyway,' she said. ' They got short little legs. They're just sawed-off little runts.'

Over the top of the old woman's head the sergeant held up six fingers. Spottiswoode held up seven. ' Feels more like ten,' the sergeant said. ' I must pay a call! '

' Hasn't she been yet? ' he whispered to Spottiswoode when he came back.

' Not her! '

' It's a wonder to me where the old girl puts it all.'

Bet was standing in front of the settee, conducting with the hand that held her glass while the private in the corner and Private Phipps vied with each other in singing *Nellie Dean*. Spottiswoode kept looking at her waving glass and he shrank back expectantly, but the old woman's hand was quite steady.

' Wot about a song from yourself, Bet? ' one of the locals cried. ' Give them *Waiting at the Church*! '

' No, me singing days are over,' she giggled. ' Still, I don't mind if I do.'

She struck an attitude in the centre of the floor, placing one hand on her hip and giving the other one a flourish. 'Music, maestro, please!'

The sergeant nudged Spottiswoode. 'It's working! We'll have to carry her home yet!'

Spottiswoode shook his head. 'Not by a jugful! She can hold a whale of a lot more yet. She's a lot tougher than I am, I must say. And look at those two!'

The other two soldiers were leaning against each other. They listened in a glassy-eyed daze while old Bet sang innumerable verses about a young bride waiting for a groom who never came. A number of locals joined in the choruses. At the end the old woman swept them an elaborate curtsey and bowed royally at the applause. 'Ooooo, that 'as made me dry,' she cried.

The sergeant weaved his way to the counter for more drinks. Phipps caught him by the elbow. 'Not for us, pal,' he said thickly. 'We can't take it! We're going home!'

Old Bet waved cheerily to them as they staggered out. 'Pore lads, they're feeling a bit under the weather,' she said. 'But you can't blame 'em, can you? It must be 'ell to be stationed in a dead-and-alive 'ole like Pomfret Pond. I knows 'ow I feel meself. If it wasn't for a drop of beer occasionally I dunno wot I would do. A drop of beer does yer good. It makes yer forget, don't it?'

'If only Kitty 'Obson would take a drop,' she said. 'Ooooo, it would do 'er good, wouldn't it? The old 'ypocrite that she is!'

She was telling the sergeant and Spottiswoode more about Kitty and about the time she had pulled Kitty's carnations up by the roots—'Just to 'ave a bit of me own back you might say!'—when the landlord cried: 'Another five minutes, ladies and gentlemen!'

'Good lordame!' Bet cried. 'Is it turning-out time already? Wot a shame! Just as we was beginning to get merry.'

'There's still time for another drink, ma,' the sergeant said.

Bet giggled and dropped a curtsey as she took her drink. 'Well, 'ere's fun, boys!' she cried. 'Ooooo, I ain't been so 'appy for ever such a long time! It's 'ateful to 'ave to go back to them old tabbies in the alms'ouses. Oooo, I do wish one of them flying-bombs would come and knock the whole place down!'

The sergeant whispered excitedly to Spottiswoode. Then he went to the bar and consulted with the landlord. He came back with six bottles of beer. 'Stuff some of these in your pockets,' he said to his pal. 'We'll go home with you, ma,' he said to Bet. 'You don't mind, do you?'

'That I don't,' she giggled. 'But wot will them old faggots say! Oooo, it will be fun! Come on, let's go!'

The sergeant and Spottiswoode each took an arm, but old Betty was firmer on her feet than they were. 'You boys better look after yourselves,' she said. 'I'm all right. See, there you go, you dopey!' she cried to Spottiswoode who had almost bumped into a lamp-post. ''Ere, let me take your 'and!'

'Oh, we won't be 'ome till morning!' she began to sing as they approached the gloomy bulk of the almshouses. 'Oh, we won't be 'ome till morning! For it's a birthday every night!'

She led them round to the back and through the yard. 'The front door's always locked at eight o'clock,' she said. 'Old Kitty 'Obson sees to that! Oooo, you'd think the alms-'ouses belonged to Kitty—she do go on so! Mind your 'eads as you come in!' she warned them, opening the back door. 'Them 'ouses wasn't built for tall men!' She chuckled as she led them along a passage. 'They wasn't built for men at all, if you ask me! Nobody but a lot of old tabbies would live in 'em.'

Spottiswoode was last, and he fumbled with the door handle. But it would not fasten properly, so he left it ajar, thinking: We'll be going out again in a few minutes. He was following the sergeant and Betty Paternoster into her room when a door along the corridor opened and a little old woman scurried out. She was muttering angrily, and she banged the back door shut and locked it. Spottiswoode heard her say : 'People should learn to close doors after 'em. Making such an uproar at this time of night! '

' Did you hear that? ' he said to the sergeant.

' Oh, was that old Kitty? ' Bet said, jumping down from a chair after turning on the gas. ' Ooooo, she will be mad! '

The sergeant put the bottles of beer on the table. ' We'd better not stop, ma! We'd better be going.'

' Oh, wot's all your 'urry? ' Bet said. ' The night is young! '

' And you're so beautiful! ' she and the sergeant sang together, then they both laughed. ' No, ma, we'd better go,' he said. ' We'd like to stop for a chat, but there's no sense in you getting yourself into hot water on account of us.'

' But wot am I going to do with all them bottles? ' Bet said.

' Throw a party! ' Spottiswoode grinned. ' Invite old Kitty and fill her full! '

' Oooo, that would be fun, wouldn't it! ' Bet's eyes glinted with merriment. ' I guess I'd end by throwing some of the empty bottles at 'er! '

' Well, good night, ma! ' The sergeant shuffled awkwardly. ' It's been a fine evening, hasn't it? We've enjoyed ourselves. Thanks a lot! '

' Thank you! ' Bet said. ' I ain't enjoyed myself so much for—oh, ever such a long time! '

' I'll let you out the front way,' she said. ' Seeing as 'ow that old tabby 'as locked the back door.'

' Brrr, it's like a prison, isn't it? ' Spottiswoode said, looking at the great stone staircase and the huge oak door with all its bolts and locks. Old Bet cackled and muttered something that he did not catch. ' How are you going to get it all shut up again, ma? ' the sergeant asked, pushing back the bolts.

' Oh, I shall manage,' Bet said. ' I'll stand on this great chest 'ere. It's 'andy for anybody as small as me. Only thing it's ever been useful for, I guess! I always calls it Kitty 'Obson's 'Ope Chest! '

' I 'ope she'll find a burglar in it one day! ' She giggled

and held the door open for them. 'Good night, boys. Thanks for ever such a lovely time.'

They stood outside and listened to her shooting in the bolts. 'You all right, ma?' the sergeant cried.

'Yes, I'm all right,' she called back, and they heard a thump as she jumped down from the wooden chest. 'Good night, boys! Be good!'

They stood for several seconds, then they began to walk slowly up the street. 'Reckon the poor old gal 'll catch it from those other old tabbies in the morning,' the sergeant said after a while.

'Ah, but she'll be fit for them, don't you fear!'

They walked a bit more, then suddenly they stopped and began to laugh almost hysterically. 'Funny, wasn't it?' the sergeant spluttered. 'I reckon it must have cost us a small fortune, and yet we didn't manage!'

'No, she had us on, boy!' Spottiswoode giggled.

'Poor old girl,' the sergeant said. 'She'd need to be tough in that great prison of a place! Come on, boy, let's get to kip!'

THE POOL

I HADN'T been at the Portobello Pool since the summer before the war, seven years ago. I realized this when I heard
my sister-in-law say it was open again, after being closed during the war. I don't know what made me want to go. Maybe
I wanted to see if I could recapture old times or something.
Maybe I was at a loose end. When you've been away from
home for over six years and you come back and find all your
old pals married or dead or scattered or something you take
funny notions.

The last time I was at the Pool it was with my pal, Ginger.
We'd been pretty young then—twenty-two. It's a long time
ago, and I've been places since then, but I remember it all as
clearly as though it had happened yesterday.

I remember Ginger saying: 'It costs two pounds seven and
a penny to get married.'

And I'd said: 'I'd look at my two pounds seven and a
penny a lot of times and then I'd put it back in my pocket.'

'You!' Ginger said.

'You would,' he said. 'If everybody was like you mankind
would soon die out.'

'Why should it?' I said. 'Because people stopped flinging
around their two pounds seven and a pennies doesn't mean
that the race wouldn't continue.'

'Marriage is a lottery,' I said.

We were standing at the G.P.O. waiting for Nelly and her
pal, Babs. It was a Sunday and we were all going to the
Pool. Ginger and Nelly were going to the Pool all right.

74

They'd got caught and they couldn't afford to get married.

I remember that we talked tough the way they talk in American movies, and all the time we were scared stiff. We didn't know at the time we were scared stiff. It's only now that I realize this. I'm seven years older, and seven years is a long time. But then we looked tough and we acted tough the same as everybody we saw around us. But all the time we were scared, and I reckon most of the people we saw were scared too. Everybody was scared at something. Maybe it was because they hadn't a job or couldn't pay their rent, or maybe it was because they'd gotten themselves into a fix like Ginger and Nelly. But mainly I think it was because they knew the war was coming. We all felt that something was going to happen in that summer of 1939.

'What do people do when they haven't got two pounds seven and a penny?' Ginger said.

'Don't ask me,' I said. 'I never had two pounds seven and a penny.'

Nelly and Babs came along then, and we stopped worrying about money. Nelly was a cute little piece with curly black hair. She had on a checked suit and one of these tennis-bandeaus. Babs was cute, too. It was the first time I'd met her. She had a towel and her bathing-costume rolled under her arm.

We got on a Portobello tram. It was packed, mostly with fellows and girls about our own age, with towels rolled under their arms. Most of the fellows wore bright blue or green sports jackets and brown and white shoes, and the dames wore little pixie-caps or bandeaus. That harsh cyclamen was a pretty popular colour then.

Everybody talked loud. The top deck of the tram reverberated with snappy wisecracks that we'd all heard in different films. A crowd of kids about sixteen or seventeen at the front of the tram were singing *Let's Fall in Love*. I'll always remember that was the song. Because Babs and me sort of hummed it at each other. 'Our hearts were made for it. Why be afraid of it? Let's fall in looove!' But Ginger and Nelly didn't sing, and they didn't say much; they were too busy doing mental arithmetic. It wasn't so much the initial two pounds seven and a penny; it was what they were going to do after that. Ginger was getting only twenty-two and six a week and didn't look as if he'd ever get any more. And Nelly was getting only fifteen bob.

Babs and I talked a lot between singing. She was a cute kid all right. The more I looked at her and the way her eyebrows slanted up like Marlene Dietrich's the more I understood how Ginger and Nelly had got themselves into such a fix. But I wasn't going to be such a fool as that, I said to myself. I had no two pounds seven and a penny to throw around.

The crowds were fairly flocking into the Pool. As we came off the tram we could see the High Dive over the cream-coloured walls and the clock on top of the Pool Restaurant. It was twenty past three.

I remember the time because it was twenty past four when I first kissed Babs. We'd been playing around in the water, then we'd come out and were sunning ourselves, and some-how or other we'd got to pawing each other a bit, and then I kissed her.

I didn't realize what I was doing until Nelly and Ginger laughed, and Nelly said: 'Do you two aim to make a public exhibition of yourselves?'

And so we got away a bit from each other. I pretended I was watching a beefy old gent doing a fancy stroke. 'Look at him!' I said. 'Kidding himself on he's a youngster!'

'I hate to see old men swimming,' Nelly said. 'I'm always terrified they'll conk out.'

'They shouldn't go into the deep end,' Babs said. 'There should be a law against it.'

'There should be a law against anybody going into the deep end,' I said, grinning.

'Caution is his middle name,' Ginger said.

Babs jumped up and caught my hand. 'Coming in again?'

'No,' I said. 'I'd rather sit here and watch.'

'He's a ghoul,' Ginger said. 'He's hoping somebody'll get drowned.'

'Yessir!' I said. 'As long as it's not this baby!'

Babs kept on pressing me, but I wouldn't go in again. I'd had enough. I didn't want to have to do mental arithmetic like Nelly and Ginger.

I saw Babs once or twice after that, but then the war came and I didn't see her any more. Once or twice I've thought about her in the past six years, but not very much. I've had lots of other things to take up my attention. I've got around and had some good times.

I was thinking about all this as I stood at the G.P.O. waiting in a queue for a Portobello tram. And I don't know what it was, but I began to feel a bit old. It was funny. I'd never had that feeling all the time I was in the Army. It's just since I came home that I've noticed it. I've noticed it especially when I've seen that the kids in our street are young men and women now. It's like the feeling I had one night in a pub when a young sub-lieutenant spoke to me. He said: 'You're Tommy Geddie, aren't you?' I said I was, wondering who the hell he was. And then he said 'I'm John Cruickshank,' and I remembered the last time I'd seen him he was a kid of fourteen delivering our milk.

The feeling got worse as I got on top of the tram. There were so many kids on it: young fellows and girls in their early twenties. Made me feel like a grandfather! And there was a crowd of youngsters singing *I Dream of You*. It was just like old times. Still . . . I wasn't dressed any different from them and I'm sure I didn't look any older, but I felt uncomfortable. I began to wish I had somebody with me, somebody I could talk to and fool around with. Somebody like Ginger. . . .

Poor old Ginger, he'd got shot down on ops over Germany. Nelly hadn't liked being a widow very much, and the last I heard she was knocking around with a Yank. I expect she's away by this time as a G.I. bride. Nelly wasn't one for waiting long.

I wondered about Babs. The last time I saw Nelly she said Babs was in the A.T.S. Probably she was married by this time. Maybe she was a G.I. bride, too. . . .

I must say those kids on top of the tram scared me a bit. They all talked so loud, and they acted so tough. They kept shouting wisecracks at each other: wisecracks I'd heard in films I'd seen in the last few weeks. I tried to tell myself they were just the same kind of people as me and Ginger and Nelly and Babs had been. They were just the same; it was just that I was a wee bit older. I'd been places and seen things those kids had never seen. That was all. They were just like me and Ginger under the skin. In fact they didn't look any different. The fellows wore bright checked sports jackets, though some of them were in uniform. And the girls wore bandeaus just the same as Nelly and Babs, only they'd arranged them a bit different. Those that didn't have bandeaus had their hair bunched on top of their foreheads and falling shoulder-length at the back. There really wasn't any difference. Seven years wasn't such a long time after all.

I took a dekko at my reflection in the tram-window. I didn't look any different from any of the other fellows. No grey hairs, nothing like that.

When the tram stopped at the Pool there was a rush to get off. A crowd of guys were bunched at the top of the stairs. I was standing, waiting for them to get down. One of them stood aside and said: 'After you, old man!'

That rankled a bit. I kept thinking about it. I suppose it was perfectly natural for the bloke to call me 'Old man.' He probably called all his pals that. I used to do the same when I was his age. But—well, it was this standing aside for me that got my goat. I'd never have done that if I'd been in his position.

It sort of took the gilt off the bright sunny day. I loafed around the Pool, watching the swimmers. There were all shades of sunburn, and all stages of nudity and semi-nudity. And almost everybody was young. There were hardly any middle-aged people at all. The only ones I saw were two elderly women, evidently sisters and spinsters, who were sitting side by side, spectating. I wondered idly as I passed them what kind of sex-thrill they got out of it. They looked kind of funny and out of place. This wasn't a place for old people at all.

Everybody seemed to have somebody else with them. Fellows and girls, fellows with other fellows, girls with girls, young men with kids, young women with kids. I stood for a while at the shallow end, watching a young bloke trying to teach his kid to swim. The kid kept calling: 'Daddy! Daddy! I'm goin' to sink!' The bloke just told him to go ahead and not be a mutt. And he grinned at me and said: 'I guess we've all felt like that at some time.'

I talked to him for a while, then his wife came up with another kid, so I moved on. But I was beginning to feel a bit strange with nobody to talk to amongst all this crowd. I don't know what it was. In the Army I'd never felt like this; I'd always had plenty of people to talk to—too many around me sometimes. But here it was as if I were walking in some sort of isolation. As if I had leprosy or something.

I leaned on the rail, overlooking the deep end, just above the spot where I'd kissed Babs. I was leaning like this when a girl in A.T.S. uniform came and leaned beside me. Something in the way she stood made me look at her again. She was like Babs a bit. It was just a bit, but something in the way she held her head brought back memories.

She saw me looking at her, and she looked away quickly. Then she looked back, and then she smiled. She was a cute kid all right. Nice grey eyes and nice fair hair, a shade darker than Babs'.

'Warm, isn't it?' I said.

'Terrible,' she said.

'Uncomfortable things, uniforms, when you're hot,' I said.

'You've said it,' she said.

'Glad to get rid of mine, anyway,' I said.

'I've three months to go yet,' she said.

'Still!' she laughed. 'I don't need to worry about spending my coupons just yet!'

The radio was playing *I Dream of You*. From the loudspeaker near us the words came rolling out: 'How can you ever know . . . the way I feel. . . .'

As if from a great distance I seemed to hear Ginger say again with twenty-two years old insolence: 'Caution is his middle name.'

'Oooooh!' the A.T.S. girl cried. 'Surely that kid's too young to go in the deep end?'

'Not him,' I said, glancing over the rail at the kid who'd taken a header into the pool. 'He knows what he's doing.'

'Maybe,' she said. 'But if I were his mother I'd be scared stiff to let him come here and do that.'

'But you're not his mother, sister!' I laughed. 'You can't learn young enough!'

'Like to come to the restaurant for an ice-cream?' I said.

'That would be swell,' she said.

I'm taking Helen to the pictures on Wednesday night. If it cost two pounds seven and a penny to get married seven years ago, what does it cost now? Not that I care. If it cost only ten bob I'd still look at it twice and then put it back in my pocket.

· GLAMOUR BOY AMONG THE NEEPS

(For Bob and Gladys)

I

ONCE or twice during the night the farmer's wife awoke and listened to the wind howling and to the soft spatter of snow on the window. The sounds made her apprehensive. Surely nothing as bad as that would happen. . . . It would be terrible if it did. They had had him for three days already. Surely they couldn't have him any longer. . . . And she snuggled down again against her husband, trying to reassure herself. . . .

But in the morning when she awoke and saw the whiteness seeping through the cracks of the blackout she knew that what she had feared had happened.

'George!'

George grunted and turned over at her nudge. 'What is it, lass?' he mumbled.

'It's nine o'clock,' she said.

'Ach, it's nae that time already,' he said. But he sat up, yawning. Then suddenly he pinched her and leaped out of bed. 'Where's my sark?' he cried.

She watched him struggling into his clothes. 'Take down the blackout, George,' she said. 'I'm feared that we're snowed up.'

'Ay, we're snowed up all right,' he said, looking out and grinning. 'Well, well, I must away and see the grieve and see what he's put the men ontil.'

Elizabeth shuddered when she saw the huge drifts. It looked worse than last winter, and then they had been snowed

81

up for three days. Heavens, if that happened again she'd go crazy!

Mr. Swanson was sitting at the table when she went into the dining-room. 'Good morning, Mrs. Dickie,' he said, looking up from a huge plateful of ham and eggs.

'Good morning,' she said, and passed on into the kitchen.

'Well, well, Jessie,' she said to the stout maid who was standing beside the cooker, making toast. 'It's some morning!'

'Ay, is it,' Jessie said. 'It looks as though that Glamour Boy 'll nae be able to get awa'.'

'Oh, don't say that, Jessie!' Elizabeth screwed up her pretty face with disgust. 'That would be just the last straw! We've had him for three days already.'

'Well, I widna be surprised if we had him for another three wi' this snaw,' Jessie said, putting two rashers of bacon in the frying-pan. 'Are ye for an egg this mornin'?'

'I don't think so.'

'His Nabs has had three,' Jessie said. 'I never saw a man wi' such a guts. I felt like sayin' til him, "D'ye ken that eggs are rationed?"'

'Never mind, Jessie, we'll soon get rid of him,' Elizabeth said, sitting down at the kitchen table. 'I think I'll just have my breakfast in here. I couldn't bear his company another morning.'

'Did he finish last night?' Jessie said.

'Yes, he got all the lights in the steading repaired. He was to go this morning. But now . . .'

'Ay, it's a blue lookoot wi' this snaw,' Jessie said. 'He'll never get his car doon the loan. The grieve says he's nivir seen such drifts. The men are a' castin', but I doot they'll nae shift it. We'll need the snaw-plough.'

'Well, let's hope it comes quick and lets Mr. Swanson away,' Elizabeth said. 'Three days of his company has been more than enough for me.'

'And for me!' Jessie said, glowering.

Elizabeth smiled and began to eat her breakfast. Mr. Swanson—nobody had ever found out what his first name was—had set Jessie's back up the first night by saying that his hot-water bottle was leaking, and he had caused so much fuss that Jessie had been forced to give him her own. 'As if I could help the bloody thing,' she had said to Elizabeth. 'I just hope ma stone bottle burns his big fat backside as often as it has burned mine!'

'It's a dreadful morning, Mrs. Dickie.'

Elizabeth looked up at the voice and saw the Glamour Boy, as Jessie had christened him, standing in the doorway. 'Yes, isn't it?' she said.

'Looks as if I'll not be able to get away,' he said, crossing to the window and looking out at the snow-covered steading. 'It would be a job if I got snowed up, wouldn't it?' He laughed.

'Still, this is a very pleasant spot to get snowed-up in,' he said. 'I couldn't have chosen a better place, could I?'

Elizabeth put a forkful of bacon in her mouth and gave a vague mumble. Mr. Swanson stood with his hands in his pockets and looked out of the window, whistling softly. He was a big, flabby, young man—what the cattleman scornfully called a 'townser'. He had a sallow, unhealthy-looking skin and blank-looking pale grey eyes, and he always looked half-shaven. Jessie made a face behind his back, and picked up Elizabeth's empty plate and carried it to the sink.

There was a stamping of feet and George came in the back door. 'Ay ay, Mr. Swanson,' he said, shaking the snow off his coat. 'Ye're up!'

'I guess I was up before you,' Mr. Swanson smirked. 'I heard you coming downstairs at nine o'clock. It's a grand life, a farmer's!'

'Ay,' George said. 'Are you having your breakfast in here, lass?' he said to Elizabeth, sitting down and kicking off his wellingtons. 'I'll just ha'e mine in here, too. Well, well, Jessie, what about ma breakfast, lassie? A working-man like me should aye get his breakfast put down til him as soon as he comes in. Isn't that right, wife? ' He leaned over and gripped Elizabeth's knee as he sat down beside her.

Jessie giggled and hurried to fetch his eggs and bacon. Mr. Swanson guffawed. George winked at him. ' Well, well, Mr. Swanson, you'll be getting ready for the road? '

Mr. Swanson guffawed again. ' You're a right comic, Mr. Dickie! Do you want my car to stick and have to get your men to dig me out? '

' Oh, it'll nae be as bad as all that, Mr. Swanson. You might manage awa' when the men have finished castin' the snow. Away out and have a look for yourself.'

Mr. Swanson gave an exaggerated shiver, but George bent over his bacon and eggs.

As soon as Mr. Swanson had gone out Elizabeth said: ' Will he manage to get away, George? '

' I doubt it, lassie, I doubt it.' George frowned over a large mouthful. ' It's as bad as I've ever seen it. The grieve says it'll take two days to clear the loan, and that's only if the snow doesn't come on again. I doubt it's nae all out yet. It was like startin' again when I came in.'

' Damn! ' Elizabeth lit a cigarette. ' What did that mannie want to get snowed-up here for? Could he not have left last night when he finished his job? '

' Well, wife, we canna help it,' George said, standing up and warming his bottom in front of the cooker. ' I'm nae looking forward any more than you are to another night or two of him sitting in the sitting-room so that I canna even let off wind! '

' Really, George, what things you say! '

' Now, lassie, what's wrong wi' that? ' George grinned at the giggling Jessie and, leaning over Elizabeth, he ruffled her hair.

' Here, George, none of that! ' She sprang up and backed away to the sink. ' Keep your hands to yourself! '

But George just laughed, his good-looking young face becoming teasingly boyish. ' That's the thing to sort her, isn't it, Jessie? Ye dinna ken what a fine fightin' wife I've got.

There's nae a better farmer's wife in the Howe o' the Mearns. Nor a bonnier! '

'Shuttup, you big baboon! ' Elizabeth said. 'And away out of here while I help Jessie to get on with the work.'

When she came downstairs, after helping Jessie to clean the bedrooms, Elizabeth found Mr. Swanson in the sitting-room. He was lounging in an easy-chair in front of the fire, staring at the flames. Elizabeth was reminded not for the first time of a huge Cheshire cat. 'I guess it's no go,' he said. 'I'll never manage to get away to-day.'

'Oh, won't you?' Elizabeth said.

'No, I guess not.' He laughed. 'Mr. Dickie and the men are trying to fix something on to the crawler-tractor to make it into a snow-plough, but I doubt if it'll work.'

'What about your work?' Elizabeth said. 'Won't your firm have something to say if you don't turn up? '

'Oh, they can whistle! ' He grinned. 'I'm due a holiday, anyway.'

Elizabeth said no more; she started to dust the sitting-room. Mr. Swanson went on staring into the fire. He made no attempt to carry on a conversation. That was the way he had sat for the past three nights. He did not read or play cards; he just sat and yawned. Elizabeth bustled about energetically, venting her annoyance at his lassitude on the furniture and hoping that she would spur him into doing something.

But Mr. Swanson sat in front of the fire all forenoon. The first movement he made was when he was called for dinner.

'Man, that's a right snow-plough we're makin',' George said, reaching for the potatoes. 'Ye'll have to come out and give us a bit hand, Mr. Swanson.'

'I guess I'm better where I am,' Mr. Swanson said. 'I don't fancy standing out in that snow at all.'

George laughed and tried to chaff him into coming out and helping, but Mr. Swanson wasn't to be drawn. After dinner he went back to the sitting-room and sat down in George's easy-chair. George looked at him, then he looked at Elizabeth and raised his eyebrows. 'Well, well,' he said. 'I'll ha'e to awa' back to ma work!'

Elizabeth followed him into the kitchen. 'If that mannie sits there again all afternoon,' she said, helping George on with his coat, 'I'll scream!'

'You've no wee jobbies you could give him to do in the house?'

'Not unless I break something!' Elizabeth smiled. 'I wonder how that would do?'

'You'd better not, lass!' George shook his head. 'He might nae be able to repair it again!'

'What about yon lamp Aunt Ina gave us? It wouldn't matter if it got broken.'

'Ay, but what would poor Aunt Ina say?' George grinned. 'Mind, lass, that I'm her favourite nephew!'

By four o'clock Elizabeth was almost desperate. Every time she went into the sitting-room and saw Mr. Swanson she wanted to throw something at him. 'Sitting there like a graven image!' she said to Jessie. 'Can he not go outside and help the men to cast snow?'

But just before tea-time he disappeared, and when Elizabeth went outside to tell George that the tea was ready she found Mr. Swanson in the turnip-shed talking to some of the land girls. 'I've been helping to hash what-do-you-call-'ems,' he said. 'Er—neeps!'

'Oh, yes, neeps!' Elizabeth said. 'The cows eat them,' she said. 'In case you don't know.'

Mr. Swanson ate his tea in silence. George talked all the time, but by the end of the meal even he was showing signs of strain. After tea Mr. Swanson disappeared again. 'Is he away back to the neep-shed to hash more neeps?' Elizabeth asked Jessie. 'I hope he cuts his head off! You wouldn't know it from the rest of the neeps, anyway!'

'No, he's in the office,' Jessie said.

'In the office?' George said. 'What's he doin' in the office?'

'He's playin' darts wi' Nellie Fowler,' Jessie said, and she lifted the tray and went out, banging the door behind her.

'Well, well!' George laughed. 'Eh, but it's fine, lassie, to get the place to ourselves for a bit. Nellie 'll keep him busy the night!'

Nellie Fowler was the toughest land girl in the county. She was the best swearer at the Mains of Pittendary: better even than George himself. And Elizabeth said that was something no one need be proud of! Nellie was a tall, stout girl with a round red face and bold brown eyes. She was a better worker than most men, carrying sacks of grain and heaving sheaves on to the mill as lightly as some women would have tossed a pancake.

'I didna think Nellie was the kind o' lassie that would ging after a man,' George said to Jessie when she came back with a fresh scuttleful of coals for the fire.

Jessie sniffed. 'Neither did I. But she's awa' after him like a ferret after a rabbit. And aince she catches him she'll worrit the stuffin' oot o' him.' Jessie nodded her head decisively. 'If he bides here long enough!'

'Jessie seems a bit peeved,' George said.

'Well, so would you be if you were her. You know fine that Nellie always comes up at nights to play darts with her. Poor Jessie! She'll have to go back to knitting yon jumper she's been trying to knit for the last six months!'

Jessie may not have been pleased, but George and Elizabeth were delighted. After three nights of the electrician's company they were glad to get their sitting-room to themselves again. They got out the cards and played Scrambled Patience until ten o'clock when Jessie brought in their tea and biscuits. The Glamour Boy appeared almost at once—Jessie raised her eyebrows at Elizabeth and nodded at the tray—and they put away the cards.

'Well, well, Mr. Swanson,' George said affably. 'I hear you've been entertaining one of our Land Army. Did you have a pleasant evening?'

'Oh, yes, it was all right.' Mr. Swanson swallowed a biscuit almost at one mouthful.

'I hope you saw the lassie home!' George winked at Elizabeth.

'Oh, I took her to the corner of the steading,' Mr. Swanson said. 'It was too cold and the snow was too deep to go any farther.'

II

'When's that mannie going away?' Elizabeth said. 'I'm sick and tired of him. I've had him on my hands for a week now. It's bad enough being shut in here ourselves, not able to go and see our friends, not able to leave the blasted farm, without having to bear his company on top of it. I'm going mad, George. I'll be sticking a knife into somebody if something doesn't happen soon. Is this damned snow never going to clear? Every day I think: Well, this is it all over now. And then when I waken in the morning I find there's been another fall.'

'Well, lassie, we canna help the weather,' George said. 'And the poor mannie canna help it either. I'm fed up with him, too.'

'But not as fed up with him as I am,' Elizabeth said sharply. 'You're outside a lot. But every time I go into the sitting-room I see him there. Doing nothing! The big slug! Can he not read or something? Can he not help the men to cast the snow?'

'Lassie, do ye want the poor man to tire himself out?' George said. 'He must have some strength left for night to grapple with Miss Nellie Fowler!'

Elizabeth smiled. 'Well, I suppose that's right. What we'd have done without Nellie and the dart-board I don't know. They've certainly taken him off our hands for three hours every night. Though that still leaves other twenty-one hours a day,' she said.

'Now, lass!' George grinned. 'Ye ken that I take up a

good lot o' them. Ye can hardly blame Mr. Swanson for what
happens to you in bed! '

' Really, George, what things you say! '

' Well, you'd rather have me saying them than Mr. Swanson, wouldn't you? '

' Of course, you big baboon! ' She sighed. ' I wonder what
the damned snow-plough's doing? You'd think it would have
had all the roads between here and Aberdeen cleared by this
time.'

' Well, it hasna, wife,' George said. ' Do you ken that
there's a war on! '

' Ay, and there'll be a bigger war in this house if that mannie
doesn't get away soon! ' she said. ' I could murder him!
He's never even given me his ration-book. If that's not adding
insult to injury, what is it? '

III

George's typist, Miss Burnett, had not been able to come to
work because of the storm. But on the sixth day she struggled
along the road from her home at Auchencairn, two miles
away. ' And if she can come,' Elizabeth said to Jessie, ' I
don't see why that blasted Glamour Boy can't get away from
here. Even though he only got the length of the hotel at
Auchencairn I wouldn't mind; he'd be off my hands.'

She was enlarging upon this when Mr. Swanson sauntered
into the kitchen. Elizabeth got such a shock, thinking he was
lounging in the sitting-room, that she dropped a bowl.

' Oh, hell! '

' Now, Mrs. Dickie! ' Mr. Swanson wagged a thick forefinger at her. ' You mustn't let the weather get the better of
your temper! '

Elizabeth and Jessie gaped at each other as he walked past
them into the office. ' Well, I'll be damned,' Elizabeth said
at last. ' The weather . . .'

At dinner-time George banged in and sat down at the table
with great heartiness. ' Well, Mr. Swanson! ' he cried. ' Our

snow-plough's got well under way this time. It looks as though you'll be able to get away to-morrow.'

'Yes, it looks like it,' Mr. Swanson said without enthusiasm. Elizabeth wondered why, and that afternoon when Mr. Swanson forsook the sitting-room for the office she wondered again. Late in the afternoon Jessie came into the sitting-room and closed the door carefully behind her. 'D'ye ken the latest?' she whispered.

'No.' Elizabeth leaned forward, eager for anything that would lighten the depth of the misery of snow.

'Miss Burnett's just been intil me,' Jessie said. 'And she says: "Will you please keep your friends out of the office to-night as me and Mr. Swanson are going to play darts?"'

'Well, I never!' Elizabeth said.

'Ye may well say,' Jessie said. 'Humph! She'll be made up wi' him. He's a bonnie-like messin'. Glamour Boy ma foot!'

'And what about Miss Nellie Fowler?' George said when his wife told him. 'Has he given her the go-by? What's she saying to all this?'

'How should I know!' Elizabeth said. 'All I know is that Jessie told me he'd asked Nellie to play darts with him to-night, too!'

'Well, well, there's going to be some fun at that rate,' George said. 'But it'll nae matter to us, wife. Get out the cards and let's get on with our Scramblers!'

They were in the middle of an exciting game of Scrambled Patience when Jessie came in. 'And here's the Ten o' Spades!' George cried, banging down a card almost on top of his wife's hand, making her yelp with fury. 'Stop the now till we see what Jessie wants! Stop when I say the word! Well, lassie, what is't?'

'Can we ha'e the dart-board in the kitchen?' Jessie said.

'Who's we?' said George. 'I hope it's none o' your followers, Jessie! This wife o' mine is very strict. She winna allow followers at all. Not even me!'

Jessie simpered. 'It's Nellie Fowler.'

'Oh, it's Nellie, is't? Well, well, ye can have the dartboard.' George grinned. 'Now awa' ye go and let's get on with our game. This wife o' mine's like to beat me! And I canna allow that. She takes a lot o' watchin', this wife o' mine—but ye're a fine wife, aren't ye, Lizzie?' he said, squeezing her knee when Jessie went out. 'There's nae a better wife in the Howe o' the Mearns!'

'Get away, you daft brute!' Elizabeth said. 'Let's get on with our game. And stop calling me Lizzie!'

They played for a while, then Elizabeth said : 'I'd fain like to know what's going on in the kitchen.'

'Now, lassie!' George said. 'That's what I call the height of inquisitiveness! Ye rave about poor Mr. Swanson. Ye call him all the names under the sun. Ye even complain about the amount he eats! Ye dinna like him in your sitting-room. And now that you've got rid of him you wonder what he's doin'.' He shook his head in mock reproof. 'Oh, lassie, lassie! That's what I call adding insult to injury!'

'Shuttup!' Elizabeth laughed. 'Or I'll throw something at you.'

'Well, well.' George picked up his cards. 'We winna quarrel about the lad. We'll wish him well. We'll get on with our peaceful game and not bother about him.' He grinned. 'But mind you, lassie, I'd fain like to ken myself what's goin' on in the kitchen. You must mind and ask Jessie all about it to-morrow!'

IV

Nellie Fowler was leaning against the cooker when Jessie went back to the kitchen. 'Are we to get it?' she said.

'Ay, he said we were.'

'We—ell?' Nellie said, looking towards the closed office door.

'Oh, I'll soon get it,' Jessie said. 'It'll be a pleasure!'

She knocked lightly on the door and almost immediately

turned the handle. 'Mr. Dickie says we've to get the dart-board,' Nellie heard her say.

She returned with the board and darts. 'I just nickit it awa' frae afore their noses,' she grinned. 'They were that flabbergasted they didna ken fut to say.'

'Huh!' Nellie took off her heavy Land Army coat. 'Well, fut about it? Will I ging first?'

And without waiting for Jessie to answer she picked up the darts and threw one at the board. It landed right in the centre.

They played until half-past nine, then Jessie began to make tea. Nellie sat and read *The People's Friend*. 'Are ye readin' Beatrice Inglesby's new serial?' she said. 'It's real romantic, isn't it? The love scenes fair make ma mouth water.'

'I suppose I'd better tell His Nabs that the tea's ready,' Jessie said. 'Or will he be ower taken up wi' Burnett?'

But before she could do anything the office door opened and Miss Burnett and Mr. Swanson came out, dressed for out-doors. They walked to the back door and said 'Good night' in a sheepish manner. Mr. Swanson was careful not to look at Nellie.

'I wonder how far he'll ging wi' *her*?' Nellie said, helping herself to a scone and biting it almost in half.

'There's his car startin' up,' Jessie said. 'I help ma God! Is he goin' to drive her hame?'

'Ay, is he,' Nellie said, listening. 'The big fat B.!'

When Mr. Swanson came back he found Nellie and Jessie playing another game of darts. 'Well, ladies!' he said affably. 'Having a little game?'

Nellie did not answer, but Jessie said: 'Ay, fut dae ye think we're doin'?'

'I wonder where my working-boots are?' Mr. Swanson said. 'I guess I'll have to get them packed. I think I'll be able to get away to-morrow.'

'They'll be where ye left them,' Jessie said. 'Here, Nellie, it's ma turn!'

Mr. Swanson began to rummage about the kitchen. 'I

thought I left them under the dresser,' he said, ' but they're not there now.' Nellie and Jessie grinned at each other behind his back.

He stood and looked around, scratching his head delicately so as not to disturb his carefully-brushed parting. He frowned and went towards the cooker. ' I wonder if they could have got behind this? '

He bent over the cooker and peered down into the hole behind it. ' Oh, here they are! Now, how the devil did they get down here? '

He heaved himself on top of the cooker, stretching over the top so that his big bottom stuck up in the air. Jessie and Nellie looked at each other, then they looked at the inviting target. Nellie lifted the dart she was holding. . . .

But suddenly she threw it down and, striding forward, she lifted her foot and gave Mr. Swanson such a tremendous kick on the bottom that he went head-first into the hole behind the cooker.

v

The next morning when Mr. Swanson went out to the neep-shed to go away from the Mains of Pittendary he found the handles of his car tied with rope, the inside of the car was full of neeps, and the exhaust was choked with rotten tatties.

TORTOISES ARE SO AFFECTIONATE

'TORTOISES are so affectionate,' he said. 'I remember once I had a tortoise and it used to sit on my lap and put out its head for me to stroke it.'

'I never had a tortoise,' I said. 'But I used to have newts when I was a child.'

'I had newts, too,' he said. 'I kept them in a small pond I made in the garden. It wasn't really a pond. It was just a hole I dug myself. In the winter the water got frozen and all the newts got frozen into the ice. Solid. I poured hot water over them and they revived a bit. But the next day the same thing happened and they died.'

We were sitting on the veranda. He had asked me to sit this one out; his leg was still giving him a lot of trouble and he'd danced quite enough for one night. I didn't mind at all. He was a nice-looking boy, a Flight Lieutenant, with fair wavy hair.

I leaned back and looked at him, at the way his hair waved back from his forehead. The moon was shining on it. I wanted to put out my hand and stroke it, but I didn't think it was the sort of thing a nice girl should do at all. I'd only met him for the first time. The band was playing *You're Mine*.

'What did it feel like when you crashed?' I said.

'Oh, I don't know,' he said. 'There wasn't much in it. It just happened and that was all.'

'I've never met anybody before who'd crashed,' I said. 'A friend of mine in the Raf has been terribly high up, though.

He told me that he thought they were never going to stop going up. I told him he hadn't needed to worry because it was the other place he was destined for. He said he didn't care, for he'd friends in both places!'

I laughed because I always think that's a terribly funny story, but the Flight Lieutenant never even smiled.

I leaned back. 'You're mine through all the years to be,' I hummed. 'You're mine through all eternity.' The stone of the seat was cold on the back of my neck. 'Tell me some more about yourself,' I said.

'I used to have a puppy when I was a kid, too,' he said. 'A jolly little chap. A wire-haired Scotch terrier. Do you like dogs?'

'We-ell,' I said. 'Yes, yes!'

'I used to have rabbits, too,' he said. 'One of them was called Susan. She was a blue Angora. I was terribly, terribly hurt when she died. I think a maid we used to have poisoned her.'

'Did she?' I said. 'Wasn't that terrible!'

'Yes, I never liked that maid after that,' he said. 'She married a policeman and they've got a pub now in the Old Kent Road. Even though I was terribly dry I'd never think of going into it.'

'But surely she wouldn't think of poisoning you,' I said.

'I wouldn't put it past her,' he said.

I laughed and laughed at that, not so much because I thought it funny, but because it gave me a chance to clutch his shoulder. But he never even smiled himself. He sat quite still, staring out at the moonlight on the rhododendron bushes.

'Go on,' I said.

'Sometimes my people left her to look after me at nights,' he said. 'But she used to lock me in my room and go out with her policeman. I used to sit and stroke my tortoise.'

'You poor thing,' I said.

I put my hand on his knee and gave him a little pat. But he didn't move. After a while I took my hand away and watched some couples strolling among the rhododendrons.

' I was sorry when my tortoise died,' he said. ' I cried for two days.'

' Were you? ' I said.

I sat back and listened to the music. They were playing *Deep in the Heart of Texas*, and I wished I were dancing.

' I cried a lot when the newts died, too,' he said. ' They looked so small and so lost. . . .'

' Did you? ' I said. ' Oh, hello! ' I said to big Bill who had just come on to the veranda. ' Are you looking for me? This is our dance, isn't it? '

' It wasn't,' he said when we were dancing. ' But since you seemed to think so——' He laughed, and I laughed, too.

After the dance we went for a walk among the rhododen-drons. When we came near the veranda I saw that that Bentley girl was sitting beside the Flight Lieutenant—the plain Bentley girl who'll never get a man, poor thing. I heard him say : ' But tortoises are so affectionate,' then I pulled Bill's arm and said : ' Let's go in. I want to dance! '

THE BRIDGE

A WET Sunday. His tobacco-stained fingers plucked
peevishly at the old-fashioned lace curtains, and he frowned
at the miniature fountains splashing on the green-moulded
stone of the window-sill. It was just like it to rain on the first
Sunday he had spent in this benighted place. He couldn't
understand why Madge had asked him to meet her parents
to-day; it would have been much simpler to have asked him
to visit them through the week. Then he could have gone
home to-day as usual. As if it wasn't bad enough to see this
fusty old parlour six days a week without having to endure it
on the seventh day, too. And alone. There was nobody left
in the place but himself and that old frump, Miss Allison.

She hadn't gone away for the week-end like the others.
Probably she had no place to go. She looked as though she
had been here for years: rather like a mummy in a museum.
Though there wasn't much chance of her ever being a
mummy! That was quite good. He must tell Baxter that
one. Baxter was the only bright spot in the boarding-house.
If it wasn't for Baxter he'd have sought other lodgings long
ago. So would Baxter. But they clung together, nourishing
themselves on the amusement they derived from the foibles of
the other boarders. They were an amusing bunch. Especially
old Watson and Miss Allison. Not that there was really anything outstandingly funny about Miss Allison; she was just a
typical middle-aged old maid. She was a civil servant, a big
stout woman with large expressionless brown eyes. But old
Watson was a yell. True blue and English and all that, with

a Union Jack tattooed on his chest—or if he didn't have, he should have one. He was so conservative that he thought if a man was a miner, his sons should be miners, too. He'd never forget the look of amazement on old Watson's face that time when Baxter twitted him. Old Watson was pretty fond of the bottle, and he'd nearly had apoplexy when Baxter said : 'Do you mean that if a man's a drunkard, all his sons should be drunkards, too, Mr. Watson?'

Baxter and he had to walk warily in this mausoleum, careful not to tramp too hard on people's toes, threading their way through the bric-à-brac of other people's minds. He crossed to the fireplace and looked down with distaste at the paper-filled grate behind the ornamental fire-screen before he switched on the electric-heater. Standing with his back to it, his lips curled at the empty semi-circle of easy-chairs. If he expounded his views now they would not be wasted any more than if the seats were filled. Empty! And as empty when the other boarders sat smugly in them with repleted stomachs. Thank heavens, the card-table would not be taken to-night from its corner for the interminable games of bridge. He stretched himself and looked at his reflection in the mirror above the piano. Balancing himself on his toes, he swayed backwards and forwards. The stool for two was pushed under the piano. No pianoforte duets from Miss Allison and Miss Baird to-night! The huge over-fed tomcat, which looked as though it were stuffed, could remain comatose on top of the writing-desk without imagining that its lovers were calling.

He heard a footstep in the hall, and as the door opened, some dead petals fell from the withered bunch of marigolds in the vase on the polished table. It was Miss Allison.

She looked flustered when she saw him. 'Oh, Mr. Davidson, I didn't know you were here. I thought you had gone out.'

'Good afternoon,' he said, moving away from the electric-heater. He tried to put some warmth into his voice. He supposed he'd have to be pleasant to the woman seeing that they were alone in the place.

She sat down in an easy-chair opposite the glow from the synthetic coals. She spread her plump white hands towards it and said: 'It's a miserable day, isn't it?'

'Yes,' he said, wondering what he could say to her after they'd exhausted the weather. They had lived together in the same house for over six months, but they had never spoken to each other beyond civil greetings at morning or at night. 'The rain looks as though it's never going to stop,' he said.

She laughed nervously, a blush spreading over her sallow plump cheeks. 'Like the war!' she said.

'Oh, I don't know,' he said.

'It's terrible, isn't it?' she said.

He nodded agreement. What else could you do with an old hag like this?

'What do you think will happen?' she said, patting her dull, permanently-waved shingled hair.

He sat down and frowned at the creases in his new flannels. 'Oh, we'll win, of course, we're bound to win.' That was the answer she probably expected. 'We're a tough lot.'

She laughed again. 'Aren't we!'

Davidson looked around, wondering what other subject he could mention. There was no sense in tramping on this big fat cow's toes. He looked up, but the glass tubes of the chandelier twinkled sarcastically at him. What was the use of talking about the war to a woman like this, a woman who would probably be militant in handing out white feathers when the time came? Maybe she would give one to him!

'But the Germans are tough, too,' she said.

'Of course,' he said. 'Of course. Still——' He laughed, trying to get the proper hearty note into it.

'How long do you think it will last?' she said.

'Oh, who knows?' he said. 'Maybe the Ministry of Information could tell us!' He added quickly: 'Have you been to the pictures lately?'

'I very seldom go to the cinema,' she said. 'The last time I was there I was terribly upset when I heard the audience cheering a troopship going to France. I just couldn't bear it;

I had to come out. All those young men going to be killed. . . .'

He took out his case and selected a cigarette, staring intently at it as though he were choosing a tie. He put it in his mouth and put the case back in his pocket. Then he drew it out again. 'Would you care for a cigarette, Miss Allison?'

'No thank you.' She bent her head. 'I—er—I don't smoke.' She watched him as he lit a match. 'I—er—I used to smoke. But that was long ago. I remember that my friend and me were asked to leave a cinema because we were smoking. But that was in the last war.'

'But you won't remember the last war,' she added. 'Of course not. You would only be a baby then.'

Damn her and the last war, he thought irritably. Why must they always drag it up? It's ancient history. Don't they realize that this is a different matter; that we're twenty-five years further ahead in time? If not in sense!

'I suppose you'll have to go?' she said.

'I guess so,' he replied. He rose and tried to laugh jocularly. 'Anyway, I'll have to go now. I'm going out for tea.'

When he came downstairs ten minutes later, she came out of the lounge with her hat and coat on. 'The rain's stopped,' she said. 'I think I'll go out for a stroll.'

He opened the door politely for her and followed her down the steps. 'The flowers are so nice and fresh in the spring, aren't they?' she said, pointing to the snowdrops and crocuses. 'You'd think all that rain would kill them, but they seem to be fresher than ever. Poor things, they don't last!'

'No,' he muttered.

'Youth's such a fleeting thing,' she said.

Walking up the street beside her, Davidson's teeth clenched with the effort of trying to find a congenial subject. Anything to bridge this gulf of age and ideas. . . .

'It's cold,' he said.

'Yes, isn't it?' she said.

'Wouldn't be surprised if we had frost to-night.'

'Neither would I,' she said.

They entered a busier thoroughfare. Numbers of young women pranced along together in their Sunday clothes, eyeing the young men, especially the ones who wore uniform. Davidson noticed that those girls who were clinging to the arms of soldiers walked unevenly; they were so busy chattering to their escorts, chattering as if they had so much to say and so little time to say it in, that they did not watch where they were putting their feet. He looked at their faces, trying to probe behind the powder and lipstick, wondering what they were feeling.

A bus swished past them through the puddles, and Miss Allison drew closer to Davidson in an effort to avoid the splashes. ' Nasty things ! ' she said.

The bus stopped to allow two young soldiers to get on it. They stood on the step, waving to the two girls they had just left. One of them hung out dangerously, singing at the top of his voice : ' The girl who loves a soldier is the girl who loves a parade. Oh, the girl who loves . . . is part of the grand cavalcade. . . .'

' They have to do that to keep up their spirits, poor things,' Miss Allison said. ' I remember in the last war my—my friend told me that they always sang whether they felt like it or not.'

She sighed and re-slung her fur over her shoulders. ' My— my friend was killed,' she said.

' Oh ? ' Davidson said.

Miss Allison kept her eyes averted; she was watching the faces of the two girls who were passing. ' He—he would have been forty-six next Friday,' she said.

' I'm sorry,' Davidson said, feeling that the words were inadequate, yet knowing that they were the first sincere words he had spoken that afternoon.

They stopped at the corner. ' Well, good afternoon, Mr. Davidson,' she said.

' Good afternoon,' he said, and he lifted his hat.

He began to walk slowly to Madge's home, feeling vaguely uncomfortable when he remembered how often he and Baxter had joked about Miss Allison being an old maid. He felt a bit foolish as though Miss Allison had been holding something out on him. And as he knocked at Madge's door, he realized suddenly that numbers of girls of her generation would become the unloved spinsters of twenty-five years hence. At the thought, he shivered with uncontrollable agony. But not Madge. . . .

MY FRIEND FEDERICO

EVERY time we come into Portlessington we go to Paddy-roosky's. Paddyroosky's real name is Miss Hilton and she is a dame about thirty-five who always wears slacks and is crazy about highbrow music. Her old man had the pub before her, otherwise I don't suppose she would carry it on. She leaves practically everything to her manager, Mr. Myles, who usually hangs about the public bar and has a lot of cronies who swap yarns with him about the last war and about what they are doing now in A.R.P. Paddyroosky herself hangs around the lounge and if she sees anybody interesting she makes for them and hangs on to them. That's how she got acquainted with us. She saw us the first time we went into the pub, and I always tell Mac it was his ginger hair that did it. She came and sat down at our table and made us take drinks on the house. 'So you're in the Merchant Navy?' she said. 'Gee, I think you boys are all swell. You're doing a swell job of work.'

Mac kidded her on. Mac's one of the world's champion kidders, though I guess he got kidded himself when he married Trudy. Miss Hilton began to speak about music. She talked about Beethoven and Brahms and Bach and Sibelius, and Mac kidded her on.

'And I just adore Rachmaninoff,' she said.

'Well, I'm not so keen on him,' Mac said. 'But I just love Paddyroosky.'

'Padereweski!' she said, and she went into a swoon. 'Oh, I think Padereweski's divine!'

And so that's how the name stuck to her. But she's a real nice dame for all that, and very generous. We always look forward to going and seeing her when we are in Portlessington.

The last time we were there Mac was in an awful daft mood. He kept speaking in broken English, mixing up all the French and German and Latin that he knew. He kept calling Paddyroosky 'Beautiful Signorina' till I thought I'd burst out laughing. It started when we went in and Paddyroosky came over and asked Mac how Trudy was. I don't think Paddyroosky likes Trudy much. I think she has a notion for Mac herself. I don't blame her. Trudy is an awful wet. She comes to Portlessington sometimes to see Mac and she comes with us to the Golden Hind, and every time she goes all weepy over a couple of beers. The last time she was there she had a row with Paddyroosky, so I think it was real sporting of Paddyroosky to ask Mac about her.

'My vife!' Mac cried. 'Ah, I have lef' her. I fall in lof with you now. Hard!'

He and Paddyroosky were going on like this when a man came into the lounge and made for Paddyroosky. I don't think she looked any too pleased to see him, but she introduced him as Mr. Liddell, and he joined the company. 'Vat vill you have to dreenk, huh?' Mac said.

'Ah, you're a Frenchman?' Mr. Liddell said, interested. 'The Free French! Vive la France!'

'No, no, no!' Mac cried indignantly. 'Me no French. Pouf! Me Spanish! Cabrinos des etos aqua pura madre de dios carramba!'

Mr. Liddell looked quite impressed at this. 'I'm afraid I don't speak Spanish,' he said.

'Ah, but I speak Engleesh good,' Mac said. 'I speak ze Engleesh better zan anybodee here.'

I sort of choked into my beer.

Mac waved a hand at me and said: 'My friend Federico—he no speak ze Engleesh so good.'

'Bella signorina,' he said, turning to Paddyroosky. 'Bella

bella! La donne e mobile machiavelli chu chin chow con amore bella vista!'

Mr. Liddell looked sort of surprised and said: 'I didn't know you spoke Spanish, Miss Hilton.'

'I don't,' she said. 'But I understand everything that my friend says perfectly.'

There were three Black Watch men that we knew by sight at a table in the corner of the room. One of them was passing me with his drink and he said: 'Ay, chum, ye're here again? D'ye ha'e a guid trip?'

'Ay,' I said.

Mr. Liddell looked even more surprised. 'It's funny,' he said to Mac, 'how you foreigners understand us. You understand us better than we understand you. That Scottie now. I didn't understand one word he said. Yet your friend seemed to understand him all right.'

'My friend Federico veree clever,' Mac said. 'But he no speak ze Engleesh so good. Me,' he said. 'I speak alla da language. Especial la bad language.'

'Do you speak German?' Mr. Liddell said.

'Sherman!' Mac said, and he indicated with a wave of his hand that nearly sent my beer flying that it was almost his mother tongue. 'Sure, I speaka da Sherman. Sprachen die deutch donner und blitzen ich lieb sie.'

'What a pity,' Mr. Liddell said. 'A friend of mine who often comes here speaks very good German. I would have liked you to meet her. But she's not here to-night, unfortunately.'

'Dat ees too bad,' Mac said.

'The next time you're here you must have a talk with her, Mr. Liddell said. 'I think you'd find her very interesting. And he looked sort of funny like at Mac. 'Very interesting indeed,' he said. 'She may come to-night yet. I hope she does.'

'Ah, but ve must go,' Mac said, drinking up his beer. 'Ve must go. Pronto!'

'Could you not stay a little?' Mr. Liddell said. 'I'm sure

my friend would be very interested in you. She is very interested in foreign sailors, especially one who could speak German.
I'm sure it would be worth your while.'

'No, ve mus' go,' Mac said. 'Adios!'

We were all fairly well lit, and Paddyroosky came to the
door with us. Mac kissed her hand and said : 'Adios, adios,
bella bella signorina! Au revoir and auz weidersein!'

I was surprised to see tears in Paddyroosky's eyes. 'Good-
bye, boys,' she said. 'See and take care of yourselves. Come
back soon!'

Mac walked backwards and kept kissing his hand to her until
she disappeared in the blackout, and even then he wouldn't
turn round and walk properly. 'C'mon, you silly son of a
bitch!' Sandy said. 'Ye'll bump into somebody if ye're no'
very careful.'

'Do not insulta my modder!' Mac cried. 'I weel slitta your
thoat. Yes!'

We took him by the arms and supported him between us
until we came to the main street. We stood and waited for a
tram to take us to the docks. Mac sang and capered, raising
quite a commotion, and we were glad when the tram came
along. When the conductress came upstairs for our fares Mac
tried it on with her, saying : 'Bella signorina, you vill give us
tree halves, yes?'

But she wasn't having any. 'Sixpence,' she said. 'And
none of your shenanigans.'

'Ah, signorina!' Mac said, putting his hand on his heart.
'Ve are tree poor sailorman. Geeve us a leetle smile, yes?'

'I'll give you a kick in the pants,' said the beautiful signorina.
Sixpence!'

'You drunks,' she said as she went downstairs.

'All our versatility wasted,' Mac said sadly. 'Some people
have no appreciation.'   ·

But it appeared that some people had. When we got off the
tram near the dock gates Mac again began to sing and dance;
so much so that Sandy said : 'If ye dinnie shuttup we'll be
gettin' run in for breach o' the peace.'

And sure enough, just then a policeman came along and said: 'What's going on here? Let's see your identity cards.'

I was preparing to do a bunk, but Mac said: 'Ah, señor polismans, you are ze von ve are looking for, yes! My friends and me—ve veesh to find our vay to ze basin.'

The bobby flashed his torch full in our faces. 'Ah, foreigners!' he said. 'Identity cards, please!'

That's done it, I thought. But Mac didn't budge an inch. He took out his pocket-book and handed his card to the bobby. You could have knocked me down with one of my mother's scones when the policeman just glanced at it and handed it back, holding out his hand for mine. I guess he mustn't have looked any farther than the outside, for surely he couldn't have thought that MacLennan was Spanish! As for Sandy's name and mine—but he just handed them back! I felt like saying: 'Your Engleesh policemen are vonderful!' but thought maybe it would be carrying the joke a bit too far.

'Where you want to go?' he said slowly, speaking in a sort of broken English to us.

'Ze grand basin!' Mac said. 'What you call eet? Ze place for ze sheeps. Ze bottom? No, no, I make naughtee shoke, yes! Ze docks!'

'Oh, yes.' The policeman began to direct us; then he started to wave his arms about. 'To-night!' he cried. 'An air raid. Biff! Bang! Boom!' He began to imitate an aeroplane. 'But do not be afraid. No! No! It is sham! It is mock! It is fake!'

We knew all about what he was trying to tell us, but it was so funny watching his antics and hearing his attempts to speak broken English that we kidded we didn't understand.

'Please?' I said.

'My friend Federico.' Mac pointed to me. 'Excuse him, please. He no speak Engleesh so good.'

The poor bobby was beginning to get desperate, but he persevered. 'Air raid!' he cried. 'Sirens. Not real. Do not be afraid!'

'But no, no!' Mac cried. 'Ve lof ze Engleesh bobby!'

And he grabbed the poor cop and kissed him on both cheeks.
' My friend Federico—he also lof ze bobby! ' And he pulled
me forward and tried to shove the bobby into my arms. But I
hung back. A joke was a joke, but I didn't intend to carry it
that far.

' My friend Federico—he is shy! ' Mac said. ' Vell, ve mus'
go. Ve mus' scoot! Ah ha! I make ze naughtee shoke
again! I am veree wicked, no? '

But we couldn't get away from that cop. He insisted upon
taking us almost to the boat's side. We were right thankful
when eventually he left us. As Sandy said afterwards : ' Maybe
he had appreciation of Mac's daftness, but he had just a damned
bit too much appreciation for ma taste! '

QUIET SUNDAY

SHE was going to have a quiet Sunday. She'd been making up her mind for it all week. Ever since she'd come home the house had gone like a fair. 'I'm fed up with folk coming to see me,' she said to her mother. 'I'm beginning to wish I was back in the W.A.A.F.'

'You should be thankful folk are botherin' themsels to come and see ye,' her mother said. 'My word, I'm real glad to see folk comin' about the house again. It's been a bonnie quiet house this all through the war with both you and Alex bein' away for so long. There's been many a week when your father and me havenie had a single visitor.'

'Well, I'm tired of folk coming in and biding for cups of tea,' Mary said. 'I just want to sit well back and have a rest. You've no idea what a comfort it is to sit well back in an easy-chair in a quiet room. It's such a change from twenty girls chattering and clattering about a barrack-room.'

She hoped that all the bustle and chatter-chatter of these old hens visiting her mother would be over before Sunday. They all had the same story. 'I just dropped in, Mrs. Nicholson, to see how Mary was.' But, of course, they stayed to blether with her mother and to gossip about a lot of people that Mary either didn't know or had forgotten existed. It was just curiosity that made them come. 'They're bothered with their noses,' she said bitterly. 'They just want to see if anything's happened to me since I went away.'

But she was going to have a quiet day on Sunday. She must write to Harold. She'd been looking all week for a letter from him. Goodness, but she wouldn't half lay into him about not writing. Wasting his time going to the local with the other fellows when he should be writing to her. She was going to write a long letter, and if anybody came in while she was writing—well, she'd just go upstairs and get on with it! She was fed up with being polite to folk she wasn't really interested in anyway. She was interested in nobody but Harold. And she wished it was time for his group to be demobbed so that they could make arrangements about getting married. It was eleven days now since she'd seen him and she'd had a funny kind of ache in her breast ever since. It wasn't a pain, what you could call a pain anyway—it was just an ache that was always there. And she kept thinking about him all the time, longing to see him.

On Sunday she was still asleep at ten o'clock when her brother, Alex, awoke her with a cup of tea. 'Are you going to get up for your breakfast, toots?' he said.

'I don't think I'll take any,' she said. 'I'll just drink this, then I'll get up and dress myself.'

She half sat up in bed, sipping her tea and thinking what she would say in her letter to Harold. She lay for half an hour, composing an angry letter, asking why he had never written. Then she turned and snuggled down under the clothes and went to sleep again.

It was one o'clock when she got up. She was going into the bathroom when her mother shouted: 'There's no sense in beginnin' to wash yersel' the now. You'll be hours in that bathroom. The dinner's almost ready. Better come and get it. I'm no' goin' to keep things hot for you.'

It was half-past two when she got herself dressed. She was putting on lipstick before the mirror above the sideboard in the living-room when her mother said: 'I wonder if ye'd run along to the chemist's for me, Mary? I want a bottle o' Lixen.'

'But he'll be shut, Ma.'

'No, he's open from two to three on Sundays. Hurry up or ye'll miss him. Just put your coat on. It'll just take you two or three minutes.'

Alex looked up from his Sunday paper. 'You might take
the pup out for a run with you, Mary,' he said. 'He needs
some exercise.'

'You and your old pup,' she said.

'Better put his lead on so's he won't run away,' Alex said.

'Well, you put it on for me,' she said. 'I'm needing all my
time. I want to write a letter to Harold.'

'Ach, it's lying under the chair in the lobby,' Alex said.
'You can surely get it for yourself.'

But the lead was not where Alex said it was, and after a
great deal of hunting Mary found it lying behind the coal-
scuttle in the scullery. 'Come on, you little brute,' she said
angrily to the pup. 'You've wasted enough of my precious
time.'

'Hear her!' Alex said. 'Lies in her bed till one o'clock
and then says we're wasting her time! What time have *you*
got to lose, lady!'

Mary didn't answer. She put the lead on the pup and went
out. She held her head well back, bracing her shoulders,
and pranced along on her high heels. Goodness, but it was
fine to have really high heels again after those *sensible* shoes
they'd made you wear in the W.A.A.F. She felt at least six
inches higher. If only Harold were walking along beside
her! He wouldn't seem so tall and up in the clouds
now!

It was a cold, clear afternoon with a nip of frost in the air.
The pup bounded along the pavement in front of her, strain-
ing at the lead. 'Here, Captain, here, don't go so quick!'
Mary cried.

The pup thought it was an invitation to play, for he turned
back and leaped upon her, almost knocking her down in his
enthusiasm. He clawed frantically at her legs.

'Stop it!' she shrieked. 'Stop it! Mind my stockings, you
little brute!'

She bent down to see that no damage had been done, and
the pup leaped up, trying to lick her face. Then suddenly he
jumped away, and before Mary could pull tighter she found

that the lead had been wrestled from her hand, and the pup was flying along the street.

'Captain! Captain!' she cried. 'Good dog, here, good doggie!'

But Captain thought it was a game, and after running back a few yards he turned again when Mary had almost reached him and scampered quickly, yelping with delight. She ran as fast as she could after him, but she hadn't yet mastered her high heels after such a long time, and she lurched dangerously.

Two young men standing at the corner laughed when they saw the pup dragging his lead. They whistled to Mary and one of them called : 'Lovely day for a run, sweetie! Training for a marathon?'

The pup had passed Ross the chemist's. It stopped every few seconds and looked back at Mary, its tongue lolling out. But as soon as it saw her coming nearer, it turned and ran on still farther. Her temples were throbbing with the exercise and with fury. 'Oh, if I could just get you!' she hissed to herself.

After they were about a hundred yards past the chemist's and nobody on the street had shown the least sign of trying to stop the pup, Mary decided to give it up as a bad job. I hope he throttles himself, she muttered angrily as she turned and began to walk back towards the chemist's. Her breasts swelled upwards with indignation, and her high heels beat an angry tattoo on the pavement.

She was going into the chemist's when she heard the rattle of the lead and the pad of the puppy's paws behind her. She held the door open for it. 'Now, I've got you!' she said, gripping the lead viciously. 'By God, you won't escape from me again in a hurry!'

But while she was waiting for the chemist to make up a prescription for another customer, Mary bent over the counter to look at some bottles of perfume, and unthinkingly she allowed the lead to slip from her fingers. A few excited wuffs from the pup made her realize what she had done. She turned at the same time as the chemist came from the back of the shop. The pup had jumped up on a weighing-machine for babies and it was tearing the feathers out of the pillow on the scales. Mary made a dive at it, and at the same moment another customer came into the shop. The pup rushed through the open door.

Mary was breathless with rage when she got home. 'You and your bloody pup!' she cried hysterically to Alex. 'I wish you'd left it with that damned fool of a soldier that gave you it!'

'Now, Mary,' her father said, looking up from his newspaper. 'We all ken you've been in the sodgers, but we're for none o' that barrack-room talk here.'

'Where is the pup?' Alex said.

Mary was nearly in tears by the time she'd ended her story. 'I don't know where he is,' she said. 'And I don't care! He bolted like a flash. Oh, if you saw the mess he made with those feathers! And if you'd seen Mr. Ross's face!'

'Never mind, Mary,' her mother said soothingly. 'There are worse losses at sea!'

Alex sighed and rose, laying aside his paper. 'I suppose I'll have to go and look for the poor little devil. He won't know his way home. I'll never let you take him out again, Mary.'

'Let me take him out again!' Mary shrieked. 'Let me—— Oh!' She flounced away for her pen and writing-pad.

'You're a damned nuisance,' Alex said, putting on his overcoat. 'I didn't want to go out. I just wanted to sit quiet by the fire.'

'Well, what do you think I want?' Mary snapped.

'I don't know what's come over you both since you came home,' Mrs. Nicholson said irritably. 'You both sit there like a couple o' mummies and stare into the fire. Not a word out of either of you! It's terrible when folk come in to see you. I'm fair black affronted. I have to do all the conversation myself.'

Mary sat down beside the fire and wrote the address, the date and *My Darling Harold*. Then she tapped her teeth with her pen, wondering how exactly to begin. She had got to be diplomatic. She'd better start in a cooing sort of tone and then work up gradually into a rage, demanding the reason why he had never written. Really, it was terribly difficult. She had never needed to write to him before. They'd always been at the same camp and letters hadn't been necessary.

Well, I'm home and things are hardly what I thought they'd be. This house has gone like a fair all week, but despite it all I've never been so lonely. I am missing you like anything. I think about you the whole time and I have a queer pain in my chest whenever I do. . . .

That was how she felt all right. Still, it was hardly the thing to tell Harold that. It might give him ideas about his own importance. Better be a bit more cool. After all, he was in the wrong. He hadn't written as he'd promised.

She screwed the paper in a ball and threw it on the fire. She was starting the letter again when she heard the click of the front gate.

' Here's the Band Wagon! ' her mother cried, looking out.

Mary looked over her mother's shoulder. ' Help! ' she said bitterly. ' It's Jean Symington and her twins! '

' Put off that wireless, Father! ' Mrs. Nicholson said. ' We won't need it now! '

' Well, Jean,' Mary said, opening the door to her old school-friend. ' Goodness, but it's nice to see you again after all this time.'

' My, but you must be glad to be home again, Mary! ' Jean said, kissing her and pushing two little boys, aged about four, into the house in front of her. ' It'll be such a fine rest for you after all the excitement of the W.A.A.F.'

' Will we see Jesus here? ' one of the twins cried.

' No, this is no' where Jesus bides,' his mother said. She grinned at Mary. ' They've been at the Sunday School the day for the first time, and they've been pestering me ever since wanting to go and see Jesus.'

' In you go,' she said, pushing the children along the passage. ' In you go and see Granny Nicholson.'

As she closed the door and followed them into the living-room, Mary sighed. She was fond of Jean, and she supposed she was fond of the twins. But, oh heavens, she said to herself, what possessed her to bring them along to-day of all days?

'Goodness me, laddie!' Mrs. Nicholson said to the biggest twin, taking off his overcoat. 'Ye get bigger and bigger every time I see ye!'

'Ay, and dozier!' his mother said. She nodded at the smallest twin, who had already taken off his overcoat himself and had folded it neatly and laid it on a chair. 'That one's a right Symington,' she said. 'But Jimmy here—ach, he's like my father. He's easy-osey!'

'Can we go and see Jesus now?' the wee twin said.

'No, away and play,' Jean said. 'Granny and Mary and Mummy are going to talk.'

Jimmy, the big twin, went dutifully into the scullery where he sat on the floor and pushed a stone hot-water bottle and two or three shoes around, pretending they were a train. But Allan, the little twin, stood beside Mrs. Nicholson's knee, listening to the three women talking. 'Look at him!' Jean said. 'He's like his grandfather Symington, this one! He'll let nothing go past him.'

'If Jock doesn't tell me any news after he's taken the bairns to see his folk,' she said. 'I aye get all the news from this one.'

'Are they still keeping his BANK?' Mrs. Nicholson said.

'Ay,' Jean said.

Mrs. Nicholson shook her head and said : 'I never heard the like!' The Symington grandparents had given Allan a bank when he was born because he was named after his Symington grandfather, and ever since all the Symington aunts and uncles had kept putting money into it. But they had not given Jimmy a bank because he was named after Jean's father. 'Fancy folk doin' that to a bairn!' Mrs. Nicholson said.

'Are ye not goin' to play with Jimmy?' she said.

'I want to see Jesus,' Allan said.

'Well, you can't see Jesus here,' Jean said. 'Away you go and play.'

'Jesus doesn't live here any more,' Mary said, poising her pen above her letter and wondering if she dare go on writing.

To hide her laughter, Mrs. Nicholson bent forward and pokered the fire. Allan watched her attentively. 'Jesus has a big fire like that,' he said. 'Jesus pokers it!'

'I doot ye're makin' a mistake, laddie,' Mrs. Nicholson said. 'It's somebody else—a bad auld man—that has a big fire like this. Jesus hasnie got a fire.'

'Has Jesus not got a fire?' Allan asked his mother.

'No, it's the Devil that has a fire,' she said. 'Now, away you go and play—or I'll scud you!'

Allan sighed and went towards the scullery. He hesitated at the door, then he said: 'Poor Jesus, he'll be cauld without a fire.'

'And now,' the radio announcer said. 'Here is a record of Deanna Durbin singing *Home, Sweet Home.*'

Mary sighed. Her father had put on the wireless when he sat down to read his newspaper after lunch and it had been blaring full blast ever since. Nobody was listening to it, but although neither Mrs. Nicholson, Jean Symington nor Mary could hear each other speak, none of them dared switch it off. If they had Mr. Nicholson would have looked up immediately from his paper, demanding to know what they were doing. Several times Mrs. Nicholson said: 'Put off that wireless, Father,' but her husband never answered; he went on reading. What with it and the noise the twins were making in the scullery, Mary found it difficult to listen to her mother and Jean. Though it was equally difficult, she found, to think about her letter.

She wondered if she should go upstairs. The trouble about this, however, was that Jean Symington would be mortally offended. She'd go around telling people: 'You know, I went to visit Mary Nicholson, and do you know what she did? She went upstairs and wrote a letter!' So that would never do. Besides, it was so cold upstairs; the coal situation was so bad that they could have only a fire in the living-room.

'You made me love you, I didn't want to do it,' she hummed

with Judy Garland, wondering what Harold was doing at this moment. 'You made me happy sometimes, you made me glad, and there were times, dear, you made me feel so sad. . . .'

But never as sad as she was feeling just now. She wanted to scream with rage and frustration. The noise and chatter-chatter were infuriating.

And now here were her brother and his pup to add to the gaiety of nations!

'I found the poor little beggar shivering in an entry next to the chemist's,' Alex said. 'You couldn't have looked very hard for him, Mary.'

For the next hour the twins and the pup rushed madly from the living-room into the scullery, and then from the scullery into the living-room. Mr. Nicholson went on reading. The wireless went on blaring. Mrs. Nicholson and Jean Symington went on talking. Alex sat and looked at his paper, getting up sometimes to rescue the pup from the twins and sometimes to rescue the twins from the pup. Mary kept looking at the writing-pad on her knee.

At last Jean Symington rose, saying: 'We'll have to go. Jock 'll be home expecting his tea. His mother would never dream of giving him it. But before I go I mustn't forget what I came for.'

'What I really came for,' she said, 'was to ask if Father could give Jock a loan of his bowler hat for a funeral?'

'Will it fit him?' Mrs. Nicholson said. 'I think Jock's head is a bit bigger than Father's.'

'Go and see, Mary,' she said. 'It's upstairs in the bottom of the wardrobe in the wee room.'

Mary was going upstairs when she heard a knock at the door. She retraced her steps. 'Hello, beautiful!' a young man said almost before she had opened the door. 'Home again! It's the great M'Kinlay!' he cried, entering the living-room. 'H'ya, folks!'

Mary clenched her fists as she went upstairs again. Bunt M'Kinlay was a pal of Alex's: a young man from a fishing

village on the fringes of Edinburgh, who must at one time
have said to himself, 'You, too, can be the life of the party,'
and had been trying to prove it ever since. He was still
mentally aged sixteen.

She took as long as she could to find the bowler hat, and
then she stood for a few minutes, leaning her forehead against
the door of the wardrobe. Oh, Harold, she moaned to herself,
why aren't you here with me to help me to bear it?

When she came downstairs she found that Jean had sat
down again and that Bunt M'Kinlay was sprawling on the
floor with the twins and the pup scrambling over him. It was
an hour later before Jean left; Allan asking if they really were
going to see Jesus this time. All through tea Bunt talked,
telling story after story to Mr. and Mrs. Nicholson who laughed
and egged him on. 'What a comic ye are, Bunt!' Mrs.
Nicholson kept saying. Mary and Alex sat, eating in silence,
occasionally laughing as politely as they could at Bunt's far
from polite jokes.

Mary said she would wash up, hoping this would give her a
respite. But Bunt insisted on drying for her. She was at
screaming point by the time they had finished.

'Well, I must go and meet the latest girl-friend,' Bunt said.

This was a signal for Mrs. Nicholson to ask about his latest
heart-throbs. It took him over half an hour to tell her, standing most of the time with his hand on the door-handle. Then
finally he put on his overcoat. Mary thought that Alex was a
bit pushing in his eagerness to stand in the open doorway,
ready to show his friend out. She settled herself in a corner
of the sofa and poised her pen over her lettter.

'By the way, Mr. Nicholson, did I tell you the bar about the
old lady and the Communist?' Bunt said.

After ten minutes of standing in the draught of the living-
room door, Alex sat down with a resigned expression. Mary
picked moodily at the hem of her dress.

'Well, I must go!' Bunt cried. 'The girl-friend 'll be
so frozen that she'll be giving me the frozen mitt!'

Alex went to the outer door with him. Mary bit her lips,

trying to recapture what she had intended her first sentence to be.

'Oh, Mrs. Nicholson!' Bunt cried, opening the living-room door again. 'Would it be all right if I bring the new girl-friend here for tea next Sunday? I'd like her to meet you. My future meet my past sort of thing!'

'You wouldn't like to bring your bed here, too, would you?' Mary said, trying to keep the bitterness out of her voice.

'What would I bring a bed for, beautiful!' Bunt chuckled bawdily. 'Could I not share yours!'

'Well, thank God, he's gone,' Mary said when Alex finally shut the door on his pal. 'If anybody else comes here to-night I'm going upstairs, cold or no cold. I'd rather sit up there with my coat on than endure any more of what we've had to-day.'

'That goes for me, too,' Alex said.

Mary settled herself to write her letter. Alex began to read. Mr. Nicholson switched on the wireless which he had been forced to put off when Bunt M'Kinlay arrived. Mrs. Nicholson got her knitting and listened placidly to the radio serial of Galsworthy's *Man of Property*.

'Listen!' Alex said suddenly.

'Was that a knock at the door?' Mrs. Nicholson asked.

Alex nodded. He looked at Mary. But already she was on her feet, writing-pad and pen clenched tightly in her hand. 'I'm away upstairs,' she said. 'Give me time to put on my coat, Ma, before you answer the door.'

YOU KILL ME

'YOU'D better strip,' the nurse said.
'O.K.,' he said.
She motioned him into a cubicle and drew the curtains.
'Must I take off everything?' he said.
'What is it that's wrong?' she said. 'Your tummy, isn't it?'
'Yes,' he said.
'Well, if you take off your shirt and upper things that should be sufficient,' she said.
He could see her through the space between the curtains and the edge of the cubicle. He was taking off his tie when she returned with a card and leaned it against the wall, poising a pencil above it.
'Name?' she said.
'James Ravelston.'
'Age?'
· 'Twenty-three.'
'Occupation.'
'Er—artist.'
He wished he wouldn't blush whenever anybody asked him his occupation. After all, he really was an artist now. Things were different from the days when he had been a shipping-clerk going to art classes at night. He had a right to be called a professional. Hadn't he designed some half-dozen book-wrappers and had a picture hung in an exhibition? True, it was only a small exhibition. But he had had press-notices, and those who professed to know about such things had boldly predicted a future for him.

A future! He smiled with studied sarcasm as he took the hospital dressing-gown from its hook and put it on. A future with this! It was just like this to happen when he was set at last on the right road. He could not help feeling sorry for himself as he slipped his hand under the dressing-gown and touched the small lump on his side. He wondered what it was. His doctor had been dreadfully vague. He had just said: 'Take this letter to the Infirmary, and they'll give you an examination.'

Probably cancer. He was certain it was something malignant, something that, if it didn't cut his career short, would certainly trouble him for years before he finally succumbed to it.

He tried to sigh philosophically. After all, all geniuses had something wrong with them. D. H. Lawrence, Keats, Kafka, they'd all had consumption or something. Well, they could say in the future, Ravelston had cancer. . . .

'Wouldn't you like to sit at the fire until your turn comes?' the nurse asked through the curtains.

'O.K.,' he said.

Self-consciously, in the grey hospital dressing-gown with its wide sleeves, he walked over to the fire where two other men were waiting to be examined. One of them, a fellow of about his own age, grinned and said:

'Another lamb for the slaughter!'

Ravelston curled his lips in what could have been taken for a smile.

'Join the merry party,' the young man said, indicating a seat between himself and the elderly man with thin grey hair and old-fashioned mutton-chops.

For a few seconds nothing was said, then the young man with the pasty face began to hum *Three Little Maids from School are We* in a voice which would have made Sullivan blench.

'Anything serious,' he said to Ravelston in exactly the same tone as he might have said it was a fine day.

'I don't know.' Ravelston saw himself as the great artist courageously denying his suffering.

YSC—I

'It's my kidneys,' the elderly man said. 'They trouble me something awful. I can't sleep at nights for the pain.'

'Cheer up!' the young man said. 'We'll soon be dead!'

He jumped up and began to skip about, holding his dressing-gown tightly around him as though he were a woman.

'I feel like a mannequin in this,' he said. He began to give an impersonation of a famous movie vamp: 'C'mon in and see my kimona!'

'He's a great lad,' the old man said, laughing.

'Yes,' Ravelston said.

He wondered how much longer he would need to wait. The pasty-faced young man was getting on his nerves with his clowning. He wished he would be quiet. Didn't he realize that he was in the presence of a genius whose sphere of activity would be cut off before it had a proper chance to flower?

'What time does the parade start, sister?' the young man called to the nurse.

She laughed and said: 'Doctor McClintock should be here any minute now. Why? Are you in a hurry?'

'Well, not exactly,' he said. 'But I promised to take my kid to see Laurel and Hardy this afternoon, and I wouldn't like to disappoint him.'

Laurel and Hardy. . . . Just about the fellow's level. . . .

'I saw a pretty good picture last night,' the young man said. 'Alan Dinehart was in it. You know, the big sort of stout bloke. Damned good actor. He kept saying "You kill me" whenever anybody told him anything. I thought it was a pretty good expression. I could have died every time he said it.'

'Could you?' Ravelston said politely.

'I like Myrna Loy,' the old man said.

'Yes, hot stuff, isn't she?' the young man said.

'That's Doctor McClintock now,' the nurse said. 'Will you come this way, Mr. Burnett?'

'The doomed man ate a hearty meal and walked with a firm step to the scaffold,' the young man said to Ravelston as the door closed behind the elderly man.

'Reminds me of a joke I heard the other day,' he said, looking round to see that the nurse wasn't within earshot.

Ravelston laughed politely at the joke. He put his hand inside the dressing-gown and touched the lump.

'Pretty funny, wasn't it?' the young man said, when he had recovered from his convulsion of giggles and coughing. 'I just about killed myself when I heard it.'

'Doctor McClintock will be ready for you in a minute, Mr. Wilkie,' the nurse said. 'You'd better calm down before he examines you.'

'You kill me, sister,' Wilkie said, laughing.

'I would if I had you safely in a ward,' she said. She sparred up to him. Wilkie beat his chest like Tarzan and put up his fists. 'So you wanna get tough!' he said.

'We'll see who's tough when I get you into bed!' she said, dancing around him playfully, poking at him with her fists.

'C'mon and referee this match,' Wilkie said to Ravelston. 'This dame's cheating. Ah, you big bully! You should go in for all-in wrestling, sister!'

'Nurse,' a voice called from the other room.

Immediately she straightened herself and became once more an automaton.

'Yes, doctor,' she cried.

'My turn now for the judge's black cap,' Wilkie said, sorting his dressing-gown and smoothing his hair.

'Is this yours?' Ravelston said, picking up a pocket-book from the chair Wilkie had been sitting in. As he handed it over, a photograph fell from it.

Wilkie picked it up. 'Thanks,' he said. He held out the photograph shyly. 'This is my kid.'

Ravelston looked at the gay, laughing face of a child about three. 'Nice kid,' he said.

'Well, so long!' Wilkie said. 'See you in church!'

Left alone, Ravelston began to think again about his trouble, worrying more about the mental strain than the physical pain. He wondered if he would need an operation. If so, he hoped that he wouldn't find himself in the same ward as Wilkie.

What a fool the man was! It was hard lines on his child
being saddled with an empty-headed father like that. Thank
God, he had no kids. Nothing but his yet unborn paintings. . . .

Doctor McClintock pressed the lump on Ravelston's side
with his forefinger. 'Does it hurt?' he said.

'Yes, very much.'

The doctor turned away and said over his shoulder: 'Come
in and we'll soon put that right for you.'

'Are there any more, nurse?' he said.

'No, doctor.'

He started towards the door, but Ravelston stopped him.

'What *is* wrong, doctor?' he said.

'It's just a cyst,' the doctor said brusquely. 'Nothing
serious. Good morning.'

Ravelston saw his whole picture of himself as the Crucified
Artist being brushed away like a jig-saw puzzle as he turned
and found the nurse at his elbow, pencil poised.

'Which ward will you be going into, Mr. Ravelston?'

'Er—I suppose the paying one,' he said.

'When can you come in?' she said.

'Any time.'

'That's O.K.,' she said. 'You can put on your clothes and
get on your way rejoicing.'

While he was dressing, Ravelston heard first the old man
and then Wilkie go out. Wilkie sparred verbally a little with
the nurse as he was going out, and the last Ravelston heard
was: 'You kill me, sister!'

When he was dressed, he said: 'That fellow was a bit of
a fool, wasn't he? There couldn't be very much wrong with
him.'

The nurse looked up from the sink where she was washing
some bandages. Her mouth flickered queerly.

'We never discuss patients with other patients,' she said.

THE PRISONERS

FOR the first two or three days Mary did not come into contact much with the prisoners. She saw them working in the fields or going about the steading, but she could not bring herself to go near them. She felt ashamed. She was ashamed because they were herded together in that camp over there behind barbed wire and put on a lorry like cattle every day and brought here to the farm to work. And she was ashamed because of Will. Some of the prisoners perhaps had been farmers in Italy, used to walking about as Will walked about, giving orders. She tried to imagine how he would have felt had he been unlucky enough to be a soldier and taken prisoner. Could he have stood docile and uncomplaining as they had to stand while strangers jabbered about him in Italian, sizing him up and talking about his points as if he were a horse? Could he have sweated and strained while another man stood by with his hands in his pockets? She felt that it was disloyal to him to think like that, but she could not help it. If only he were a bit more sensitive; if only he had enough imagination to think *There but for the grace of God go I.* . . . She wished that he would stay inside, that he would not stride about amongst them like that, head and shoulders above them, pushing his way through them as if they were cattle or slaves. It was like the old Roman days you read about in the novels of Naomi Mitchison . . . only now the Romans were the slaves. . . .

She realized that she was being unfair to Will. He really did not look down upon the prisoners—he couldn't help being

125

so tall. He wasn't like lots of farmers, looking on the prisoners merely as cheap labour. Actually he had been very good to them. He had had the barn swept out and tidied up for them to sit in at dinner-time, and seats had been put in and a fire-place built. And he gave them as much milk and potatoes as they wanted to supplement the rations they brought with them. They needed that, of course. Will was wise enough to see that they couldn't be expected to do a hard day's work in his fields on the rations the Government allowed them.

But she was being nasty again. Why should you be so nasty? she asked herself. If you weren't in love with Will, if you didn't adore him, I could see the force of it. But you know fine that you worship him. You know that you'd let him walk over the top of you. . . .

And by God he would walk over the top of you, too, if you gave him the chance. He walks over the top of you often enough and you not asking for it.

It was just his manner. He couldn't help looking so sulky and dour. It was just the way he was made. Even with his own men he hardly ever unbent. She knew that it was a certain shyness, an unsureness, that made him like that. He was aggressive because he was really at sea within himself. All the psychology books said that. He was still a little boy play-ing at being a man. And like a little boy he could be so charm-ing when he liked. He needed only to look at her and all the hard things she had been thinking about him were swept away.

There were sixteen prisoners. They all looked very young, little more than boys; the average age would be twenty-two. At first they all looked alike : just small dark figures in a chocolate-magenta coloured uniform with a blue circle sewn on the back of the tunic and on one leg of the trousers. But after a few days she began to know individuals as she knew the other men who worked on the farm. There was the very short, broad-shouldered youth who came to the back door every day at dinner-time for boiling water for their coffee, and there was the tall one with the forage-cap pulled far down over his eyes, who was always singing and who gave pennies to the children about the farm. She heard from the maid that his name was Luigi. '' That means Willie in Scotch,' Bella. said. ' He tellt Geordie that.'

Most of them had been captured at Tobruk or Benghazi. 'They dinna like the Australians ava,' Bella said. 'They stole their watches and their rings. ✓ They even cut off their fingers if they couldna haul the rings off. Fancy onybody doin' that! Oh, they're wild, cruel devils, thae Australians. And they tore up their photographs.'

' Surely not, Bella! ' Mary said.

' Ay, they did that,' Bella said, nodding her head solemnly. ' Luigi tellt Geordie that. They tore his photo o' his wife. I ca' it a disgust for onybody to dae that—even though they are Italians.'

' But one can hardly blame all the Australians for something that was done by one or two ruffians,' Mary said. ' After all, there are rough elements in all armies. In the British as well as in the German or the Australian.'

' I dinna believe that ony o' *oor* boys would dae things like that,' Bella said.

' There's no knowing what men 'll do when they get together and get out of hand,' Mary said.

'Och, maybe some men. But ye could nivir imagine the likes o' Geordie—or Mr. Murray—doin' things like that even to Italians,' Bella said.

' No, I can't imagine Geordie being so cruel,' Mary said.

Once or twice Mary saw Geordie standing with the gang he was in charge of, talking, while they leaned on their spades, listening and laughing. ' Whether Geordie's speaking Italian to them or whether they're understanding his Mearns tongue, I don't know! ' Mary said to her husband. ' But he certainly lays off plenty to them! '

Will laughed. ' Geordie's nae speakin' Italian whatever he's speakin'! He's been teachin' them a grand lot of auld Scots words beginning with F and B. It's awfa funny. I heard Geordie say to one yesterday, " Mussolini no effing good."

But the lad was quick; he laughed and said, "Churchill no effing good." '

Will roared and laughed at the remembrance, slapping his thigh like a schoolboy. Mary could not help smiling. After two years of marriage she was still in awe of her huge husband; more afraid of him than in love with him. But at times like this, when his eternal boyishness showed, she felt almost maternal and protecting towards him. Perhaps it was this maternal feeling that had made her leave her teaching and marry him; it must have been that. What else could have made a woman of her education come and bury herself on a farm, even a farm as large as this? Sometimes when she was feeling bitter and angry against him, remembering the things she had given up when she married him, she wished that his boyishness would assert itself oftener; it gave him that charm that never failed to win her round. But unfortunately his other side, the dictatorial, patriarchal, father of his people side, was almost always on the ascendant.

Often she made up her mind to have a row with him, but as soon as she saw him she could not say all the things she had rehearsed. When he wasn't there, when he went away as he so often did without saying where he was going or when he would be back she would rage and say to herself all the things she was going to tell him when he came back. But as soon as she saw him she could not bring herself to say anything. She knew that it would have been hopeless, anyway. He would just have laughed. Or—what was worse—he would just have ignored her, treating her like a child. Or he might have lost his temper so much that he would not have listened, no matter how reasonable her complaints might have been. He would listen to nobody. 'I will not be dictated to by you or by anybody else,' he had once said to her. It was the same when any of the men complained about anything. It was not that he bullered and swore like so many of his farmer neighbours. Their men knew what to expect from them, and they swore back, knowing that the next day they could speak to them as if nothing had happened. But Will Murray was

different. His word was law. He was the Big White Chief.
He had been used to getting his own way ever since he was
a child, and like a child when he first hears the word 'No',
he could not understand. As a child he had been a bully—
Mary knew that indirectly from the stories his mother and
sisters had told her about his childhood. He was still a bully.
He loved to pinch her or slap her bottom, and he would laugh
delightedly when she made to pinch or slap him back. But
she did not do that often, because she always came off worst.
'I'm like Churchill, I'm still a schoolboy,' he said once to her.
'Only I'm not as fond of fighting as he is.'

But usually his sadism was much more subtle than his
boisterous pinching and slapping. He kept her guessing
about things; she never knew where she was with him. She
could not imagine what he was thinking. He never told her
anything. And like every other woman she wanted to know
the ins and outs of things; she wanted him to confide in her,
to ask her opinion about things. But he never did that. He
never spoke about his business. He could be going to build a
new byre or sack the whole lot of his men—it was all the
same; she would never have known from the expression on
his face. 'The Sphinx!' she sometimes said to him. 'The
Sphinx! I bet it would be more communicative than you!'
But he just smiled—that slow, mocking smile that made her
furious. She wanted then to slap his smooth, plump cheeks.
To make *some* impression on him. . . .

It had been like that about the Italians. She had not known
that he was getting prisoner-of-war labour until the morning
the Italians came and she saw them going about the steading.
And when she asked him how they were shaping as workers
he merely said: 'The grieve thinks they're all right.'

Mary tried to speak to those who came to the back door, but
she found that they knew only a few words of English. So
she tried them in French. But her '*parlez-vous français?*'
elicited no response beyond a shrug and a smile. She realized
then that most of them belonged to the peasant class. Like
Geordie and the other men on the farm who would also have

stared uncomprehendingly if they had been prisoners in Italy and somebody had said: '*Parlez-vous français?*'

They had one weary-looking guard with them. 'A damned nuisance,' Will said. 'He's no bloody good at all. He does nothing. He's never with them. He spends all his time in the dairy, putting off the land girls' time. I must see what can be done about him. I don't see why they send him at all.'

'But if one of them should try to escape?' Will's mother said anxiously.

'They'll nae try to escape. Where could they go? And what would they try to escape for, anyway? They've got plenty of freedom about here. They get to move about as they like. They get a loan of the men's bicycles and cycle up and down. I even saw one of them playing with the guard's rifle and steel helmet yesterday!'

'But surely that isn't safe?' Mrs. Murray said. 'I mean, they might be quite desperate characters for all we know. And after all, they're our enemies. I don't think it's right to give them such freedom at all.'

'Dinna be daft, mother!' Will said. 'They're all quite harmless, and they all look happy enough. What would they want to escape for? They're better here than in that camp behind barbed wire. They're better here than in Libya. I bet they're all glad to be out of the war. No, no, they'll nae try to escape. They all look quite happy.'

'Maybe they *look* happy,' Mary said. 'But that isn't quite the same thing.'

'Ach, there's nothing coming over them,' Will said. 'They get leave to wander about as they please. They're as free as you or me.'

'I wonder,' Mary said. 'Bella tells me that that Luigi one has a wife and a baby that he's never seen.'

'Now, Mary, you're just getting sentimental about them,' Mrs. Murray said. 'It's a great mistake. Remember that they're our enemies.'

Often Mary felt that next to throttling Will she would have liked to throttle his mother. Indeed she would have preferred

to throttle his mother. For, after all, his mother had none of
Will's endearing points. She was a small, thin woman with
an eager face. She was always rushing about after Will—
rushing after him as she had rushed for the last twenty-five
years. She was so eager to please him. She had spoiled him
so much, ran after him and waited on him hand and foot, that
she had quite spoilt him for any other woman. Even yet when
he had a wife who was in her way as eager to please, to make
a footstool of herself, Mrs. Murray could not refrain from
rushing about, jumping at his slightest command. Will would
just come in, slump down in his chair, and both women were
on their toes. ' Bring me my cigarettes from the office, Mary,'
he would say, and before Mary had time to move, Mrs. Murray
would be away for them, half-running. ' There you are, dear,'
she would say brightly, and she would look at Mary as much
as to say : See now, you're far too slow. What my boy needs
is somebody who'll anticipate his every wish.

Mrs. Murray was very concerned about the guard lounging
about. ' If he's not needed to watch the Italians,' she said,
' he could at least do some work himself. I think it's scandalous. Why can't he bring his mending with him or something
like that? '

'Dinna be daft, mother! ' Will winked at Mary.

' I'm not being daft at all,' Mrs. Murray said. ' It's scandalous. The Commandant at the Prison Camp had the cheek
to ask the ladies of the Women's Guild if they'd do the men's
darning and mending for them.'

' The prisoners? ' Mary said.

' No, the guards.' Mrs. Murray shuffled about on her chair
like an indignant hen on eggs. ' I think it's perfect cheek!
He wants to send fifty or sixty parcels to the Guild every week
after they come back from the laundry.'

' Well, well, it'll give the Guild wifies something to do,'
Will said. ' They're all that keen to poke their noses into
other folk's business, anyway. This 'll be a grand chance for
them.'

' I think it's scandalous,' Mrs. Murray said. ' The ladies

have all got plenty of other war work as it is. And almost all
these men have got wives of their own. What's to hinder them
sending their mending home? For that matter, what's to
hinder them doing their own mending? I'm sure all these
poor sailors and the lads in the Middle East do their own
mending. These men at the Camp have nothing else to do.
Guarding a puckle poor Italians! '

' Who might try to escape! ' Will grinned.

' The guard who comes here could easily bring his mending
with him instead of lounging about, putting off the girls' time,'
Mrs. Murray said.

' And get the girls to do it! ' Will said. ' Or maybe you'd
like to do it for him? '

' Don't try to be funny, Will. I'm perfectly serious. There's
nothing to hinder the man doing his darning while he's sitting
out there in the barn. It would give him something to occupy
his attention.'

' What about the prisoners? ' Mary said. ' Who's going to
do *their* mending, poor things? '

' Ach, they've nothing to mend,' Will said.

' Now, don't you get sentimental about them, Mary,' her
mother-in-law said. ' I'm as sorry as you are for them, and
all that, but—remember they're our enemies! '

But Mary could not help feeling a little bit sentimental
about the Italians. Even in their captivity there was something romantic about them. They sang, and when they spoke
or shouted to each other, their voices had a lilt. They brought
an exotic note into the drab life of the farm. You felt that
they should be going about with gold rings in their ears, that
there should be bright sunshine and laughter and a full ripe
moon and love. . . . She felt a fellow-feeling with them, she
told herself. For after all, she was as much a prisoner as they
were. A prisoner bound by her love and fear of Will.

Every day about lousing-time she began to stand near
the sitting-room window, waiting to see the tractors bringing
them up from the fields. But she could not watch them as
she would have liked. She remained tense, ready to move

away quickly from the window at the first sounds of her mother-in-law coming into the room. That was the only good thing about Mrs. Murray—she gave you good warning of her approach! Although a small body, she made a tremendous noise, banging down her heels and singing as she rushed about. A sign of her good temper, she said. ' I've always been sunny and on the go,' she would say. ' Nobody has ever been able to say that I sulked or wasn't full of beans! I'm sure I don't know where Will gets his silence and moodiness from.' She infuriated Mary with her brightness—especially in the mornings when she came downstairs to breakfast, singing, and insisting upon chattering all through the meal. Mary and Will would sit and eat, never answering her, staring at the table-cloth or out of the window. And their silence would in its turn infuriate Mrs. Murray, so that after a few remarks about some people having got out of bed on their wrong sides and about their unsociableness the morning meal usually ended in either a quarrel or in repressed tempers—Mary and her mother-in-law brushing past each other in the passages, each of them looking at something over the other's shoulders.

Mary was standing like this at the window one forenoon when Will came into the room silently and came up behind her. ' Well, are you watching our Italians? ' he said, pressing his forefingers under her armpits.

Mary shifted uneasily. She felt dwarfed and insecure when Will stood like that behind her; he was so huge and solid. She felt that sometime without warning he might reach out and crush her.

' Yes,' she said. ' But I must away and see about the hot water for their coffee.'

It was a new one who came for the water to-day. A tall youngster Mary had not seen before. ' Excuse me, madame, you speak French, yes? ' he said, smiling and handing her the pail. ' *Les autres me dit que vous le parlez.*'

Mary blushed. ' *Mais . . . oui. . . .* '

He grinned. ' *Ah, bien!* ' And he began to speak rapidly in French. Mary could catch only a word here and there, but

she was able to make out the sense of what he was saying. He
wanted to have conversations with her every day. He would
speak in English and she would speak in French.

He came close to her, looking down at her almost flirta-
tiously. 'I speak good English, too. Yes!'

'*Oui*,' Mary said. She spoke slowly in her pedantic school-
mistress French that she would be delighted to speak with him,
but not *à ce moment*; she had work to do. Perhaps she would
see him at night before he went back to the camp?

'*Ah, mais oui, mais oui*,' he said, and he drew himself up
and clicked his heels, bowing to her as she backed out of the
kitchen.

Mary went back to the sitting-room, smiling. Of course,
he was too charming—like all Southern people—and he was
probably a rogue into the bargain. Still, she liked it: all this
heel-clicking, these half-bows from the waist. The Polish
soldiers they had had for the harvest last year had also had it,
but with them she had felt that it was just put on. There was
a coldness about them, a superiority, that she did not feel with
the Italians. Of course, the Poles were a free people; maybe
they had every right to be arrogant—whereas these Italians
were prisoners. But this one was more like a Pole than
the others; none of them had that heel-clicking and half-
bowing; they were more like children, warm and natural and
gay.

Mary opened the sitting-room window as wide as it would
open. It was the first sunny day they had had for several
days, and the Italians were taking full advantage of it. Some
of them had brought out their dinner and were sitting around
the barn-door. The tall French-speaking youth was in the
centre, speaking and gesticulating to those around him.

Mary opened the gramophone. 'What are you going to
do?' Will asked.

'I'm going to put on some records. Italians like music.'

Mrs. Murray sniffed. 'Pampering them, that's what it is.
I bet nobody does all these things for our own poor boys in Italy
or Germany. My word, they'll be made to work and slave.

They won't get fires built for them in barns and coffee boiled for them and gramophones put on at dinner-time. . . . Really, Mary, I whiles think you're not wise.'

Will winked at his wife. 'It's only the auld wife! Never let on you hear her!' he said. 'But see and dinna put on any of your highbrow dirt. None of your Beethoven and Bach! Give them something cheerful.'

'But Beethoven's quite cheerful,' Mary said, putting on the *Emperor Concerto*. 'What could be more cheerful than that? It's like a parade. You can imagine you see horses prancing and nodding their heads and trumpets blowing and flags flying and people cheering. . . .'

'See here,' Will said, searching among the pile of records. 'Here's something more like the thing. *The Muckin' o' Geordie's Byre*. That'll make them cock up their lugs! I hear that Geordie has been trying to teach them it, anyway.'

But Mary did not take the record. 'Don't be daft, Will,' she said, and she selected Elisabeth Schumann singing *Batti, Batti, O Bel Masetto* to put on after the Beethoven.

'It's just pure nonsense,' Mrs. Murray said. 'It's scandalous, pampering them like this. Remember they're our enemies. I'll never forget that it was the Italians who first used poison-gas against the poor defenceless Abyssinians. Really, what between having to do the darning and the mending for their guards and letting them cycle about the steading as they like and play with the guard's rifle. . . . This country 'll soon be run by Italians! And it's people like you and Will that encourage it. All your silly Socialist nonsense. . . .'

'Is the dinner near ready, Mary?' Will cut into his mother's chattering.

They were sitting at dinner when the telephone rang. Will was away for a long time in the office, answering it. 'Who was it, dear?' Mrs. Murray said when he came back.

'A man,' he said, shovelling his food quickly into his mouth and not looking up from his plate.

'I knew it must be a man,' Mrs. Murray said, trying to be arch. 'I hoped it would be a man, anyway. Mary would have something to say if it had been a woman, wouldn't you, dear?'

Mary looked at her plate, too. She would have liked to have struck Mrs. Murray. Did you ever see such a fool! Not even after all these years did she know when to hold her tongue. No wonder Will was so silent. He must have been driven into this silence in self-defence. His mother's inane questions would drive anybody daft.

'Who was it, dear?' Mrs. Murray said again.

Will heaved himself round and put his empty plate on the sideboard behind him. 'It was Mr. Johnston of the Prison Camp,' he said. 'He phoned to tell me that our Italians are to be cut down to ten on Monday. Now, are you satisfied! What about shouting for the rest of the dinner, Mary?'

Throughout the remainder of the dinner Mrs. Murray chattered angrily about the injustice of cutting down the number of their prisoners to ten. 'After Will taking them all this week when he wasn't really needing them! And then next week when the harvest's starting and we're needing them —to be cut down! It's not fair at all. If I were you, Will, I'd complain to the Executive Committee. You have the biggest farm around here. Surely you need more labour than any of your neighbours? I think it's scandalous!'

Will ate his pudding as quickly as possible, then he rose and went out in the middle of his mother's chattering. Mary would have liked to have risen and followed him, but she knew that if she did, Mrs. Murray would take offence. So she sat silently and let the old woman air her grievances.

I babble, babble, babble . . . just like Tennyson's Brook. No wonder Will was moody and queer sometimes—after putting up with this for twenty-five years. Mary did her best to protect him from his mother's possessiveness and nagging. She knew that she was possessive about him, too, but not in the same stupid way, she hoped. She realized that he was a man and that he had all a man's outside interests. But his mother still thought of him as a little boy. It was undoubtedly Mrs. Murray with her endless stupidities who was the cause of so much of his childishness. Mrs. Murray always boasted that she had never thwarted him in any way—and see the result! A pocket dictator! She said, too, that she had always tried to get his confidence—and again see the result! This secretiveness that would drive anybody crazy. Once in a moment of expansion Will himself had blamed his mother for his secretiveness. 'When I was a loon she was aye wanting to know where I'd been or what I'd been doing, and so I got into the habit of telling her as little as possible.' Mary had always remembered this, and so she never questioned him—or if she did she was more furious at herself for asking than she was at him for not answering—and she never nagged at him in the way his mother did when he would not answer.

He was sitting listening to the one o'clock news when she went into the sitting-room. 'We'll have to pick the ten best of our sixteen Tallies,' he said. 'I'll tell the grieve to get their names and we'll send a list back with them to the Camp. After training them and getting them into our ways it would be a pity to send them to somebody else—especially if we got some duds.'

.   .   .   .

That afternoon Mary went on her bicycle round some of the neighbouring farms to collect for the Red Cross. She returned home at lousing-time. Some of the Italians were speaking to Geordie's two children. The French-speaking youth was down on his hunkers, with his arms round one of them, laughing and talking in a mixture of Italian and English. He sprang up when he saw Mary, clicking his heels and bowing. '*J'aime les enfants,*' he said, smiling. '*J'aime tous les gens.*'

Mary leaned against her bike, smiling from him to the children. 'I like children, too,' she said. 'And I also like all people.'

'You do not like this war?' he said, beginning to speak so rapidly in French that she could not follow every word, although she understood the gist of what he was saying. 'It is horrible and useless. Our leader is swollen up with ambition.

YSC—K

I do not like our leader. Me—I would not go to the war. I had to be taken. I hate war. I am not Fascisti. I hate Fascisti. I had to run away from the police. I am not well known—but still I had to run away in my own country. I shall not go back to Italy after the war.'

'*Après la guerre* . . .' she said slowly.

He shrugged. 'It must finish some time. In 1944 I think. It must finish then. Then I go to America. I have friends there. Rich friends. They will help me. I shall not go back to Italy.'

' But your family ? ' she said.

He smiled sadly. 'They must come to America, too. I shall not go back to Italy.' He took a pocket-book from his tunic and opened it, taking out some photographs. 'This is my mother and my sister-in-law. And this is my fiancée,' he said, handing her another.

' *Très jolie*,' Mary said.

It was not a very good photograph of a very ordinary-looking Italian girl. Mary was disappointed. He was a good-looking youth and deserved better. '*Elle est très jolie*,' she said, handing it back. ' The Australians did not get this! '

He sighed. 'No, but—they got other things. Oh, madame, how I hate this war! How glad I am to be here, away from it. This work '—he waved his hand around—'I am not used to it, but I am not afraid of it. It is better to work. Work helps you to forget. In South Africa I was a prisoner for six months and all that time I did nothing. In the camp we just slept. It is not good. Our muscles, they got soft. Our brains —they get soft, too! No, it is very bad. But now here we are in Scotland. We can work. We are not behind barbed wire all the time. Soon when we are able we will be able to work very good.'

' Farm work is hard,' Mary said. ' To those who are not used to it.'

' Ah, but I am not afraid of work, madame. I only say that we are not fit yet for it.'

All the time he was speaking and gesticulating with a purely

Southern charm of manner Mary kept telling herself that he was a fraud. He was too plausible, too charming. Watch yourself, she said, don't let yourself be tricked. He's going to ask for something, sure as fate.

'*Après la guerre*,' he said, 'I shall not go back to Italy. I shall go to America. But I shall need a good friend in this country to help me. You, madame—you will be my friend?'

'*Oui, oui*,' she said, unable to explain that, of course, she would be willing to help him in any way, but with reservations. Who knew where either he or she would be after the war?

He smiled happily and took a piece of paper from his note-book. '*My name*,' he said, writing it down. 'Mario Belavito. Compagnina, Sicily. After the war you will write to me there. Yes?'

She nodded, thinking that 'after the war' was such a long way away that it was quite safe to promise anything.

'Your name?' he said, handing her a piece of paper. 'Write, please.'

She wrote 'Mrs. Mary Murray, The Braes of Lunan, Auchencairn, Scotland.' Handing it back to him and watching him put it in his pocket-book beside his photographs, she felt her face go fiery and then go cold. She knew she'd done something foolish. All sorts of ideas rushed through her imagination. If anybody saw that slip of paper! After all, he was a prisoner. An enemy. Suppose anything happened to him at the camp and he was searched? How did he come to have her name and address? They'd never believe that she'd given it to him in a purely friendly way. She might be arrested as a spy. In any case, what would Will think? The prisoner might show it to any of the men. They'd say she was carrying on with him. . . .

'Excuse me, I must go,' she said quickly. 'My husband will be in for his tea soon.'

All evening Mary kept thinking about that scrap of paper. It was 'trading' with the enemy . . . wasn't there a law about it? Heavens, if the man got caught with it on him? What a fine speak for the folk of the Howe o' the Mearns! It was a good job that man, Grassic Gibbon, who wrote the books about the Mearns folk and who was so disliked by them because of it, was dead, or what a story he'd have made of it! Should she tell Will? Or should she wait and ask the Italian for the paper back to-morrow? If the Italian came back to-morrow. . . . Heavens, what if he didn't. . . .

She was so worried that she had nightmares about it, waking at last in a sweat because she was standing in the dock with both Churchill and Mrs. Murray scowling down from the bench at her.

‘   ·   ·   ·   ·   ■   ■   ▲   ■

The next day Will said : ‘There's a Tally here that speaks English and French.’

‘I know,’ Mary said. ‘I've been speaking to him.’

‘The grieve says he's no bloody good,’ Will said. ‘He talks too much. We don't want him back.’

‘Oh, but Will!’ she cried. ‘The poor thing—he was so pleased to get somewhere where somebody understood him. You can surely find something for him to do.’

‘There's nothing he can do,’ Will said. ‘Except talk! We don't want him back.’

He put on his cap and went out. Mary sighed. The poor devil of an Italian—just when he had come to some place where somebody understood him—somebody of his own kind —for obviously he was not a peasant like the others—to be driven away because he was not a good worker. And why should Will be allowed to judge, anyway, whether a man was a good worker or not? He was as strong as two men himself —though he would not have lifted a finger to help a man of half his strength and size lift anything too heavy for him. ‘And why should I?’ he would have said if he'd been tackled about it. ‘I'm paying him to work, amn't I? If he can't manage it, then it's his look out.’

Mary seethed with rage, and she seethed more because she had nobody she could talk to about it. She knew that it was hopeless to mention it to Mrs. Murray. She felt like speaking

to Bella, but was terrified lest in some way it came back to
Will's mother.

About four o'clock that afternoon Will came in and said:
'Mary, you might get in that boy that speaks English. He's
got a list of the ten best Tallies. You copy it out and we'll
send it to the Camp with them to-night.'

'But he'll want his name on it, too,' she said. 'I don't
like . . .'

'Och, we can easy make out another list and keep his name
off it,' Will laughed. 'We'll send it in an envelope!'

Mary did not like the job, but she went to the field where
the Italians were working. The tall one smiled and drew himself up straight when he saw her coming. *'Pouvez-vous venir
avec moi?'* she said. And she added, smiling: *'S'il vous
plaît?'*

He spoke rapidly to the Italian sergeant who was in charge
of the squad. The sergeant nodded to Mary, then he started
to come with them. All the way to the house she spoke in
French, and the tall prisoner translated it into Italian to the
sergeant.

She sat down at the kitchen-table and dipped her pen in the
ink. 'I will write down the names,' she said slowly in
French. 'Will you read them out to me, please?'

He leaned over her, and she shifted uneasily. All the time
she was writing she was acutely aware of the little black hairs
on his brown fore-arms. 'ANTONINI,' he spelled. 'GIOVANNI.
English? John! French, Jean!'

The sergeant stood back a little, frowning. He looked
enquiringly from Mary to the tall prisoner when they spoke.
Every now and then Belavito spoke quickly to him in Italian,
and occasionally they laughed. Mary felt embarrassed and
very defenceless. She wished desperately that Will were there.
Even Mrs. Murray would have been a comfort. . . .

'Je vous donnerai . . . the list,' Mary said slowly, *'quand
vous avez fini le* . . .' She snapped her fingers. 'Work,
work, work! What's the French for work?'

'Ah, *quand nous avons fini le travail!'* Belavito grinned.

Then he drew himself up, clicking his heels. 'Monday—you and me—we will speak more, yes?'

She nodded, feeling sick at her deception. God, how she hated Will for making her do this!

He saluted. 'Good-e-night.'

'Good night,' she said.

She waited for the sergeant to follow him out, but he stood still. Mary glanced at the clock and saw that it was almost five o'clock, time for them to go. The sergeant took the two slips of paper which had to be signed every night from his pocket.

Mary was panic-stricken. She knew that he was waiting for the list of names. 'Excuse me!' she cried. She rushed outside for Will. He was standing with his hands in his pockets, watching the cattlemen branding numbers on the horns of some cows; making no attempt to help them. 'Look!' she cried. 'I've made out a list of names and that boy's name's on it. He insisted that I put it on. I was going to write out the list again, but the sergeant's standing waiting.'

Will laughed. 'What are you worrying about? I'll soon settle things.'

'What's the lad's name?' he said, following her in. She pointed it out on the list. 'Mario Belavito,' he said, writing it in his note-book. He whistled cheerfully as he signed the slips for the sergeant. 'Good night, sir!' he said in his hearty way, handing back the slips and the list.

The sergeant saluted and went.

Will picked up the telephone. 'Is that the Prisoner of War Camp? That you, Mr. Johnston? Well, I've made out a list of the names of the prisoners that I want back. But there's one man's name on it that I don't want. What's his name again, Mary? Belavito—Mario Belavito. Don't send him back at any price! What's that? Oh, my wife put his name on the list to please him. You know what women are, Mr. Johnston! Right, you'll see that he doesn't get sent back. Yes, send anybody else you like—but not him!'

.   .   .   .

All evening Mary had thought about the poor Italian and the way they had tricked him about the list of names. Every time she looked at Will she hated him. He was so callous, so cruel, so unimaginative. . . . What in God's name had made her marry a man like this?

Wearily she rose, her mind numb with all the thought and venom that had been spinning through it since the afternoon. 'Eleven o'clock,' she said. 'I'm going to bed.'

'Right, dear, I'll be up in a few minutes,' Will said.

She was opening the sitting-room door when he spoke. 'You know,' he said, looking past her, 'I've been thinking a lot about that poor bugger of an Italian all night—you know the one I mean? The one we told the camp not to send back. The one who spoke French, but who's no bloody good. He must have thought he was on velvet when he came here and got you to talk to. It's a pity, but . . . Well, I suppose war's war and work's work, and that's an end of it.'

THE MEETING

THE artist hadn't been in touch with Culture for over two years. So he thought he'd go to the Annual General Meeting of the Scottish Art and Literature Society in Edinburgh. He hadn't paid his subscription, but he felt that didn't matter. He would be representing Art. He wrote to Margaret Westwater, the short story writer, to meet him at the two o'clock train.

The Society had been started by Catriona Andrews in an attempt to put Scottish Art and Culture on the map, but before very long ' society ' had wormed its way in in search of culture. The artists and writers who had found the Society a meeting ground for the expression of their views had been pushed to the wall. The last meetings the artist had attended had been rather like meetings of the Women's Rural Institute or a Women's Guild. He wondered if the War would have changed this in any way.

The train was half an hour late. The artist dashed along the platform, looking for Margaret at the barrier. It was eighteen months since he'd seen her and he'd no idea what she'd have added to her wardrobe. But, as he pushed past two elderly ladies, he saw her old red velvet cloak, and he guessed that she would have her coupons still untouched. And he wondered if he'd manage to get any from her.

The meeting was to be held in an old house in the High Street, once the home of some antique Marquis or Earl. The Scottish Art and Literature Society had had it all renovated. The artist and Margaret reached it about a quarter past three.

'We're pretty late, Scrubby,' she said as they went up the outside stone stairs.

'What does it matter?' he said. 'We'll make a good entrance!'

The meeting was being held in a small room which seemed to be packed with old women. David Mackenzie, the young novelist, was sitting in the middle of a row of empty seats at the back. He looked relieved when he saw them. 'I was beginning to think I'd come for nothing,' he said, as they sat down beside him.

Scrubby crossed his corduroy-trousered legs and took a look round. All the old and familiar faces, he thought. All the Dear Old Ladies of Edinburgh in search of Culture. They were sitting with earnest faces, listening to Catriona Andrews. Catriona, beautifully dressed, beautifully sun-tanned, was reading her report of the year's progress in her beautiful English voice. Scrubby did not bother to listen to her; he had heard her so often before. He looked about for his Dear Friends. But except for David and Margaret and Jimmy Grant Ruthven, who was squashed among some old women at the front, he couldn't see any. He was yawning with disappointment when the door opened noisily and Hetty Frayne, the novelist, bounced in.

Hetty Frayne had been engaged once to a Red Indian. The *affaire* must have made a great impression on her, for every year she looked more and more like a squaw. She was a large blowsy woman with bare legs and a battered red felt hat sitting on top of her frizzy grey hair. She was carrying a large canvas bag sewn with a design of bright yellow marigolds.

''Lo, Scrubby, you're looking well,' she boomed as she sat down beside him. 'That sun-tan didn't come out of a bottle, anyway.'

'You're lookin' well yourself, darling,' he said.

'Not feeling well, though,' she said. 'Cough.'

She put down her bag which held several library books, a bundle of knitting, and a stone hot-water bottle. 'Like this?'

she said, pointing to the knitting—a mass of black, orange and red stripes. ' A new hat.'

' A bit waspish,' he said.

' Suits me, though.'

' Like the cows and the tatties and the neeps? ' she said, after she had taken a quick look round to see who was there, nodding to a few people who had turned round to ' Ssh! ' and shouting ' 'Lo, Margaret, 'lo, David! ' past Scrubby.

' They're all right,' he said.

' Painting any? '

' No,' he said. ' But, Hetty, I'd love to paint you looking over a dyke between two cows, both of them wearing your hats. I'll call it " Hetty Frayne and Her Hats : A Composition by George Crichton." '

' Hope I'm dead before it's hung,' she said. ' Either that or you're hung first.'

' That could easy be,' he said.

' Twig old Walter,' she said, jerking her head backwards.

Walter Porteous, the aged and honoured Royal Scottish Academician, was sleeping in the corner of the back row. His head rolled over his chest, and every now and then he snored, blowing out his sandy beard and whiskers. Next him, young Peter Reid-Brown of the B.B.C. was playing with a bunch of keys and stroking his little fair moustache. He was trying self-consciously not to be aware of old Walter.

' And so we come to the end of another year of cultural progress in Scotland,' Catriona was saying. ' And we look forward to many more years when we hope the promise of this year will be fulfilled. Before I finish I would like to say how pleased I am to see so many of you here—the faithful who keep this Society and all it stands for going! Thank you.'

There was loud but polite applause as she sat down. She crossed her slim silk-clad legs, smiling sweetly, then she leaned forward and whispered something to Andrew Burnett, the President. He rose, put his fingers in his waistcoat pockets, and began a long, rambling speech. After the first few minutes of strain, Scrubby could not be bothered listening. He looked about him, whispering to Hetty and listening to the conversation David and Margaret were carrying on in loud whispers. Occasionally they wrote down things on a note-book David was holding, giggling to each other. Scrubby squinted, but he couldn't make out their writing, but he knew that it was probably scurrilous comments about the dear old ladies in front.

Suddenly the sound of bagpipes being tuned up in the High Street came through the open windows. Old Walter Porteous gave a jump and then an extra loud snore. Hetty winked solemnly at Scrubby.

Several members looked round, but most of them listened attentively to Andrew. 'We often say "Puir auld Scotland",' he was saying. 'But do we ever ask ourselves who is to blame for this state of affairs? Who is to blame because most of our young writers, our young artists, our young poets and our young musicians make for London? Do we ever pause to think when we are reviling them? Do we ever ask ourselves what encouragement we give them? We keep wondering why we have no Scottish music, no Scottish novels, no Scottish paintings, but do we ever ask ourselves why?'

Hetty and David and Margaret and Scrubby applauded loudly at this, but most of the old ladies were too busy looking irritably in the direction of the bagpipes, which were warming up. One or two of them whispered indignantly to each other. Hetty winked again at Scrubby.

'It is for this purpose that we try to keep this Society alive,' Andrew shouted. 'We keep it alive—difficult though it is in these troubled days—not only to encourage art and music and letters by our contemporaries, but to keep alive the glorious traditions of the Scottish past.'

There was some polite applause at this. But it was drowned by the droning of the bagpipes bursting into *The Muckin' o' Geordie's Byre*.

Scrubby chuckled. People whispered to each other, nodding at the open windows. Peter Reid-Brown straightened his tie, then he rose and closed them. Andrew blew his nose, smiled pathetically, and went on with his speech. But his remarks about the glories of the Scottish past were almost unheard below the loud screeching of the pipes.

'Vulgar, what?' Hetty whispered, with a bawdy chuckle.

'. . . and for this reason this room in this historical house in this most historical street in Scotland has been bequeathed to the Society by an anonymous donor,' Andrew shouted.

For a moment loud applause vied with the bagpipes, then the bagpipes won. They charged into *The Diel's Awa' Wi' the Excisemen*. People spoke angrily to each other. Then a large woman in a tartan skirt, her full paps panting under a white silk blouse, rose and hurried outside.

'A zealous member away to give him half a crown to move on,' Hetty whispered, giving Scrubby a nudge.

He handed her a cigarette. She coughed slightly as he lit it for her.

'We are hoping,' Andrew shouted, 'we are hoping, therefore, to use this room for small intimate exhibitions.'

'Shocking,' Hetty said with a leer.

She and Scrubby began to laugh, then in trying to restrain her laughter Hetty began to cough. She coughed and spluttered, but she couldn't stop. People looked round at the sound of the high gasps. Scrubby began to feel alarmed. He was sure that Hetty was going to choke, and he patted her on the back. Her bronchial whoops punctuated the drones of the pipes as they faded down the street.

'Must go out,' Hetty spluttered, and she rose and made for the door.

Scrubby was going to follow her, but Margaret put her hand on his arm. She followed Hetty outside. In the doorway they passed the lady in the tartan skirt, who was beaming with success.

Scrubby moved along beside David. 'Trust our Hetty to do things in a big way,' David whispered.

The Treasurer read her report. Two or three people went outside to ask for Hetty. Margaret came back and said : 'She's sitting on the steps, entertaining an audience of small, dirty-nosed children.'

By the time Hetty came back, Catriona had got down to the real business of the afternoon: the re-election of office-bearers. The Treasurer and another earnest young woman dashed about, asking people to propose this member or to second the proposal of that one. ' A beautifully put up job,' David whispered. ' You've got to hand it to Catriona. She's got this Society in the hollow of her hand.'

' Mr. Mackenzie, will you second the proposal of Mr. James Grant Ruthven as a member of the Council? ' the Treasurer whispered to David.

' With pleasure,' he said.

' The only thing that'll give me any pleasure this afternoon,' he said to Scrubby.

' What are you grousing at? ' Scrubby said. ' You've had the bagpipes, you've had Hetty, and now you're having this. I think it's been a great afternoon! '

After the election of the office-bearers the meeting broke up for tea in a room downstairs. On his way down, Scrubby stopped to speak to Jimmy Grant Ruthven, and by the time he got down the tea-room was swarming with people. ' The zoo isn't in it! ' Jimmy said, chuckling. ' Come on, let's get into the fray! '

With a cup of tea in one hand and a bun in the other, Scrubby began to make his way to the corner where David was standing. He was squeezing between two elderly women who were screaming at each other in upper-class voices when he saw Jane Guthrie standing alone. Jane had once had a pash for him when she was in her first year at the Art College, and he supposed he'd better go and speak to her. He didn't want to have anything to do with her; still it was manners.

' Hello,' he said.

' Hello,' she said, giving him a vague stare and then a bright smile in case perhaps she knew him. Scrubby realized this at once and wished he'd passed on.

' Busy? ' he said.

'Well, I'm waiting for Peter Reid-Brown,' she said. 'You know, he's in the B.B.C.'

'Yes, I know him very well,' he said.

'I know you, don't I?' she said. 'But it's such a long time. . . . You know, I can't remember your name! Silly, isn't it?'

'No, it's not,' he said. 'It's George Crichton.'

'Of course,' she said, but he knew that it didn't mean anything to her. After all, three years is a long time, and anyway, he was one of the kind that people had made up their minds they didn't want to know.

'Still writing poetry?' he said.

'Poetry?' She frowned. 'But—you know that I don't write poetry! I paint.'

'Oh, of course,' he said. 'I used to paint, too—a long time ago. Well, I must move on. I must go and speak to Catriona. S'long.'

'S'long,' she said.

But Catriona was so busy speaking to Lady Weir and the Hon. Betty Dalrymple that Scrubby just said 'Hello' and moved on to the corner where David had been joined by Margaret and Hetty and Jimmy Grant Ruthven.

'Enjoying yourself?' Hetty was saying to David.

'No,' he said.

'Our little Davie didn't come here to enjoy himself,' Margaret said. 'This is all going to be kept for a story, isn't it, darling?'

'Nobody would believe it,' he said gloomily.

'You're right,' Scrubby said. 'Look at them all! Edinburgh's Four Hundred! Come on, let's all go and have a drink in some nice stinking pub. I'll be glad to get back to my cows and pigs on Monday.'

'Scrubby and I are two or three ahead of you all,' Margaret said when they were in the pub. 'The first thing he said to me when he got off the train was, "Let's go and have a drink before we go to this bloody meeting."'

'No, darling, that wasn't the first thing,' Scrubby said, finishing his whisky and shouting for another.

Margaret giggled. 'No, neither it was.' She sipped the fresh drink that had been placed before her. 'When he got off the train,' she said, 'he dashed along the platform and threw his rucksack at me and shouted: "Just a minute! I must away to the Gents!"'

'Well, it was a non-corridor train,' Scrubby said.

'What about the windows?' Hetty said, giving him a nudge.

'The carriage was crowded,' he said.

'I always remember that time you were going to Lanark,' Margaret said, 'and you and that man you got speaking to did it out of the windows. I always wanted to write a story about it. I think it's lovely you saying to him did he mind if you did, and him saying no, he'd just been on the point of asking you.'

'What a lovely story,' Hetty said, leaning back and closing her eyes.

'It's mine,' Scrubby said. 'If anybody writes it it'll be me.'

'But, darling, you're not a writer,' Hetty said.

'No, but I might be one of these days,' he said. 'I sometimes think I might write.'

'But, Scrubby, how could you ever find time to write on the farm if you don't find time to paint?' Margaret said.

'"I dunno,' he said. 'Still, I might. It's my story, so don't any of you go and put your claws on it.'

'Of course not,' they said, but he knew perfectly well that each of them was itching to do something about it. 'They're all right,' he said to Margaret before he left her to get on the train. 'They're all grand people—just now when we're all drunk! But as soon as the drink begins to wear off you'll see them more clearly and you'll wonder whether you really like them as much as you think you do just now. I wouldn't trust one of them an inch. I'm going straight back to try to write that story.'

'Right, darling,' she said, shaking hands with him at the barrier. 'So am I.'

HUNTING BUFFALO

WITH growing trepidation Kathe climbed the three flights of worn-in-the-centre stone stairs. What would it be like? The Refugees' Committee had given her no inkling; they had hoped she would be happy and had turned briskly to the next case.

A dog barked inside when she rang the bell marked *Macrimmon*. The barks made her heart beat faster than ever. A voice shouted: 'Shuttup, Twist, for the luvva mike!' And then the door opened, and a young man with a shock of black hair and huge horned-rimmed glasses peered out at her. 'Yes?' he said.

She drew her breath and released the words she had been practising for so long: 'Please, I am come. I am Kathe.'

'Oh!' The door opened wider and a broad shaft of light flung itself over the dim landing. 'Come in. Skipper's out just now, but she won't be long.' He reached out and took her case, and she followed him in. 'Down, Twist, down!' And he kicked the door shut with a red-slippered heel.

Kathe looked down apprehensively at the big bulldog that was sniffing at her legs. 'Here we are!' the young man said, leading her into the kitchen, and he laughed nervously as he put down her case.

'Here ve are!' she said, and she laughed, too.

He was very tall and very thin. His lean jaws were pock-marked, and his eyes blinked nervously behind the big glasses. He wore a bright yellow polo-sweater and blue corduroy trousers. 'Just make yourself at home,' he said. 'Skipper

152

shouldn't be long.' And he picked up a book that was lying face down on the table amongst a litter of dirty dishes, and went into the next room.

Kathe took off her hat and fluffed out her short fair hair. With relief she saw the bulldog follow the young man out, and she bent and examined her neat silk-clad legs to see if the dog's snuffling had done any damage. She looked about her as she took off her coat. A number of silk stockings hung on a pulley on top of sheets of *The Daily Worker* and *The Scottish Daily Express*. The newspapers were sodden beneath the stockings, and a pool of water lay under them on the dirty linoleum. A red jumper was drying on the back of a chair in front of the grey ash-strewn fireplace. Some newspapers were sticking from beneath the rug at the fireside. Later Kathe discovered that another jumper was laid between these sheets; it was Skipper's favourite method of pressing her clothes. Improvised book-cases were in odd corners, filled with ex-library copies and Penguins. An empty bottle of South African sherry stood on top of the Singer's sewing-machine. Clippings of white silk had been pushed beneath the treadle; some of them were lying in the dog's dish beside the machine. Kathe looked at her neat typist's hands, then she looked at the tableful of dirty dishes and sighed. She would have to begin those horrid ' domestic duties ' some time. . . .

She was drying the last cups when the front door opened noisily. The bulldog barked loud welcome and floundered across the linoleum into the hall. ' Is that you, Skipper? ' the young man called.

' Yes, it's me. Who did you think it would be? Your Uncle John Simon come to collect your back Income Tax? Get down, Twist, get down, you ugly brute! '

A woman of about forty-five came in, trying to fend off the amorous dog with a full message-basket. She wore a suède jerkin with a zip-fastener, and a black-and-white checked shirt. Her black curls bobbed up and down beneath an absurd little red ' Pixie ' bonnet. She nodded affably to Kathe and banged down the basket on the table.

'Whew, it's warm climbing those stairs!' she exclaimed, sinking into the chair before the fire and knocking down the red jumper. 'Old age doesn't come itself! Got a fag, Abby?'

'That's seven you owe me,' the young man said gloomily, taking two or three loose cigarettes from his trousers-pocket and handing one to her.

'Oh, well, you'll get them back at the end of the week.' Skipper winked at Kathe over the match-flame. 'If I remember!'

'You'd better,' Abby said. 'This household never smokes anything but O.P.s. I hope you don't smoke,' he said to Kathe. 'Or if you do, I hope you buy your own.'

'Nice bloke, isn't he?' Skipper said. 'I don't suppose he'd introduce himself? He's too modest!' She grinned at him. 'Fräulein Kathe Sturt, Mr. Gavin McLellan Malcolm, otherwise Peter Abelard, called Abby for short.'

Abby scowled at Skipper, then with a nod to Kathe he slouched into the other room. Skipper grinned, the firelight glinting in her dark devilish old eyes. 'Abby's bark is worse than his bite,' she said. 'He's a nice kid really. Studying French Literature at the 'Varsity. Though God knows what good it's goin' to do him—unless he's goin' to help the Entente Cordiale to win this bloody war!'

She looked quizzically at Kathe. 'You're much younger than I expected. And much prettier!' She rose and stretched, the cigarette dangling in the corner of her mouth. 'Suppose we'd better get the supper set,' she yawned, picking up the red jumper and throwing it on to the already untidy sofa. 'That's the worst of keepin' a boarding-house, you've got to have meals ready at certain times. Those other hooligans 'll be in directly, howling for meat.'

'Now,' she said. 'Will you peel some potatoes while I clean the fish? Or will we do it the other way round? I don't know which job I hate the worst!'

Kathe was laying the table under Skipper's direction when two young women came in. Mrs. Macrimmon introduced them as Doris and Esther.

'How are you, comrade?' Doris, who took big strides and whose fair Eton-cropped hair had a home-cut look, leaned over the table and shook hands firmly. 'I hope you'll like it here.'

'I am sure I shall,' Kathe said, smiling.

'You'll find it a bit different from Vienna, I guess,' Esther said, throwing her hat on the sofa and taking out a small comb and mirror to arrange her gleaming auburn hair.

'But, yes!' Kathe shrugged. 'That is to be expected. Do you know Vienna?'

Esther hunched one shoulder in the manner of Greta Garbo. 'Well . . .'

'No, she doesn't know Vienna,' Skipper said. 'She's never been farther than Newcastle.'

Esther pouted peevishly. 'There you are again, Skipper! Why do you always go and spoil my effects?'

'You shouldn't try to make effects, comrade,' Doris said, putting a bundle of forks and knives on the table and beginning to arrange them. 'You know what Marx says. . . .'

'Aw, quit quotin' Marx,' Esther said. 'I'm sick of hearin' about him. What the hell do I care what he said? All the hot air he spilled doesn't make things any better for me, does it? It doesn't help me to get away from that telephone switchboard.'

'But it will, comrade, it will.' Doris leaned on the table and waved a knife at Esther. 'Just wait until the Social Revolution!'

'Ach!' Esther shrugged and took a cinema magazine from under a cushion. 'You make me tired.'

Doris looked at Kathe and shook her head. 'There's a lot of her kind,' she said. 'Too many of them. They've got no faith, that's what's wrong with them. They want everything to be lovely just now; they're not willing to work for it. I expect there are a lot like that in Austria, too?'

'I do not know,' Kathe said.

'But didn't you find that in the Party?'

'The Party? Please?'

Doris nodded. She spoke slowly, picking her words carefully, and raising her voice. ' You had to leave Austria on account of your Party activities, hadn't you? '

' But, no! ' Kathe looked bewildered. ' I am leave my country because I am Jewess. I am not in Party.'

' Well, I'll be damned! ' Doris whistled.

' I wish to hell Julian would hurry up,' Skipper said. ' He's late.'

' Probably he's seen somebody he's just had to follow,' Esther said cattishly.

' More than likely somebody's been following him! ' Skipper laughed. ' Really, those young men nowadays have as sad a time as we girls had when I was young! '

They were half-way through supper when the door opened. Kathe, sitting opposite, stared at the young man framed in the darkness. A mouthful of fish and potatoes lay on her tongue. She made no move to take out the bone that was biting into the roof of her mouth.

A pale oval face loomed out of the darkness. Everything that was perfect in Greek sculpture was chiselled on its framework. Dark hair streamed back, cutting itself off from the blackness of the hall as Julian entered the kitchen.

' Hurry up, you're late! ' Skipper cried, waving her fork at him. ' Your supper's in the oven. See if you can manage to get a place between Esther and Kathe.'

' We'll need to get a bigger table, Skipper,' Abby said.

' Go to hell! ' Skipper said. ' This is fine. I've seen ten people sitting down at this table.'

Kathe wondered how they had managed when Julian put down his plate and squeezed in between her and Esther. She had never seen so many people sitting at such a small table. She felt crushed between Doris and Julian, but the pressure of Julian's dark sleeve against her arm made her tremble with pleasure.

' B' the way, this is Kathe,' Skipper said. ' She's come to help me with the house.'

' I guessed that,' Julian said pleasantly. ' I hope she's a better housekeeper than you are, darling.' He winked at Kathe, and she blushed.

'There's nothing wrong with my housekeeping,' Skipper said, laughing. 'It's you hooligans who upset things. Look at those knickers of Doris's on the pulley! What other respectable landlady would allow the like of that?'

'That reminds me,' Abby said, swallowing his last mouthful and rising. 'I want to do some washing, so I hope none of you galoots want the sink.'

He put a pile of handkerchiefs, socks and underwear on the board beside the sink. He was running hot water and swirling soap-flakes in the sink when Skipper said in a cooing voice: 'Darling, I wonder if you'd . . .'

'I haven't any fags left,' Abby said without looking round.

'It's all right,' she said. 'I've got fags of my own.' She took a packet from her pocket and lit one. 'I was wondering if you'd do me a favour, darling.'

'You might give me a fag anyway,' Abby said. 'You don't scruple to smoke mine, but you never offer me one of yours.'

'She's a capitalist, comrade,' Doris said, pushing back her empty plate. 'What else can you expect from one of the non-working classes?'

'Somebody's got to be a capitalist in this house to keep things balanced,' Skipper said. 'Haven't they, dear?'

Kathe nodded and smiled, but she did not understand what Skipper was talking about. She did not understand anything about this strange household. Unless, perhaps, it was Julian. Handsome young men were common to all countries, and the feelings they aroused were universal. She watched him as he ate steadily. He was so beautiful that it pained her. She had an all-devouring impulse to take his dark head and press it to her breast.

Her emotions became so uncontrollable that she was forced to move her chair away from him and watch Abby. The French scholar had the sleeves of his yellow pullover rolled up and he was plunging his thin hairy arms into the soapy water.

Doris was crouching in front of the fire, her shiny nose almost touching the inside of a thick Left Book Club book. Esther was polishing her nails. Nobody was making any move to clear away the dirty supper dishes. Skipper, who had been hunting beneath the sofa, brought out a dirty pair of stays. 'Darling,' she said to Abby, 'I wonder if you'd give those shoulder-straps a wash? Then maybe you could iron them when you iron your own stuff. There's no hurry.'

'Thank you,' Abby said sarcastically.

'Not at all,' Skipper said. 'It's a pleasure.'

The bulldog was sniffing at Kathe's legs. It tried to scramble on to her lap, but she pushed it down. But Twist was determined and tried again. Julian was the only one who noticed the girl's difficulty. He picked up his plate and cried: 'Here, Twist, good dog!'

Kathe smiled gratefully at Julian. The bulldog shifted the remains of Julian's fish and potatoes with two wallops of its pink tongue, then it looked up expectantly. 'You were well named, you ugly brute,' Julian said, taking some potatoes from the dish and throwing them down. 'You're never satisfied.'

'A perfectly human failing,' Skipper said.

Doris looked up from her book. 'It's not a human failing at all, comrade. It's because people haven't been educated properly.'

They began to argue about this, all shouting at the pitch of their voices. Even Esther stopped polishing her nails to join in. And in the middle of it Doris brought out a typewriter from under the sofa and began to type, stopping every now and then to deliver a short speech. Kathe thought of the respectable quietness and tidiness of her Viennese home, and her eyes dimmed. Those strange Scottish voices. . . . But she must remember that she was an enemy alien; here only on sufferance because she was a refugee. To try to combat her homesickness she watched Julian, admiring his straight nose and his wide brow, looking eagerly at his dark blue eyes which blazed with excitement as he argued with Abby.

And so in the following weeks whenever she thought of

Vienna and the people she had known, Kathe tried instead to think of Julian. It was not difficult. And presently she found that she thought more often of him than she thought of those she had loved in her own country. She thought of him whenever she felt that the strange housework—and the even stranger household—was beyond her and she couldn't go on.

Skipper left most of the housework to Kathe. Skipper liked to lie late in bed, and when she did get up she spent most of her time reading and smoking and arguing. She was always in a muddle, and she was incapable of organizing either herself or the rest of her household. Esther never did anything to help. Doris occasionally took spasms of working in the house, but usually she spent all her time reading or typing long letters ' to the one great love of my life '—a Labour Organizer in Birmingham who already had a wife and three children. Doris was always weeping because he wouldn't leave his wife and her good cooking, and she would sit and snivel for hours in front of the kitchen fire, telling the others about him. Esther never did anything but grumble about her work and talk about the cinema. Julian was usually shut in his room, working; he was in his last year at Medical School. Kathe became very friendly with Abby, and it was he who told her what he felt she should know about everybody—except Doris who was not long in disclosing her own most intimate feelings. It was Abby who told her that Skipper's husband had gone away years ago. ' He went hunting buffalo,' he said, ' and he forgot to come back! '

It was Abby, too, who told her that Julian had applied for a commission in the army and that he was waiting to be called up. Kathe was horrified. ' But he is so young,' she said. ' And so beautiful. It is not right. It is a sin.'

Skipper looked at Abby and laughed. ' That boy's got something that must appeal to refugees! '

Kathe flushed. But she was stubborn in her point: ' It is not right that he should go and be killed. There are many, many more who are ugly and who would not be missed.'

'They're all somebody's kids,' Skipper said. 'Somebody
loves them, ugly phizzes or not.'

Abby smiled and quoted:

> 'He turned her ower and ower again
>   O gin her skin was white!
> "I might ha'e spared that bonnie face
>   To ha'e been some man's delight."'

'To ha'e been some man's delight,' Skipper said, and she
smiled at Kathe.

Kathe repeated the quotation to herself whenever she looked
at Julian. And she looked at him often. She waited upon
him hand and foot. No matter how much she disliked housework, she did not dislike it when she was doing it for him.
But no matter how much she did for him, he never treated
her in any way differently from the way he treated Skipper
and the other girls. He appeared not to notice whether she
was there or not. And the more indifferent he was, the greater
her love grew. She had read often in novels that this was
the case, and she had said to herself that even if it were true
she would never be such a fool as to be in the same boat. But
now here she was! And hopelessly, passionately in love—so
much in love that she would have allowed Julian to walk
over her.

Not that he ever showed that he wanted to do that. He
never showed that he was very much aware of her. As a
refugee domestic, the others treated her like a long-lost sister.
But Julian always treated her in the impersonal way in which
he would have treated a servant.

Doris and Abby especially tried to bring their political and
social beliefs into practice. In fact sometimes Doris embarrassed Kathe by her desire to help. The Eton-cropped member
of the Y.C.L. took her beliefs much more seriously than any
member of the Y.W.C.A., and she did some of the dirtier
kinds of jobs for Kathe. Then one day she heard the Austrian
say that she couldn't afford to buy new stockings because her

pay was so small. And she said: 'But you get eighteen and six a week, comrade, and your food. Surely that's enough?'

'But, no, it is very small,' Kathe said. 'In my country I get five pounds a week.'

Doris stared, then she threw her tolerance overboard for a few minutes and said: 'Do you know how much the unemployed get in this country, comrade? Fourteen shillings a week, and they don't get any food!'

After that Doris did only what she felt was strictly comradely for Kathe. Not that Kathe noticed any difference; she was so busy watching Julian, looking for a thawing in his attitude towards her. But there was none. Until one night about six weeks after she came.

Julian brought home a human brain, which he said he was going to study. He asked Kathe if she would put it in some safe place for him. She looked with horror at the grey sponge-like matter and drew back. Julian laughed and said: 'Have you a tin or something?'

He put the brain in a pail and put the pail in the bathroom. All through supper he entertained them with imaginary accounts of the person to whom the brain had belonged. 'I bet it was a dirty old man who dealt in the white slave traffic,' he said. 'He was probably so ashamed of his past that he left his body to science to try to make amends.'

'Maybe he had a split personality and wanted to see if the dissectors would find that out,' Abby said.

'I wonder what he looked like,' Skipper said. 'The brain's so ugly that you can hardly believe that it ever belonged to anybody who was good-looking. Yet maybe it did. I wonder if your brain looks as ugly as that, Julian?'

He shrugged. 'Nobody knows. I can imagine what it's like, but I don't suppose anybody else could.'

Kathe shuddered at the morbidity of the conversation. She could not believe that the beauty of Julian's head encased a mass of grey matter like that in the pail in the bathroom. And yet maybe on the battlefield . . . a shell perhaps would . . .

She had to make an effort to swallow what was in her mouth, and she made no move to go on with her meal. She was glad when Abby said: 'By the way, I saw Benny Learmouth to-day.'

'Oh!' Julian looked up quickly. 'I didn't know he was back in town. Were you speaking to him?'

'For two or three minutes. There was another bloke with him, and they seemed in a hurry.'

Julian frowned. 'What sort of a bloke?'

Abby yawned. 'The usual. A nice-looking bloke. Tall and fair. He looked the rugby type.'

Julian lit a cigarette. He rose and stood with his back to the fire, his hands in his pockets. 'I wonder when Benny got back?' he said. 'I thought he would have let me know.'

'Maybe he thought you had been a bit too busy with refugees!' Abby winked at Skipper, and they both laughed.

Kathe looked from them to Julian, uncomprehending. She noticed the angry flush on Julian's cheek-bones and wondered what they had said to annoy him. The door being pushed open by Twist created a diversion. Kathe watched the bulldog's ungainly slither across the floor. 'Here, Twist!' she cried, and she placed her half-empty plate on the floor.

But Twist did not bound towards it with his usual exuberance. He lay down in a sickly way before the fire, his tongue lolling drunkenly out of his mouth.

'So you can't take it!' Abby said. 'What's wrong with you to-night, me fine fellow?'

Twist opened his mouth and retched. Abby shrugged. 'You're not living up to your name to-night! Where have you been? Hunting buffalo?'

'Mrs. Seymour downstairs must have given him something,' Skipper said.

'But he couldn't get out or in,' Doris said. 'The door's shut.'

They looked at each other, then they looked at Julian, realization breaking suddenly upon them. 'Hell!' Julian rushed to the bathroom.

A few seconds later he brought in the empty pail. He stood and looked down at Twist who was groaning and twisting on the rug. 'You dirty dog! I hope you get a lot of complexes because of this.'

He sighed. 'Well, that's my evening ruined. Guess there's nothing else to do now but go to bed or go to the pictures. Anybody like to come with me?'

'To bed, darling?' Skipper laughed.

Everybody had something on. Except Kathe, who looked down at the table. She was afraid to look up in case she would betray her eagerness. She was the only one who had not laughed at Skipper's remark. 'What about you, Kathe?' Julian said. 'Would you like to come to the flicks?'

In the cinema they sat silently side by side. Kathe's mind was in such a chaotic state that she could not follow the film. But beside her Julian laughed every now and then. He sat hunched down in his seat, his dark head sticking out of the wide collar of his overcoat. Kathe kept glancing at him, then finding that she could not follow the film at all, she looked all the time at him. She shifted slightly so that her shoulder rested against his. He turned and smiled. But he made no move in response. She wondered why. They were in the back seats, and all around them amorous couples were busy with their own affairs. *Ach Gott*, but he was shy. This English reserve. She could not understand how Englishmen ever managed to get married at all if they all took as long about the preliminaries as Julian. She must do what she could to quicken him up a bit.

She tucked her hand into his arm. He looked round and smiled, and he gave her hand a little squeeze against his side. But he looked again at the film, laughing at the wisecracks of a famous blonde comedienne. Kathe turned almost sick with the love-surge that welled up in her. She tried to will him to put his arm around her, but she could do nothing; his dark

head kept being thrown back, and loud laughter volleyed from
his white throat.

He took her arm in the blackout on the way home, but anything he said might as well have been said to Skipper or Doris
or Esther. She was intensely disappointed. Those Englishmen were so stolid and cold. Englishmen . . . but, of course,
no, he was Scottish! Perhaps that accounted for it? In her
bedroom she stood for a long time in front of the mirror,
wondering what was wrong. Surely she was pretty enough,
young enough. . . .

Two or three nights later she was surprised when he asked
if she would go out with him again. And her surprise merged
quickly into delight as she rushed to get ready. So! They
took a long time to make up their minds, those Scots, but when
they did there were no half-measures!

She put on a white velvet evening dress that she had thought
she would never get the chance to wear again. Dear little
frock, she thought, touching it tenderly, are you going to see
life again, the life you were used to in Vienna? Her eyes
sparkled with excitement, and she took great pains with her
toilette. Julian was beginning to grow impatient, but when
she appeared he whistled with admiration. 'Gee, I wouldn't
have known you, Kathe! You're a clinker!'

They went to a fashionable restaurant. Edinburgh was
becoming very gay and cosmopolitan these days with so many
Polish and Czechoslovakian and French soldiers. There was
a sudden feverish gaiety about Julian which Kathe found
difficult to understand. She could not reconcile it with his
past quietness. Possibly it was the war. Skipper had told her
that she didn't think it would be long now until Julian was
called up. No doubt that explained this sudden abandon.
Poor boy, he wanted to have a last fling. Her heart melted
with tenderness and yearning as she smiled at him. How easy
it would be to give him all that he wanted. To give was said
to be better than to receive, but it was in no sense a martyrdom
when it was Julian who was to receive.

Kathe looked about proudly. No other girl had such a good-looking escort. No other couple was attracting as much attention as they did.

Julian ordered wine. 'Let's eat, drink and be merry!' he cried. 'For to-morrow . . . But we won't talk about to-morrow, will we, Kathe?'

'But, no,' she said.

'To-night's the night!' he cried.

Kathe smiled in a slightly bewildered way. She never knew where she was amongst catchwords. She translated it slowly to herself. *Lieber Gott*, she would be more than ready if it meant what she thought it meant. She smiled and said: '*Sie sind herzig.*'

Julian did not understand her any more than she understood him, but he laughed and held up his glass. Why shouldn't they be happy? Life was short. Better enjoy themselves while they could. It was the eve of Armageddon. . . .

Julian was so drunk that they had to take a taxi home. Kathe herself was unsteady on her feet. In the taxi Julian leaned drunkenly against her, his head on her shoulder. 'Good old Kathe,' he mumbled. She slipped her arm around his neck. 'You're a nice kid,' he mumbled. 'A hell of a nice kid.' But when she leaned her head on top of his, he made no response. His head lolled drunkenly. When they got home everybody was in bed. Kathe helped Julian to his room, and he fell sprawling over the bed. His eyes were closed, and she saw that he was almost asleep. 'But, Julian, your clothes!' she cried. He groaned and turned over. She turned almost sick with longing at the sight of his dark head on the pillow, and she put her hand lightly on his forehead. He mumbled something that she couldn't catch, and he turned over on his face. 'You must take off your clothes,' she said. 'Look, Kathe will help you.' She started to peel off his jacket, but he lay immobile, making no move to help her. She tugged at the jacket, but she found that it was useless, she could do nothing. He was already asleep.

She did not see him the next morning; she was out shopping when he got up. All day she wondered how he would greet her. Would he be ashamed of his behaviour? Poor boy, it was excusable, of course. Still, with such a good beginning there was no reason why the evening should have ended as it had done. She sighed. Ah, but it was a beginning . . . and a beginning was always a beginning. . . .

She was laying the supper when Skipper said: 'What are you setting six places for, dear?'

'But there are always six,' Kathe said, counting on her fingers. 'Julian, you, Doris . . .'

'Julian left this morning, dear.' Skipper yawned and stretched. 'Didn't you know that he was away?'

Kathe put down the pile of plates she was holding. 'Away? But where has he gone?'

'Hunting buffalo!' Abby winked at Skipper and laughed. 'I wonder what fascination that gink had for refugees?'

Kathe flushed. Although she did not wholly understand the meaning of his words, she understood the tone they were spoken in. She did not listen to Skipper saying that Julian had been called up. She looked at Abby and said: 'What do you mean? Many times you have said that about refugees. Please?'

Abby lit a cigarette. He tried to ignore Skipper's out-stretched hand, but she took the packet from him. 'Damn you, Skipper,' he said.

'What do you mean?' Kathe said insistently. 'Please?'

Abby looked helplessly at Skipper, but she blew out a cloud of smoke and laughed. 'You asked for it, darling!'

'I thought I told you about him,' Abby said. 'I thought you knew.'

'You thought I knew what?' Kathe said, sinking into a chair beside the table.

'Och, you know.' Abby shrugged, blinking like a sympathetic owl. 'You must have known about him, kid.' He patted her shoulder clumsily. 'You shouldn't take on like that about him. It was hopeless, anyway.'

Kathe bowed her head on her hands and whispered: 'Why?'

Abby looked at Skipper, but she was blowing cigarette-rings and watching them vanish in the air. He gulped and said: 'I can't think why I didn't tell you before. He married a refugee in London last year so that she would get British nationality.'

ATROCITY STORY

FAT Mrs. Moore was leaning on her elbows, looking out of her window at the tenements opposite, when she saw young Mrs. Grey trundling her pram up the street. 'It's cauld, isn't it?' she shouted.

'Ay, it's terrible.' Mrs. Grey did not show any sign of halting. 'I'm hurryin' to get in in time to hear the news.'

'I hope it's no' like the six o'clock news last night,' Mrs. Moore cried. 'I couldnie listen to the like o' thon again.'

'Wasn't it terrible?' Mrs. Grey pulled back the pram and leaned on the handle-bars. 'I couldnie sleep a' night for thinkin' aboot it.'

'Ach, that was daft,' said Mrs. Moore. 'Ye're daft to let it excite ye to that extent.'

'What's daft?' Mrs. Rafferty said, coming out of the entry.

'It's a' right.' Mrs. Moore laughed. 'We didnie mean you!'

'We were talkin' aboot the Japanese atrocities at Hong Kong,' Mrs. Grey said.

'Oh, weren't they terrible!' Mrs. Rafferty leaned on the railings and prepared for a long gossip. 'Thae Japanese! They're no' like us at a'. They're just barbarians.'

'Fancy if they landed here!' Mrs. Grey said. 'Just think if they turned Calderburn into a brothel. Wouldn't it be terrible. I couldnie sleep a' night for thinkin' aboot puir Mary Mackinnon frae Whitten Street. She was in Hong Kong wi' her man. Just think o' a' thae terrible things happenin' to her.'

'She was such a nice lassie, too,' Mrs. Rafferty said.

They shook their heads and were silent for a moment, thinking about poor Mary Mackinnon, relieved that they were not in her position.

'Just think if they came here,' Mrs. Grey said after a while. 'What would ye dae?'

'I'd—I'd jump oot the windy!' Mrs. Rafferty cried. 'I couldnie bear to let yin o' them touch me. What would you dae, Mrs. Moore?'

'Oh, I suppose I'd just take ma chance wi' the rest o' them. While there's life there's hope, ye ken!' She laughed. 'And who would want to bother wi' an auld wife like me, anyway? Naebody would bother to look twice at me.'

'It's a guid job it's yersel' that's sayin' it.' Mrs. Grey sniffed. 'If ony o' us had said it, ye wouldnie ha'e been long in goin' off the deep end.'

'Never mind,' Mrs. Rafferty said. 'Thae Japs 'll get it in the neck yet. The dirty heathens! Vengeance is mine, saith the Lord.'

'I will repay,' Mrs. Grey added piously.

Mrs. Moore shifted the position of her elbows. 'Well, ye ken, we ha'e oorsels to blame in a way. Ma lodger says we were sellin' guns and oil and ammunition to the Japs right up to the time the war started.'

'I dinnie believe it,' Mrs. Grey said.

'Your lodger had better look out,' Mrs. Rafferty said. 'If he goes about sayin' things like that, folk'll think he's a fifth columnist. It's no' true, anyway. Where did he hear that?'

'He says he read it in a paper.'

'I dinnie believe it,' said Mrs. Rafferty. 'I think he made it up. What decent paper would print things like that?'

'That's right,' Mrs. Grey said. 'It's a pack o' lies.'

'Well, I'm just telling ye what ma lodger tellt me,' Mrs. Moore said. 'I'm no' askin ye to believe it. But he's a real decent chap and I dinnie think he'd tell me ony lies.'

'It's awfu' some o' the things ye read in the papers,' Mrs. Grey said. 'Did ye see about yon wee laddie in Russia? His

YSC—M

mother and his father had both been killed, and the Germans tortured him to make him tell where the Russian sodgers were. Isn't it terrible? Fancy doin' things like that to a bit bairn.'

' Still, I dinnie think the Germans are as bad as the Japanese,' Mrs. Rafferty said. ' The Japanese are just barbarians. The Germans at least are kind o' like oorsels. After a', they are Christians, too.'

' Oh, Mrs. Rafferty! What a like thing to say! '

' Well, I dinnie believe that they're as bad as the Japanese. We're a' entitled to oor ain opinions, ye ken.'

' But I read it in the paper,' Mrs. Grey said.

' Well, of course, that's a different story. If it was in the paper it must be true.'

' In that case, why'll ye no' believe what ma lodger tellt me? ' Mrs. Moore said.

' That's a different story entirely,' Mrs. Rafferty said, drawing herself up belligerently. ' That was a pack o' lies. Our Government would never do a dirty thing like that.'

Mrs. Moore sighed. ' Well, I must get awa' in and listen to the news. It's just on six.'

' Michty! ' Mrs. Grey gave her pram a violent push. ' I'll ha'e to run. I wouldnie miss the news for onythin'.'

And run she did. But before she could get to her entry she heard from dozens of open windows the booming voice of doom: ' This is the B.B.C. Home and Forces' programme. Here is the news. . . .'

HE CALLED ME GIRLIE

AS soon as she got into the dressing-room she took a flask
from the large handbag with L.D. on it and put it to her
lips. After that she felt a bit better. She took off the small
ridiculous black straw hat that her milliner had assured her
was so *chic* and threw it on a chair. It looked as if it were
meant for a monkey or a child. It was so different from the
large hats with feathers that she used to wear when she was
in her hey-day. Ah, these were the good old days. . . .

She sighed and sank into the chair in front of the dressing-
table. Her knees cracked slightly. She screwed up her face
at the pains that shot up her thighs. Damn those rheumatics!
Let's hope they didn't crack during the broadcast!

She had just got into her tights and was winding the frilly
feather-boa around her neck when the door burst open without warning. A young man with glossy black hair looked
round it. He gaped when he saw her.

'Oh, excuse me, girlie!' he cried. 'The wrong dressing-
room.'

And he shut the door before she could say anything. Lily
glared at the shut door. Girlie! Girlie indeed! The cheek
of some of these young puppies. . . . The younger generation
was really appalling. Her grandson now. . . . She sniffed
when she remembered the letter she'd had from him yesterday. 'Good old girl, I'll be listening to your broadcast, but
candidly, darling, between you and me, don't you think it's
about time you gave up the stage?'

Give up the stage? She began to rearrange her curls. Her

hair had been dyed and re-dyed so often that now it was a far brighter gold than it had been when she was young. She stood back and looked at herself critically. You know . . . it did look a bit wiggy. She smoothed her eyebrows and put another dab of lipstick on her mouth.

Give up the stage. . . . Really, John was impertinent. Yes, that was the word. It was sheer impertinence for him to suggest it. A young whipper-snapper like him. Give up the stage indeed! Where would he be now, where could he have got such fine education, if it hadn't been for her and her stage-work?

She took another drink from the flask and jerked her knees up and down several times, flexing the muscles. Better get ready. God, how she hated these midday concerts for war-workers. Things were different in the old days when you didn't need to work until the evening, except for occasional matinées.

She fixed the smile on her face and went along to the concert hall.

That woman, Katherine Monkhouse, was compèring the show. Lily sniffed disdainfully. Kitty Monkhouse was legit. and she'd always looked down on people like her. Kitty was intensely respectable; she'd been married only once. And now that her actor-husband had been made even more respectable by a knighthood . . . Lily shrugged, thinking that although she'd been married three times one of them had been a Duke's son, anyway, and look at the fun she'd had! She chuckled bawdily, then she winked at Patric Reismer, the producer, who was standing beside the microphone, talking to Kitty.

The audience were already seated, whispering and giggling among themselves. The orchestra was tuning its instruments. A boy hurried on to the middle of the stage and held up a placard with SILENCE. A few seconds later the red light appeared. At a sign from the conductor, the orchestra blared out a few chords. Another wave of the baton, and Patric stepped closer to the microphone and said:

'To-day we present the eleventh of our lunch-time concerts

for war-workers. This concert comes to you from a factory somewhere in a great industrial city, and to-day again we are privileged to have that famous actress, Miss Katherine Monkhouse, with us to compère the show. Ladies and gentlemen— Miss MONKHOUSE!'

The boy held aloft another placard with APPLAUSE on it. The audience cheered and clapped, and there were a few whistles. Kitty went close to the microphone, a saccharine smile on her faded face. The boy held up SILENCE.

'My friends!' Kitty threw her arms wide, but remembering that she was holding her script she brought back her right hand quickly to within a few inches of her face. 'My friends,' she cried. 'It may be a privilege for you to have me, but it is a far, far greater privilege for me to be with you to-day. None of you will ever know how much I appreciate being here with you all. It thrills me to the bottom of my heart to be in the centre of this great factory, this humming hive of industry, to feel that for a moment I am one of you—to feel that I, too, am contributing something—even though in such a humble way— to our great war effort. None of you will ever know what great joy it brings me to be here with you all, fighting shoulder to shoulder——'

'And none of them will ever know what joy it gives you to take the B.B.C.'s whopper of a cheque home with you!' Lily said to herself grimly, and she fluffed up her feather-boa and at a sign from Patric she pranced forward and stood behind Kitty.

'—fighting shoulder to shoulder against the barbarian HUN,' Kitty cried. 'Oh, how my heart bleeds for our lads at the front, but then I remember that we, too, are all doing our bit. Rich and poor, men and women, we're all doing our bit. You're doing yours, and I'm doing mine. Yes, I'm doing mine, too—even though it's in such a poor, poor way. I'll never forget what a common working man said to me after the last concert I was at. It was the proudest moment of my life. He said: "You were swell, mate." Mate! He called me mate! That's something I'll never forget. It means more to me than all the money or honours I could ever get. He called me MATE! '

The boy held up APPLAUSE, and the workers applauded lustily.

'And now,' Kitty cried, 'now I have great pleasure in presenting a very dear and very *old* friend of mine to you. Miss Lily Dalgleish! ' She turned and showed her teeth at Lily. 'Come along, dear.'

'Thank you, Miss Monkhouse,' Lily said stiffly.

'Call me Kitty, dear,' said Miss Monkhouse, showing her teeth again.

'Thank you——Kitty! ' said Lily.

'Lily is a very dear and very valued friend of mine,' Kitty gushed. 'And I'm sure she needs no introduction to any of you. She must have been known and loved by you all for many, many years. To-day she is going to sing some of her famous successes from pantomimes.' She placed her hand on her bosom and sighed. 'Ah, those wonderful pantomimes that Lily used to appear in! None of you who have ever seen Lily Dalgleish in a pantomime will ever forget, I'm sure, what a *sight* she was as a principal boy! And now she is going to sing one of her best-known old successes *Knees Up, Mother Brown.* Come along, dear! '

'Thank you, Kitty——my pet! ' Lily gushed at her and edged in to the microphone.

Lily's voice had always been slightly raucous, with a jolly, warm coarseness. Now it was thinner, and the warmth had mostly gone. But the orchestra, by playing loudly, was able to drown much of the tinniness. Lily pranced up and down behind the microphone. Hands on hips, smile set. Automatically she winked every now and then and gave her head a knowing toss——though there weren't any stage-door johnnies now to wink back at her.

An old foreman sitting near the back of the audience leaned forward with excitement. Good old Lily! Wait until he went home and told the wife he'd heard Lily Dalgleish! Many and many's the time they'd gone together to hear her in the old days. Good old gal, she didn't look a day older than she looked in the old Palace days. A bit stouter maybe, but then Lily always was buxom. Nice and cuddlesome, that's what she'd always been. He applauded frantically. A couple of young girls sitting along from him nudged each other. 'Look-it old Joe,' one whispered.

What was she going to sing now? Joe leaned his head slightly to the side to listen better. And he nodded and mouthed the words silently. *Who were you with last night, out in the pale moonlight? It wasn't your sister, it wasn't your ma. . . .*

'Come on now, come on! All together!' Lily cried at the end of the next chorus. 'Hold your hand out, naughty boy!'

'Hold your hand out, naughty boy!' Joe sang, unmindful of the giggling of the girls near him. 'We've seen you with a girl or two, oh, oh, oh, oh, we are surprised at you!'

Lily kept the smile fixed on her face, listening fearfully for her joints to crack. She was relieved when she was able to prance away from the microphone and the boy held up APPLAUSE. There was a sharp, shooting pain in her thigh, but she held her lips stretched in their tight smile.

'And now from one of yesterday's favourites to one of to-day's,' Katherine Monkhouse gushed. 'I have great pleasure in presenting a young man who has just completed a successful tour before the troops in the Middle East. A young man who is loved and appreciated by you all—Bertie BUCKLEY!'

'Excuse me, girlie!' Somebody gave Lily a slight pat on the haunch and brushed past her. It was the young man with the black glossy hair. This time the boy with the board hadn't time to put up APPLAUSE before the audience became wildly enthusiastic. Katherine Monkhouse stood, smiling graciously from the young man to the cheering factory girls. Buckley grinned and held up his hands, then when the cheering showed no sign of abating, although the board for SILENCE was being thrust forward grimly, he turned round and winked at Lily.

She felt herself blush, and she drew her lips together tightly. Then she chuckled, and she winked back at him and gave him a wave. Why not? He had called her girlie, hadn't he? If that wasn't one better than Kitty Monkhouse and her man who'd called her mate. . . .

She stood for a few minutes and watched his act. Queer how like Tommy he was. Tommy had an act just like this in the old days. He still had the same act, she believed. The last she'd heard of him he was touring with ENSA, still singing *You Made Me Love You* and *She's a Lassie from Lancashire*. Tommy!—still acting the way this young man with the glossy hair was acting. And this young man would still be acting like this, singing *I've Got Spurs that Jingle-Jangle-Jingle*, fifty years after this, long after she and Tommy were dead. . . .

The dear, kind British public . . . it took you to its heart and it never forgot its old favourites. . . .

She sighed and turned away, not waiting for Buckley to finish his act. Her joints creaked painfully as she went upstairs to her dressing-room. She stood for a while before the mirror, scrutinizing her face and touching her forehead and cheeks.

'Girlie!' she said aloud.

She pulled off her feather-boa savagely and threw it into a corner.

'Girlie!' she cried again.

When she went downstairs to get her taxi she looked about hopefully, but there was nobody in the entrance-hall except the porter.

Some work-girls standing outside the factory-gates began to wave and cheer as Lily's taxi came out. Lily adjusted her face into the smile, and she waved back graciously.

'Thank you—mates!' she called.

Then as the taxi went on she opened her large handbag. She held the flap in front of her face, between herself and the driver's back, and she bent forward and took a swig out of her flask. Then she leaned back with satisfaction and allowed the muscles of her face to sag comfortably.

ALLOW THE LODGER

OFTEN when one of her sons took more than his share, Mrs. Wright would say : ' Allow the lodger ! ' It was one of the sayings of the house : part of the Wright family : as much their stock-in-trade as ' I thank you ! ' and ' What would you have done, chums ? ' are the stock-in-trade of two famous radio comedians. It was something amusing that they hoped their visitors would laugh at. But it wasn't amusing any longer. It stopped being amusing when Mrs. Wright did get a lodger.

That was after the boys went away to the war. Robin joined the R.A.F., Arthur went into the Navy, Bill was in the Merchant Navy, and Charlie was a Conscientious Objector and had to do land work. ' All shades of opinion ! ' Mrs. Wright said. ' There's nothing like it ! '

A lot of the neighbours were sniffy about Charlie. And Mrs. McIntosh next door, who had thought for years that he was the white-headed boy, stopped waving to him. She had been in the habit of nearly breaking her neck to rush to the window to wave to him when he passed, but all that stopped as soon as Charlie said he wasn't going to the war. Mrs. McIntosh would fain have picked a quarrel with his mother about him, but Mrs. Wright said : ' It's nobody's business. The laddie's free to think what he likes. And he's my son as much as the others.'

' I wish folk would mind their own business,' she said. ' If they did, the world would be a better place, and they might be able to do away wi' wars then.'

That was one of the first things that annoyed her about her lodger. He was inquisitive. And he was inquisitive in a pawky, prying fashion that irritated Mrs. Wright. 'If only he'd come straight oot wi' it,' she said to her husband. 'But he goes speirin' all round the corners. Ye ken fine what he's wantin' to know, but he never comes direct to it.'

Mr. Bertram was working in Edinburgh in munitions. When somebody asked her to take him, Mrs. Wright thought at first that it would be a good idea. The boys were all away, and the house seemed empty. 'It'll be somebody young comin' in about,' she said. 'The house is awful quiet without the laddies.'

But Mr. Bertram did not make the house any noisier. For one thing, he was not as young as she had expected; he was forty-two or forty-three. A large fleshy man with a smooth round face and almost bald, he gave the impression that he would be heavy on his feet. But he slipped about quietly, and he never banged doors. That to Mrs. Wright, who had been used to four young men racing up and down stairs and clamping about the house, was almost an unforgivable sin. 'What a Creepin' Jesus if ever there was one!' she complained. 'He's aye slippin' aboot in his stockin' feet. I get many a fright frae him. Whiles I'm standin' in the scullery and when I turn round there he is standin' at ma back!'

'However, I suppose I'll just ha'e to get used to him,' she said. 'There's a war on—and he'll be ma war-work!'

Often she made up her mind that she would tell him he would have to get digs elsewhere, but somehow she never brought herself to the point of doing so. On nights after she had become particularly irritated with him she would lie in bed, thinking of the many plausible excuses she could make for asking him to look for other accommodation. But somehow when morning came and she answered his soft 'Good morning, Mrs. Wright,' she could never bring herself to say the sentences she had repeated so glibly in her thoughts. And three years after he came, he was still with them. 'Like a sair back ye cannie get rid o',' Mrs. Wright said.

On the fourth Christmas of the war all her sons were to be home on leave. It would be the first time they had all been together for more than three years. Mrs. Wright was as excited as hell. 'It'll just be like auld times again, faither,' she said.

Father just grunted and went on reading the *Evening News*.

'What are ye goin' to do aboot His Nabs?' he said after a while, jerking his head in the direction of the lodger's room. 'Where are we all goin' to sleep?'

'Och, we'll manage somehow,' she said. 'We've aye managed yet. Bill and Charlie can sleep on the put-u-up in the livin'-room, and Robin and Arthur 'll have their ain rooms. The wives 'll be here, of course. My, what a houseful!'

Robin and Arthur had got married since the war started, and their wives lived with their own people but came to the Wrights every Sunday for tea. Robin's wife, Nell, worked in an office, and Arthur's wife, Jenny, worked in the Grainger Street branch of the Co-operative Store.

Robin arrived first, two days before Christmas. Nell had got holidays to coincide with his leave. But Jenny hadn't been so fortunate. She was getting only Christmas Day. 'That's the worst of you plutocrats in offices,' she complained to Nell. 'Gosh, I wish I was working for the Government.'

Charlie was the last to arrive, late on Christmas Eve. They had not known what time his train would come in, and they were all at supper when they heard a car draw up at the gate. 'This must be him in a taxi!' Nell cried. 'I help my kilt, it takes him! Trust our Charlie to do things in style!'

Mrs. Wright rushed to the door. 'Hello, ma!' Charlie put down his case and two huge parcels and kissed her. 'How's the auld wife?'

'Oh, she's still got as much gas as ever,' Bill said, lifting his brother's case after giving him a smack on the back.

'What have you got in all the parcels, son?' Arthur said, lifting them and taking them into the living-room.

'Watch now!' Charlie cried. 'There's eggs in one of them. I've had the most god-awful job in the train protecting them.

What way do sodgers have to take as much paraphenilia aboot
wi' them when they travel? There was one bloke in the
carriage with me and he had as much stuff on him! Decked
like a bloomin' Christmas tree! '

'Hello, Dad!' he said, shaking hands. 'How're you
feelin'? That pain not been botherin' you lately?'

'No, I'm keepin' fine,' Mr. Wright said.

'Well, toots!' Charlie gave Nell a hearty kiss. 'As much
lipstick on as would sink a battleship!'

'Howya, Jenny!' He kissed her. 'Like your new hair-
style, kid. Suits you!'

'Do you really?' She squinted at herself in the mirror
above the fireplace. 'Robin doesn't like it very much.'

'Ach, Robin's daft,' Charlie said, squeezing his brother's
elbow as he passed.

'Well, Mr. Bertram,' he said.

Mr. Bertram gave him a soft, limp hand. 'How are you?
Had a pleasant journey?'

'Och, it wasn't bad.' Charlie flung his coat on the put-u-up
and pulled off his scarf and flung it on an easy chair. 'The
train was packed and I had to stand in the corridor until we
got to Dundee—after me buying a first-class ticket, too! But
I got a seat after that.'

Mr. Wright had reseated himself at the table. He looked
from Charlie's coat to Charlie's scarf. 'Ay, it's easy seen you're
hame, my man,' he said, shaking his head. 'The place looks
like a pawn-shop already!'

'It's all right, I'll put them away just now,' Charlie said.
'Let me get in first!'

'What have you got in all the parcels, son?' Robin said.
'Surely to God you don't need all that luggage for five
days!'

'You're an inquisitive lot!' Charlie said, beginning to undo
one of the parcels. 'Don't you know that I come from the
land of plenty! I don't bring you manna and gold and frank-
incense or whatever it was, but I bring you something better—
butter and eggs and twa chickens and twa wee rabbities.'

'Listen to his accent!' Jenny giggled. 'You're getting to be a real Aberdonian!'

'Ay, lassie, I'm aye speakin' aboot wifies and mannies and loonies and bairnies.'

'Sit in and get your supper,' Mrs. Wright said. 'The parcels can wait.'

'No, I want to open them,' Charlie said. 'I'm feared I've got some o' my eggs broken. I was terrified all the road in the train in case some muckle sodger would knock his rifle against them. That's why I took a taxi down from the station. I was feared to ging in a tram.'

'Ging!' Jenny giggled again.

'Surely got plenty of money for taxis,' Robin said. 'If you had a soldier's pay, son, you wouldn't be able to afford taxis.'

'Ach well, it's Christmas,' Charlie said. 'And Christmas comes but once a year, and when it comes we'll have——'

'Good beer!' they all shouted, and then they laughed.

'Never heed them, Mr. Bertram,' Mrs. Wright said to her lodger. 'Get on wi' your supper and never let on you hear them. They're all daft!'

'Ay, see who we get it off!' Arthur cried. 'She knows!'

But Mr. Bertram was uneasy. He sat with a half-smile on his face, listening to the chatter and the chaff that flew from one side of the table to the other. His eyes darted from Robin's sweeping blond moustache to Charlie's weather-beaten face and laughing green eyes, on to Arthur's wide mouth with the perfectly-shaped white teeth and then back to Bill's raised eyebrows and long inquisitive nose. They were alike, and yet they were un-alike. Four different drawings made from the same model. Four different artists had done them, and each artist had put his own individual stamp upon them. And in between stood out Jenny's dark vivacity and Nell's sleek blondeness, and the more worn edges, the more mellowed oils, that were the parents. Mr. Bertram sat beside Mrs. Wright, and inwardly his timid mind shrank against her warm bulky flesh for pro-tection against these six young hoydens. But even while he got some sense of protection from her, even though it was only in the nearness of their ages, he could feel that she was much nearer akin to the young people; they were flesh of her flesh, bone of her bone. It was from her they derived their vivacity, their coarse animalness, their charm and their good looks. He glanced furtively at Mr. Wright at the other end of the table. Yes, and from him, too. He was picking the flesh from the bones of a kipper with his fingers, laughing gaily at Jenny as he did so. ' It takes the old man to pick a kipper clean, doesn't it? ' he was saying.

' Ay, there'll be no' much left for the cat by the time you're done! ' his wife said.

' Allow the——' Charlie gulped and giggled. ' Allow the burglar! '

As soon as he could, Mr. Bertram excused himself. He closed the door behind him with relief, shutting it on their noisy good nights. There was silence for a few seconds, then as he began to go upstairs, the babble of their voices broke out. . . . His hands were sweating so much that he found it difficult to turn the handle of his bedroom door.

' Thank goodness he's gone,' Mrs. Wright said, taking the cosy off the tea-pot and pouring herself another cup of tea. ' He fair gi'es me the jitters.'

' Well, what do you have him for then? ' Charlie asked.

' What do you think! We cannie afford to pay the rent unless we keep a lodger. This house is far ower big for yer father and me.'

' Och, but surely we could help to pay the rent between——'

' Listen to who's talkin'! ' she cut in quickly. ' Spendin' money on taxis and first-class tickets! You dinnie need to speak, ma man, you that never has a penny to bless yoursel' wi'. I ken you, Charlie Wright! You've maybe got a pocketful of money on ye the night, but I bet by next Thursday when it's time for ye to go away ye'll be askin' me for the loan o' twa pounds! '

' Ach well, money was made round to go round,' he said plaintively.

'Ay, but not to go round as quick as you make it. Goodness knows what'll happen to you, ma man, when your father and me are no' here to help ye.'

'He'll get married to some rich auld wife that's half-blind,' Bill said.

'She'll have to be half-daft, too,' Arthur said. 'Won't she, son?'

'No, it's me that'll have to be half-drunk,' Charlie said.

'Mr. Bertram's a nice enough felly, ye ken,' Mrs. Wright said. 'But—well, there's just somethin' aboot him that gi'es me the creeps. I don't know what it is. He slips aboot the hoose that quiet-like, and—och, there doesnie seem to be ony gumption in him at all! Even the night—well, you'd have thought wi' you all bein' at home that he would have loosened up a bit and spoke. But he didnie. He sat there as quiet and mi-moo'ed as an auld hen.'

'He's a bit of an auld wife, I think,' Robin said, twirling his moustache.

'Ay.' His mother laughed. 'And you leave yer moustache alone, ma man! We've all seen it, so ye dinnie need to draw our attention to it. If ye're no' careful ye'll have it twirled off!'

'Are you not thinking about growing one, son?' Bill nudged Charlie.

'No, it's a beard I'm goin' to grow! It'd give the cows and the horses a surprise, wouldn't it? They'd think it was a new kind of hay!'

'You'd better no' bother,' Mrs. Wright said. 'We're for no beards here. Ye're queer enough, Charlie Wright, wi'oot growin' a beard.'

Charlie sniffed and made a funny face. 'Oh, has anybody been talking lately?'

'Oh, just wee pug-nose up the road. She said she wouldnie gi'e ye house-room.'

'She did, did she?'

'Ay, she did.' Mrs. Wright flushed with anger. 'And then the impiddent wee bitch had the nerve to say "Good mornin'" to me in the Store the other day. I just looked right through her.'

'That was right, lady!' Bill grinned. 'Give her the good old frozen mitt!'

'Tell her to mind her own bloody business,' Robin said. 'Tell her to go and fight herself if she's so bloody keen about it.'

'How's my old pal, Mrs. Mac?' Charlie said.

'Oh, she's comin' round the corner a bit,' his mother said. 'She actually asked if you'd be hame for Christmas. In fact, she's comin' in to see ye the morn.'

'Oh! Let me die on your bosom!' Charlie leaned melodramatically towards Nell. 'This is too much!'

'Give him a whiff of smelling salts, duck!' Bill grinned.

'No, keep them for later.' Charlie sat up and passed his empty cup to his mother. 'I'll need them when I go to bed with him. Do your feet still sweat as much, son?' he asked Bill. 'I hope not. I forgot to bring my gas-mask with me!'

'There's a bloke in our Mess whose feet smell like nothing on earth,' Robin said. 'Oh, boy, there was one night——'

'Oh, for God's sake!' Mr. Wright said, pushing back his chair. 'What do ye aye want to start thae kind o' stories for at meal times? Ye havenie improved one bit, not one o' ye!'

'Ay, that's enough,' their mother said. 'Mind that yer father has a weak stomach.' She helped herself to another piece of cake and laughed. 'And so have I!'

'You've always been the same ever since I've known you, Robin Wright,' Nell said with pretended disgust. 'I know when I used to come here for tea on Sundays years and years ago—you wouldn't believe it, Jenny, but often I was so disgusted when they all got talking that I had to go away to the scullery to eat my tea in peace.'

'You were never disgusted,' Charlie said. 'You were aye in hysterics.'

'Ay, we've had many a laugh,' Mrs. Wright said, shaking her head reminiscently. 'Them were the days, as the man said! Still, maybe thae days 'll come back again. Let's hope so!'

'Och ay, lady, we never died in winter yet,' Charlie said with a grin. 'Though I've been damned near it sometimes when I've been spreading dung in the fields.'

All the same, the presence of Mr. Bertram put a damper on their Christmas Day. He had to go to work; his factory was working at top speed. 'So they say, onyway,' Mrs. Wright said. 'But it seems to me that he spends a lot o' his time makin' cigarette-lighters and wee nicknacks.' And so instead of spending Christmas Day like a Sunday, as they'd have done had they been by themselves, Mrs. Wright had to get up early to see about his breakfast. And she had to prepare a midday meal. Robin and Arthur and their wives appeared downstairs just shortly before it was ready, having had cups of tea in bed earlier. But Bill and Charlie were bundled out of their bed by their mother early in the forenoon. 'Come on, get up!' she cried. 'I want to get this put-u-up made up and the living-room cleaned. Mr. Bertram 'll be here for his dinner before we can say Jack Robinson!'

'Ach, this lodger's a damned nuisance,' Charlie said.

'You're a damned nuisance yourself, Charlie Wright,' she said. 'You've been a damned nuisance all your life! Come on, get up!'

At dinner-time Mr. Bertram came in the back door silently. Charlie and Bill were in the scullery, making their mother laugh with tales of sailors and land girls, and they did not notice Mr. Bertram until he had been standing for a few seconds behind them.

He jerked his head bashfully at them and grinned before he went to the bathroom to wash. He re-entered the living-room as silently and sat down at the table. Mrs. Wright put his food in front of him, and he began to eat, apparently oblivious to the chatter and laughter that was going on all around him, although the Wright family were perfectly aware that he was listening to everything that they said. Several times during the meal Mrs. Wright did her utmost to bring him into the conversation, but he just smiled and ducked his head.

They all sighed with relief after he had gone. 'Whew!' Charlie exclaimed. 'I can unbutton my stays now!'

'Is he aye as quiet?' Bill said.

'Och ay.' Mrs. Wright took a cigarette from Robin's case. 'He fair gets on my nerves whiles; he's that quiet. He sits there and ye never ken what he's thinkin'.'

'That must be a blow to you, lady!' Arthur said, winking at the others.

'Well, I like to ken what folk are thinkin',' she said, laughing. 'I cannie be doin' wi' thae silent knights!'

'And the queer books he reads, too!' she said, blowing out a cloud of smoke. 'What blethers! Of course, he's got a dirty mind, aye talkin'—when he does talk, and mind you, whiles he opens out to yer father and me when we're oorsels—talkin' aboot nudism and spiritualism and a lot o' havers. There's a book on his dressing-table that I want ye to look at. I cannie make head nor tail o' it.'

Charlie and Bill raced each other upstairs to fetch it. Bill grabbed it first and started to look through it. After trying to snatch it from his brother, Charlie began to look around the room. It was the one he and Bill used to share. 'God-almighty!' he cried. 'Look at this!'

He pointed to a text on the mantelpiece, *Service not Self.* 'Surely he's never heard of Samuel Smiles!' he said.

'Och, that's nothing,' Bill said. 'Listen to this!' He guffawed and was starting to read, but Charlie grabbed the book from him.

He looked curiously at the title, *Guide to Self-knowledge Through Space and Time.*

'Good God!' he said. 'C'mon, let's go downstairs. It's cold up here, and those pictures and texts of his give me the willies.'

He stood inside the living-room door and cried: 'Now, brethren, listen to this!' And he began to read in a ministerial voice:

' " Another experiment that you can carry out is an experiment with a candle and a piece of tape, whereby one can concentrate by the art of relaxation until one's thoughts gradually disappear." '

' Well, that's no good for you ! ' Robin snatched the book. ' You've nothing in that noddle of yours that could disappear.'

' " Gradually you forget everything," ' Robin read, ' " and your thoughts are gradually vanishing until there is nothing to see and nothing to think of. You go into a coma, your mind becoming a blank. . . . It may take from ten seconds to half an hour, or perhaps three quarters, to do this, but persist until you succeed." '

' Why? ' Jenny said with a giggle.

' That's from a chapter called " How to Develop Clairvoyance ",' Charlie said, grabbing the book again from Robin.

' We got a candle, lady? ' Robin said.

' I'll candle ye! ' his mother said. ' Come on, drink up yer tea and let's get this table cleared. We'll have to hurry if we're goin' to the pictures.'

.   .   .   .

The next morning when she came downstairs, yawning, Jenny said : ' It's terrible me having to get up and go to work while my man lies warm in his bed! '

Bill and Charlie grinned at her from the put-u-up. ' That's the kind of wife to get, son,' Charlie said, giving Bill a dunch with his elbow and sitting up to drink the cup of tea his mother had placed on the floor beside him.

' I'm only a working gal! ' Jenny sung, rouging her lips before the mirror above the sideboard.

Bill pushed back his tousled hair and reached for his cup of tea. ' Never mind, hen,' he grinned. 'Lookit the big pay-packet you'll have at the end of the week. We'll all come out in force to meet you, won't we, Chuck? '

' You bet! Can I get to carry it for you, duck? '

' I can carry it quite well myself, thank you! ' Jenny looked around vaguely. ' Anybody seen my hat? '

'Hat?' Bill raised his eyebrows at his brother. 'Oh, you mean yon wee brown thing like a saucer with a lump o' veil hangin' at it! It was kicking about last night.'

'It's hanging in the hall,' Mrs. Wright shouted from the scullery. 'If you lassies would take care of your things better you might be able to find them again when ye want them. I found it lyin' under the gramophone.'

'Oh, have we got any new records?' Charlie said. 'What about putting it on before you go out, Jen?'

'I'll gramophone ye!' their mother shouted. 'At this time in the mornin'! None of yer shennanigans! Come on, both of ye, get up and let me get the living-room tidied!'

'What, at this time in the morning!' they shouted.

But they had to get up. They sat crouched in front of the fire, their overcoats over their pyjamas, while Mrs. Wright bustled about with a Hoover. About ten o'clock, after repeated shouting from their mother, Robin and Arthur and Nell joined them. Robin tried to take up a stance with his backside to the blaze, but he was hauled away. 'As the only lady I think I should get priority on the fire,' Nell said.

'Come on, less o' yer nonsense!' Mrs. Wright cried. 'Ye'd think ye were a pack o' bairns. Sit in and let's get our breakfast.'

She sat at the head of the table, drinking tea, while the four young men wired in to ham and eggs. 'Well, ye've still all got good appetites, I'm glad to say,' she remarked. 'Whatever else's changed about ye, there's still nothing wrong wi' them!'

       .   .   .   .

That evening when they were all sitting round the fire, there was a soft tap at the living-room door. 'Come in, Mr. Bertram,' Mrs. Wright called.

He opened the door only half-way and sidled in. He hadn't on a collar, and he touched his stud and smirked. 'Excuse me being in a state of undress,' he said. 'I'm just going to clean my shoes.'

'Och, that's nothing,' Mrs. Wright said. 'I'm used to it! It used to be nothin' for thae laddies to run aboot here in their shirt tails!'

'Oh, lady!' There was a chorus of shocked protest. 'I'm sure we never did anything so ungentlemanly,' Robin said in an exaggeratedly mincing voice.

'Did ye no'!' Mrs. Wright laughed. 'I mind once ye were standin' here in front o' that fire in yer semmit and pants—ye must ha'e been waitin' for me to mend yer shirt or somethin' —and there was a crowd o' wee laddies playin' with a ball out on the road, and the ball came in the garden, and I asked ye to shout out at them, and ye said: "Oh, I can't, I'm in my négligé!"'

'Négligé, mind ye!' She gave Nell a nudge with her fat elbow. 'That's the man ye've married, m'dear!'

'Ay, and then she went to the window herself and bawled out at the kids,' Robin said, laughing. '"Don't you put your ball in here again! I'll keep it the next time! Away and play at your own gardens!"' he screeched in a high falsetto, imitating his mother, shaking his fist at imaginary urchins. '"You bad boys that you are!"'

Mr. Bertram hovered at the scullery door, an uneasy smile on his face, listening to their chatter. 'Well—er—excuse me,' he said. 'I must get on.'

Bill and Charlie winked at each other as they heard the noise of brushes being applied to shoes. Charlie put his head coyly to the side and patted his hair. 'I'll get you!' he whispered. 'And if I don't get you the cows will!'

'Shuttup!' Mrs. Wright hissed, nudging Bill as he tried to stifle a hysterical giggle.

'Well, that's a good job done,' Mr. Bertram said, coming in with his clean shoes in his hand. 'I must hurry. I'm going to a meeting. I—er—I won't be back until rather late, I'm afraid.'

'Och, that's all right,' Mrs. Wright said cheerfully. 'We're no' likely to be in our beds! See and have a good time!'

Mr. Bertram smirked and stood with his hand on the handle

of the door. 'I—er—I must try to keep elders' hours,' he said.
'Er—good night, everybody!'

'Good night,' they chorused.

A few minutes later they heard him come downstairs and
shut the front door quietly behind him. As soon as they had
heard the light patter of his feet disappear on the gravel of
the path, they all seemed to relax. 'Thank goodness, he's
away!' Mrs. Wright said, voicing the relief they all felt.
'He fair gi'es me the creeps. Even though he's safely shut
up in his own room, I never feel at peace while he's in the
house.'

'Why not get rid of him, Ma?' Robin said.

'I've tellt ye already,' she said impatiently. 'We need the
money to help pay the rent—and besides, if it wasnie him it
would have to be somebody else. Thae Government officials
have been goin' all round the houses, askin' how many are in
each. If they think ye havenie got enough for the size of the
house, they gar ye take somebody—and I'm for none o' that!
Poor auld Mrs. Whittaker in Number Eleven was garred take
in a lassie that works in a Government department that's
been evacuated from London—a painted hissy wi' painted
legs!'

'Oh, boy!' Bill slapped Charlie on the knee.

'Ay, the paint all comes off on poor auld Mrs. Whittaker's
sheets.' Mrs. Wright sighed and took a cigarette from a
packet on the mantelpiece. 'Whae's fags are they? I'm
helpin' myself, onyway!'

'So ye see,' she said, lighting her cigarette, 'although he's
not much o' a catch, we're better wi' him than wi' somebody
the Government might foist on us. He's a decent, clean bloke,
and well meaning and all that. There's nae bother wi' him—
though he's a bit o' a jessy and gets on ma nerves sometimes
wi' his creepin' aboot in his stockin' soles.'

'Ye ken, I feel sorry for him sometimes,' she said, leaning
back in her chair and puffing smoke towards the electric-light
bowl. 'He's got nobody. No place of his own and nobody
that wants him. He should have got married long ago and

had a nice wee house o' his ain and sat down in it in comfort instead o' gallivantin' away to one o' thae queer meetings.'

'Ay, he should have got married long ago,' Mr. Wright said. 'That would have been the makin' o' him.'

'Maybe his mother wouldn't let him!' Charlie grinned.

'Maybe no'!' Their mother laughed.

'See you and not be so daft, son.' Robin gave his brother a slight kick on the foot.

'No, he'll be coming home with a muckle heifer of a land girl,' Arthur said. 'You'd better watch yourself, son, and not get caught!'

'Like us!' Robin winked at Nell.

'Ay, it would be a job if you got somebody that would keep you under her thumb!' Jenny said.

'Like me!' Arthur pulled a doleful face.

'I would be Cæsar in my own home!' Charlie scowled ferociously.

'Home, Cæsar!' Bill said.

They all laughed at the worn old joke, and then Jenny got up and began to take the nicknacks off the top of the cabinet gramophone, saying: 'What about a tune?'

'Ay, it's years since we played the gramophone,' Mrs. Wright said.

'Any new records?' Charlie asked.

'What do you think!' Bill laughed. 'You can see from the dust on top of it when it was played last!'

'There's a duster in the cupboard, Jenny,' Mrs. Wright said. 'Goodness, it's gey stoury! It must be years. . . . I never open it.'

Arthur came staggering in from the hall with a pile of old records. No new records had been bought for years; not since the days when the boys were all at home and Charlie had spent most of his money on records, always trying to slip furtively into the house with them. 'He aye had them under his coat,' Mrs. Wright said. 'I mind once I popped my head out the door into the hall and he got such a muckle fright that he dropped it.'

'That was *Tell Me To-night*,' Charlie said. 'I aye mind it.'

'Ay, for she told you a lot more than you wanted to hear about spending your money, didn't she?' Bill laughed.

'Have we still got it, Jen?' Charlie stood up and began to look through the pile of records with his sister-in-law. 'It has a wee chip on the side.'

'A wee chip like hissel'!' Mrs. Wright laughed. 'He was aye spendin' his money on some trash or other. If it wasnie records it was books. Books! Books! Just look at them! My word, Charlie Wright, you'll end your days in the poor house.'

'It'll need oiling before ye put it on,' Mr. Wright said, looking up from his newspaper.

'Ach, we'll try it first and see,' his wife said. 'There's bound to be some life in it yet!'

She leaned back comfortably and listened to all the old, well-known tunes. *An Old Spanish Tango* . . . *I Was Strolling on the Beach at Balli-Balli* . . . *Falling in Love Again* . . . *Old Faithful* . . . *Empty Saddles* . . . They all brought back memories: memories of happier days when the boys were young and war was far off. . . .

'Empty saddles in the old corral,' she hummed. 'Where do you ride to-night? Empty boots covered with dust. . . . Are there rustlers on the border? . . .'

Suddenly she felt old and forlorn and tired. And underneath her nostalgia, under the warmth and comfort she felt in having her family all around her again, there began a gnawing at the back of her mind. It was all very well just now when the boys were here. It was all very well for this one short week. But what was she to do when they all went away again?. What was she to do about Mr. Bertram? At the moment she could laugh at his creepiness and joke with the boys about his mannerisms, but when they were all away again . . . when there was nobody here but her husband safely entrenching himself behind his newspaper or snoring quietly while having forty winks. . . . What was she to do then?

She sighed as the record finished. Ah, well, she would just have to make up her mind. She would tell Mr. Bertram to look for other lodgings. And as Charlie put on *Stormy Weather*, she began to rehearse what she would say to Mr. Bertram in the morning.

SAILORS, BEWARE OF WITCHES

I

THERE was consternation in Pantomime Land when most of its inhabitants got their Calling Up Papers. But there was even greater consternation when suddenly one cold bleak morning they found themselves standing outside a factory gate, surrounded by grim chimneys and tall buildings that had obviously never been made by any stage carpenter. The Sleeping Beauty was especially furious because she'd been wakened out of her long sleep to do munitions. 'I thought the war was finished,' she said. Little Red Riding Hood grinned maliciously and said: 'If you thought that, darling, you can't have been as sound asleep as you led us all to believe. Besides, it says on this gate SILKWORMS, LTD., so we must have been brought here to spin.'

'To spin what?' Beauty asked crossly. 'Uniforms for the next war? Or parachutes?'

'I don't see why Bo-Peep isn't here,' Little Mary said angrily. 'She's got exemption because of her sheep. I don't see why I can't get exemption too.'

'You can always put your little lamb in a crèche, darling,' said the Queen of Hearts. 'Though it must be getting quite a big lamb now.'

Little Jack Horner was practically the only one who remained in a good temper. 'I put my finger in my pie,' he said, 'and instead of pulling out my plum I pulled out a single for Bickerington!'

'Bickerington!' D. Whittington said scornfully. 'Whoever heard of the place! Bow Bells told me to turn, and so I turned, and before I knew where I was I was here! Where is Bickerington, anyway?'

'It's an island somewhere in the middle of England,' a voice cried from the other side of the factory gates. 'You'll soon know all about it, my hearties!'

And the gates swung slowly open and Long John Silver peg-hopped out and leered at them. He wore a bowler hat, but he was carrying his famous three-cornered pirate's one in a box marked Aage Tharrup. 'Ho, ho, my hearties,' he chuckled, taking his cigar out of his mouth and spitting. 'Didn't expect to find me here, did yer? You thought the old dog was finished, did yer? Get into line now, every jolly jack tar of yer! You're here to work, and work I'm jolly well going to make yer.' He scowled so ferociously that they scuttled to do as they were bid. 'Now I'll check the roll,' he said. 'Answer your names promptly.'

'Robin Hood!' he shouted.

'Present.' Robin stepped forward. 'All my Merry Men deserted me to join the Merchant Navy, and now I've been directed by the Ministry of Labour to come here and spin. I want to protest about it. If I have to spin, I want to spin in an aeroplane.'

'Spin inside them there gates and get busy!' Long John roared. 'Aladdin!'

'All plessent and collect,' Aladdin said, shuffling forward. 'Alas, I've lost my magic lamp and my genie—they're working on the Atomic Bomb—so I can be of no use here, I fear.'

'Cut the cackle and get inside!' Long John aimed a kick at him with his wooden leg, and Aladdin rushed inside the gates after Robin Hood.

'Peter Pan!'

As Peter Pan stepped forward, Long John said: 'Are you alone?'

'Alone, all alone!' Peter said sorrowfully. 'The Lost Boys are all in the R.A.F. and Wendy's in the W.A.A.F. But they wouldn't take me. The Air Force wallas said I'd be a bad influence. They wouldn't even let me be a Bevin Boy. They said I might try to fly too high! '

' Well, don't try any of your flying stunts here,' said Long John. ' Machine number three for you.'

' Dick Whittington! '

' Richard, if you please,' Whittington said haughtily. ' Sir Richard to you, varlet.'

' None of that, none of that,' Silver said. ' We're all alike here, prince and commoner, all in the same boat. If there's anyone better than another, then I'm the one, for I'm the fore-man here. Where's your cat? I've got him listed.'

' Alas, I don't know. Poor pussy—every time I go past a butcher's I turn my eyes away and wonder.'

' Machine number four,' Long John said. ' Goldilocks and the Three Bears! '

' If you please, sir,' Goldilocks said, stepping forward. ' As there are four of us, can we take it in turns to do the work? '

' Well, I never heard the like,' Long John shouted. ' In you get, the whole lot of you. I'll put you on double shifts if I hear any more of your nonsense. Machine number five! '

' But my long hair,' Goldilocks protested. ' Even though it's not one of Mr. Clarkson's best wigs—it's only a utility model—it'll get caught in the machine! '

' Wear one of them snood things then,' Silver cried, giving her a push. ' Then you'll be in the fashion like all the other factory-girls.'

He shouted name after name, and each one of the famous Pantomime Land inhabitants had some kind of protest to make against being directed, but one after the other he chased them into the factory. Then when the last one had disappeared in-side he leaned against the gate and took out another cigar. As he lit it, his eye caught the sign *No Smoking*, but he hawked and spat contemptuously.

II

An hour later Long John Silver was still leaning against the gatepost, humming *I'm the Man who Makes the Thing that Makes the Thingymybob*, when Old Mother Hubbard rushed up and demanded his Clothing Coupon Book. 'Hurry up,' she cried impatiently. 'Or I'll miss the bus. I don't want to be like Mr. Chamberlain and 'ave to wave me umbrella to the bus-conductress. Most of them conductresses won't stop the bus for old lidies like me, anyway. If I was a man it would be all right. Ooooo, they'd stop the bus quick enough then! Stop it for anythink in trousers they would! '

'Well, why don't you wear trousers, me dear? ' Long John said, searching in another pocket.

'What do you think I want your coupons for? ' Old Mother Hubbard snapped. 'I saw a lovely pair of green corduroys in the Co-op's window last week. Oh, do 'urry up, Johnnie. Where 'ave you put it? '

Long John began to look desperate. 'I can't think what I've done with it, dear. I'm sure I put it in this pocket. I must 'ave lost it. Yes, that's what must 'ave 'appened. I've lost the bloody thing.'

'Lost it! ' Old Mother Hubbard put her hands on her hips. 'Now, John Silver, don't you try any of them funny tricks on me. No, no, me little chicken, you 'aven't lost it. You've given it to another woman—that's wot you've done. A little bird whispered to me that you were in the Wagon and Horses the other night with the Widow Twankey. So you gave it to her, did you? '

Long John backed inside the factory as she advanced belligerently upon him. 'No, me dear, no, no,' he protested weakly, 'I haven't seen the lady for weeks and weeks, dear.'

'Don't you tell me any of your lies, you—you Casanova! ' she screamed, brandishing her umbrella. 'Go and get that coupon book back from her just as quickly as you can. If you don't, I'll—I'll——'

And she rushed at him, but as soon as she saw that he was peg-hopping furiously in the direction of the Widow Twankey's, she stopped. She rearranged her feather-boa and nodded amiably to the girls at the nearest machines. 'That's the way to settle him, gals,' she said. 'If ever you want advice on 'ow to treat a 'usband you come along to Old Mother 'Ubbard. The Citizens' Advice Bureau 'as nothink on me. In fact it was me wot started the Citizens' Advice Bureau in Bickering- ton. I wrote a little book *How to Get Your Man—And How to Hold Him*. It sold out in two days. Regular little best- seller it was.'

She chatted amiably to them, looking every now and then at her gold wristlet-watch. 'My, wot a time Johnnie's taking to get that book,' she cried. 'If he don't 'urry up I'll miss the next bus, and I don't want to go down into 'istory as The Woman Wot Missed Two Buses.'

As she strode majestically in the direction of the Widow Twankey's, Cinderella and her two Ugly Sisters rushed through the gates. 'We're late,' Trixie was shouting. 'I told you we'd be late. If that little slut, Cinderella, had had all her wits about her and had set the alarm properly we'd have been whisked here in time with the others instead of having to depend upon that fool of a rat-coachman and his six white mice. You must give him the sack, Cinders. He's getting far too old and doddery for the job. Besides, he's out of fashion. We must move with the times. If you weren't always so busy dreaming and mooning about that prince of yours you'd have realized that long ago.'

'Please, sister, please,' Cinderella wept. 'Please leave my poor Charming out of this. He's dead and gone now, poor boy, and, alas, I am a widow, and Mr. Bevin's got his eye on me.'

'I wish Mr. Bevin had his eye on me,' Bunty giggled.

'Well, he has, hasn't he?' Trixie snapped.

'But not the right eye,' Bunty said dolefully. 'I don't like the look in the one I've seen.'

'If only you'd played your cards right with the Lord Chan- cellor last year at Blackpool you mightn't be here now,' Trixie said. 'In fact, none of us might have been here. We might be dishing out cups of tea in a Forces Canteen and driving to work in an Army Staff Car.'

'Or a Jeep!' Bunty cried. 'Ooooo, these Americans!'

'That's one thing you can always say about Cinder's poor Prince Charming,' Trixie said. 'He did his best to try to get you off his hands! The chances you've had. There was the Lord Chancellor, and there was that Lord High Executioner at Brighton—the one who did a Houdini act on the smaller halls. Oh, but you've missed all your chances!'

'Never mind, I might get another one here.' Bunty winked and pointed to Idle Jack, who was pottering among the machines with an oil-can. 'I won't be the first girl who's gone into a factory and bagged an executive for a husband.'

'What's the meaning of this?' Long John Silver cried, clumping towards them. 'Don't you ladies know that this factory starts at seven a.m. prompt every morning?'

'I'm sorry, sir,' Cinderella said, fluttering her eyelashes at him. 'It's all my fault. My sisters were depending upon me to waken them, but I couldn't sleep last night for thinking about my poor husband who died six months ago, and then I feel asleep just as it was time to get up and I didn't hear the alarm. I do hope you'll forgive us.'

'Well, the usual thing is to fine you for absenteeism,' Long John said. 'Still, I don't like to be too hard on pretty young gals like yourself. So you're a widow, eh? Well, me dear, we'll be as kind as we can to you here. Come over to this machine and I'll show you personally how it works. I believe in the personal touch, don't you?'

'Yes, as long as it's not too personal,' Cinderella said, shrugging off the hand he had laid on her arm.

'Hey, you!' Long John shouted to Idle Jack. 'Come 'ere and show them two dames wot to do.'

Idle Jack was doing this, and Trixie and Bunty were squabbling about which of them was to have first choice of his favours, when a young sailor came into the factory, whistling *The Whistling Sailor*. He was trying to appear jaunty, but there was a woebegone air about him. 'Lookit this, ducks,' Trixie whispered. 'Familiar look about him, ain't there?'

'Looks a bit balmy to me,' Bunty said. 'See, he's talking to himself.'

'Must be some ham actor rehearsing his lines,' Trixie said.

They craned their necks, straining to hear what the sailor was saying as he passed their machine. He was looking about and muttering: 'What place is this, I wonder? What strange shore have I been cast upon? It looks familiar, and yet I can't place it. It might be Morocco—the setting's much the same as the setting we had two years ago when we played at the Palace in Glasgow. Gee, that was a swell job. I wish now I'd stayed there and hadn't sailed away down the Clyde with Will Fyffe. My poor old granny was right when she warned me never to go to sea. "Sinbad," she said. "Take a tip from me. If you want to be a sailor, be a dry-land sailor. Never get your feet wet." But, alas, I didn't take her advice, and look at what's happened to me to-day. Cast away yet once again on a strange inhospitable shore.'

He stopped beside Cinderella's machine and gazed at her as if in a trance. 'But perhaps not so inhospitable,' he cried, putting his hand on his heart. 'Who is this beautiful damsel, I wonder?' He struck an attitude and began to sing: 'Maiden, fair maiden, oh dream divine!' 'Haven't I seen you somewhere before?' he said, leaning against the machine and giving her the glad eye.

'No, I've never been there,' Cinderella said, giggling coyly. Then she recollected that she had been married into Society, and she said in her best Mayfair accent: 'Sir, this is not the proper approach to a proper friendship. Surely you should know better than that. Or perhaps you are an American and don't know any better?'

'I beg your pardon, girlie,' Sinbad said, preparing to move on. 'Wrong number!'

'Stop!' Cinderella cried, coming around her machine. 'Now that I look more closely I think we've met before. Where was it?'

'I know!' Sinbad snapped his fingers. 'It was in Leeds

three years ago. You were playing at the Gaiety with Prince Charming while I was playing at the Alhambra.'

'It's a small world,' Cinderella said.

'Fancy meeting you,' he said.

This was a cue for a popular song, but they didn't have time to sing it. The factory executives frowned upon singing unless it was official Breaks for Music sponsored by ENSA and the B.B.C. So they contented themselves by going into a huddle and telling each other all that happened to them in the interval. And when Cinderella told him how Prince Charming had died six months ago as a result of her bad cooking with Reconstituted Eggs, Sinbad immediately proposed that he take over the job as her Principal Boy.

'That would be lovely,' Cinderella said, swooning against him.

'You and me together,' Sinbad sighed romantically. 'You and me—and Tilly!'

'Oh, yes, Tilly,' Cinderella said, drawing herself away and rearranging her hair. 'How is she?'

'Well, to be honest, I don't know,' Sinbad said, taking out a packet and offering her a Gold Flake (free advertisement). 'I've sort of lost trace of her at the moment. We were clinging to a raft together when the ship went down, but I got washed off by a huge wave, and after I'd swum and swum and landed on the shore here, there was no sign of poor Tilly. I wonder what's become of her?'

'Oh, she'll turn up all right,' Cinderella said, puffing crossly at her cigarette. 'Trust that bird. She has nine lives.'

Just then there was raucous screeching outside the factory gates, and a voice called: 'Hello, cocky dear! Where's pore old cocky!'

Sinbad took his arm away from Cinderella's waist and rushed to the gates shouting: 'Tilly! Tilly, where are you?'

'Use your eyes, can't yer? Use your eyes!' And Tilly the Toiler, an enormous parrot, the size of a smallish man, came wandering into the factory. 'Pore old cocky!' she screeched. 'Scratch Tilly's poll!'

YSC—O

'Oh, Tilly!' Sinbad cried dramatically, raising his eyes in the hope that there was a Gallery in the factory. 'Oh, Tilly, I wondered what had happened to you.'

'Scratch my poll!' the parrot screamed. 'Dammit, man, can't yer do wot a lidy tells yer!'

'Okay, okay,' Sinbad said, obliging vigorously. 'Sssh now, Tilly, remember there's a lady present and she doesn't like to hear such language.'

'Lidy?' Tilly cried. 'Wot lidy? I don't see nobody but that little gal Cinders wot we used to see every night in the bar of the old Pig and Whistle. Hello, cocky, hello!'

'Hello,' Cinderella said stiffly. 'How are you?'

'I'm okay, toots,' Tilly said. 'Got a bellyful of seawater, but that's all the damage. Oh, wot a time I 'ad on that raft! The things one does for Basil Dean. I clung here and I clung there. And all the time the sad sea waves were saying "We'll get you! We'll get you—and if we don't Ernie Bevin will!" But they didn't. No, they didn't. Trust old Tilly to do them one in the eye.'

'Well, Tilly, now that you're here in Bickerington, what would you like to do?' Sinbad asked.

'I wanna eat,' Tilly said. 'And I wanna eat quick.'

'I'm a bit peckish myself,' Sinbad said. 'But we can't eat until we find work.'

'Work, work, work!' Tilly cried. 'Never 'eard of the word. What does it mean?'

Sinbad laughed and said: 'Good old Tilly! She hates the sound of the word. She'll toil not neither will she spin.'

'But she'll have to spin here,' Long John Silver said, clumping up to them. 'We'll have no slackers in this factory.'

'Mr. Silver, this young man is a friend of mine,' Cinderella said. 'He's just been shipwrecked.'

'Ah, a sailor!' Long John cried. 'Been shipwrecked a lot in me time, too, matey.' He glared suspiciously at Sinbad. 'Are you sure you were shipwrecked? Are you sure you weren't put ashore off one of them U-boats? We got to be very careful here, y'know. Fifth and Sixth Columnists and all that. Maybe Seventh Columnists by this time for all I know. I ain't read the papers for two or three days. After all, we're doing some very important work here in Bickerington. Oh, very secret work. On the hush-hush system. It's so hush-hush that even some of the workers don't seem to know anything about it.'

' 'Ello, old cock!' Tilly cried, nipping his wooden leg. 'Scratch Tilly's poll. Come on! Lord love a duck, you ain't afraid of pore old Tilly, are you?'

'Call off this bird, sir,' Long John screamed, retreating before the parrot's amorous advances. 'Call her off immediately —or I'll send for the police.'

'Tilly! Tilly! Where are your manners?' Sinbad cried.

'Ain't got any.' Tilly made another peck at Silver's peg-leg, chuckling bawdily. 'Left them behind me on the raft with me clean underwear. Reckon some of Neptune's young women 'ave got 'em now. Fat lot of good they'll do 'em! Weren't any fully-fashioned silk stockings amongst 'em!'

'I must apologize, sir, for Tilly's behaviour,' Sinbad said, at last managing to hold the parrot back. 'She hasn't been very well brought up, I'm afraid. She's always lived in cheap third-rate theatrical lodgings.'

'Coo, listen to 'im!' Tilly cried. 'You'd think he'd been used to living in the Ritz 'imself.'

'Can you give us a job, sir?' Sinbad said.

Long John looked meditatively at Tilly, and then he said: 'Um, well, maybe. . . . It's not often we get people coming here *asking* for jobs. Most of the people we get are *directed* and they spend all their time and their energy moaning about it. Yes, I think I could find a job for you—but as for that bird, no, no, a thousand times no!'

'Suits me, old cock!' Tilly said. 'I'd rather be a bird in a gilded cage any day than only a working girl!'

Here again was a cue for a song, but even if there had been an audience to sing it to, none of them could have got the chance. For just then there was a vicious flash of lightning, and Priscilla Prickler, the Witch of Power, soared through the factory roof on her broomstick. She screeched malevolently as they cowered away from her, and she shouted: 'Cower away as much as you like, my pretty ones, cower away! You're all in my power and you'll stay here until I give the word.' And she slapped the bag that was slung around her waist, a bag with £ marked on it.

'Begone, old witch, begone!' Sinbad cried, remembering that he was a hero.

'Oho, what a brave young cockerel,' the Witch cried. 'Somebody needing his wings clipped, I can see!'

'Begone, vile old dame, begone,' Sinbad cried again, feeling secure because the Witch was hovering a good seven feet above him. 'You cannot frighten me.'

'Oho, can I not?' she screamed. 'See them all cowering there! And yet this young cockerel says I can't frighten them! I have you all in my power, my brave little man, and you'll stay in my power as long as I want—until it's all in the bag, my pretty sailor, and then as soon as it's all in the bag— well, maybe I'll let you go then.'

'If I don't have another bag I want to fill by that time,' she screeched, and she set spurs to her broomstick and soared away up through the roof, cackling sardonically.

They watched her go with relief. Long John Silver wiped his brow and said: 'The old gal fairly scared me for a time. And coo, here's another old gal that scares me even more!'

He was making to hide behind a machine, but Old Mother Hubbard swept down upon him, crying: 'Just a minute, you! I want you!'

'But I'm busy, me dear,' he protested.

'Busy? Since when? Don't make me laugh. Foremen have always plenty of time for everything. No, no, ducky, you stay here with me.' Old Mother Hubbard gripped him firmly by the sleeve. 'You're not going with that girl Cinderella. I saw you making eyes at her, you nasty old man!'

'I wasn't making eyes at her at all,' Long John said indignantly. 'It was Sinbad the Sailor who was making eyes at her.'

'Nonsense,' Mother Hubbard said, fluffing up her feather-boa. 'He was making eyes at me. Nice-looking young man! And a sailor, too! I think I'll get off with him. Just wait until he sees me in my new green corduroys!'

She unwrapped the parcel she was carrying and held up a pair of trousers. 'Lovely, ain't they? Got them at the Bargain Counter at the Co-op. Only three coupons because they're W.W.X.'

'W.W.X.?' Long John said. 'What does that mean?'

'Wait, watch, and exercise your intelligence,' she said, 'if you have any!'

'Did you see anything exciting in town?' Long John asked.

'Yes, I saw some lovely Americans in them Jips. Oooo,' she said, 'they did give me a thrill! I was that excited that I purposely missed the bus and started to walk back. But I thumbed and thumbed—and now me thumb's got rheumatics, and me corns are bothering me!'

'Did you see any A.T.S.?' he said.

''Ats?' Mother Hubbard said. 'Ooooo, yes, I saw some lovely 'ats in a shop. One of them would 'ave suited me a treat. Only three pounds ten it was.'

'I don't mean hats, gal,' he cried. 'I mean A.T.S. Women in uniform. You know. Girls.'

'Girls!' Mother Hubbard held up her pants and examined them critically. 'That's all you men ever think about. Just let me catch you looking at one of them A.T.S. and then there'll be trouble. Or let me catch you looking at anything else—that Widow Twankey for instance—and there'll be even more trouble! Gracious, 'ere she comes now! All dolled up like a dish of tripe! What can she be wanting 'ere?'

'Good morning, Mrs. Twankey,' she said graciously. 'Where did you spring from?'

The Widow Twankey advanced belligerently. 'Nowhere,' she answered. 'I haven't sprung yet. But I'm going to!'

'Here, you!' she called to Long John, who was backing behind a machine. 'I want you, you long slimy worm.

What do you mean by coming into my house this morning
and pinching my clothing coupons when I was asleep?'

'Clothing coupons?' Long John stuttered. 'What clothing
coupons? I swear I never saw your clothing coupon book in
my life.'

'Oh, didn't you?' Widow Twankey cried. 'I know perfectly well it was you that took them. Only you could 'ave
known where I kept them.'

'Oho, only he could 'ave known, could he?' cried Mother
Hubbard. 'You worm!'

Both the dames advanced menacingly and Long John retreated as best he could. The inhabitants of Pantomime Land
watched the scene with interest, glad of any opportunity to
leave off work for a little. Though some of them glanced
around to see that no stage-managers were hovering behind
machines, ready to dock their salaries for slacking.

'You saw me put it there last night after you gave it to me,'
Widow Twankey cried.

'He did, did he?' Mother Hubbard said. 'And what
right, may I ask, had he to give you his clothing coupons?'

'The right of every man in this country,' Widow Twankey
retorted. 'The right to turn everything belonging to him
over to his lawful wedded wife.'

'Lawful wedded wife!' Mother Hubbard shrieked. 'See
here, you—you viper in a fur coat! Don't you stand there
and 'and me any of your old-fashioned buck! Lawful wedded
wife indeed! Do you know who I am?'

'You're the woman who had the little dog, aren't you?'
Widow Twankey smiled graciously. 'Poor little thing, I
heard you couldn't keep it any longer, you were too mean to
give it any of your rations.'

Mother Hubbard raised her umbrella threateningly, but
Widow Twankey continued: 'Otherwise I don't know you.
I never have any truck with the women the Ministry of Labour
direct here.'

'Women that the Ministry—oh!' Mother Hubbard paused
a second for breath. 'Oh, I never heard the like! I'd like

you to know, Mrs. Twankey, that I am the Queen of Bickerington, Mrs. Hubbard-Silver. I don't think I have had the
pleasure of having had you officially presented to me.'

'Well, it's never too late to put you on to something good,'
the Widow Twankey said majestically. 'Allow me to introduce myself, madam. I am the Empress of Bickerington—
Mrs. Twankey-Silver.'

The looms were silent, Long John Silver was silent, and the
fairy factory-workers were silent for the next few minutes
while the two ancient dames went at each other hammer and
tongs. Only Tilly the Toiler snored peacefully through it all
in a corner beside a loom where she had snuggled down.

'He's mine, I tell you!' screamed Widow Twankey. 'He
was married to me three years ago in a pantomime in Cardiff.
Only he was the Demon King then.'

'He's still the Demon King as far as a lot of the young
women here in Bickerington are concerned,' said Mother Hubbard. 'Only he's got the Ministry of Labour on his side
now.'

'Unhand me!' Long John shouted, struggling frantically
between them. 'I can explain all this.'

'We'll do all the explaining that's necessary, ducky,' Widow
Twankey said. 'Don't you remember, sweetie? Don't you
remember singing "Oh, give me one night in June" to me
every night for six weeks at the Hippodrome in Cardiff?
Surely the Blitz 'asn't done all that damage! I'm maybe the
Widow Twankey now, but then I was the Fairy Queen and
you were my MAN!'

'Well, he's not your man now,' Mother Hubbard cried.
'He never was anybody's man—unless Robert Louis Steven-
son's! I married him last year when he was playing Puss in
Boots at Birmingham. Didn't I, me little kitten?'

'If you'd just let me go I'd explain everything,' Long John
shouted.

'No, no, sweetheart, we're not letting you go,' they cried,
clinging tighter.

'Not on your life we ain't,' Mother Hubbard said. 'We're

going to thrash this thing out—even if we have to thrash you in the process with your own wooden leg! You bigamist!'

Before she could say any more there was a diversion. Idle Jack rushed down the factory, zigzagging through the machines, followed closely by the Ugly Sisters. 'What's this?' Widow Twankey cried. 'Looks like another unhappy little triangle.'

'It was me he asked,' Bunty was shouting.

'Yes, but it was me he got!' Trixie cried triumphantly.

'Well, I couldn't help it if that stupid old parson didn't know which of us he was to marry,' Bunty wept. 'Why did we have to choose a parson with cross-eyes? When he said "Do you take this awful man to be your lawful wedded husband?" I didn't know whether he was looking at me or——'

'And so I chipped in and said "I do,"' Trixie said jubilantly. 'Well, why shouldn't I? After all, I saw him first. My little tootsie-wootsie!' she said to Idle Jack. 'Let me crush you to my bosom.'

'Oh, leave me alone,' Jack cried. 'Why can't you leave me alone? I've never had a minute's peace since you women appeared on the scene.'

'Be a man, Jack, and stand up to them,' Long John shouted. 'Tell them where they get off.'

'Why don't you take that advice to yourself?' Jack said petulantly. 'You don't seem to be doing so good.'

'Alas, I am the victim of circumstances,' Long John said dramatically.

An impasse appeared to have been reached, but as so often happens with impasses in Pantomime Land there was a sudden diversion. A blackout descended upon the factory. There was wind and hail and snow and lightning, and above it all the high cackling shrieks of Priscilla, the Witch of Power. The factory-workers clung to each other, too dazed to rush for the nearest air-raid shelters. They heard the Witch shrieking: 'Where's that bird? I saw a bird when I was here a while ago. A very strange-looking bird. I must have it.

Now that my poor old cat's dead, it's lonely sailing through the clouds alone on my broomstick. I must have something to talk to—and a little bird would be just the thing. Ah, here she is!'

'Leave pore old cocky alone,' Tilly the Toiler screeched. 'Sinbad! Sinbad!'

'Are you coming quietly, or will I get the M.P.s to you?' the Witch screamed in the blackout. 'Or must I use my pistol?'

'Lay that pistol down, babe, lay that pistol down!' cried Tilly. 'I'll go like a good little girl. But golly, if you get tough . . .'

III

The Witch's abduction of Tilly the Toiler settled all other disputes in Bickerington for the moment. The factory fairies stopped grousing about being called up, and they allowed themselves more or less willingly to be directed into Home Guard units to search for the captured bird. The Navy happened to come to Bickerington at that time, so perhaps the arrival of so many pretty sailor boys helped the fairies to make their decision. The Fleet was under the command of the bold Admiral Neddy Nelson, and he was not long in persuading Old Mother Hubbard and the Widow Twankey to forget their differences and to form a Woman's Home Guard.

Admiral Nelson had a cast in his eye, which he skilfully hid with a monocle. Before the war he had been a dummy in a Savile Row tailor's window, and he still retained most of his pre-war elegance. Not even all the thrilling adventures in submarines and cruisers that he continually talked about could alter this. The Ugly Sisters were fascinated by him; so much so that they forgot to quarrel about which of them was legally entitled to Idle Jack. Not that it would have made any difference if they had, for Idle Jack had gone. He had taken advantage of the gloom into which the Witch had plunged the factory, and he had decamped. It was rumoured that he had taken the train to London, but as this was founded solely upon the testimony of Rip Van Winkle, who had been awakened from a light nap by a stranger enquiring the way to the railway station, too much credence was not laid upon it.

In the meantime, in her cave in the hills, the Witch was sitting on top of a step-ladder, gazing through a spy-glass into the valley below. Behind her in the darkness of the cave, Tilly the Toiler was struggling in a web which Snow White and the Seven Dwarfs were weaving around her. The Witch watched Tilly's efforts to get out of the web and she cackled madly and sang a song that she had composed herself in imitation of Mr. Auden :

> ' Spin on, me pretty ones, spin on !
> Spin yourselves into a daze,
> For now we have the parrot in a maze !
> Spin and toil, and work and sweat—
> No matter how hard you work,
> The War won't be over just yet ! '

She put her telescope to her eye again and sang :

> ' He seeks you here, he seeks you there,
> The Home Guard are seeking you everywhere.
> But no matter how hard they look—
> I've gotcher ! '

IV

In the local Lovers' Lane it was evening. Courting couples passed and repassed each other, forgetting for the moment that there was anything as important afoot as the rescue of Tilly the Toiler from the Witch of Power. The affairs of the world must rest while Youth has its Fling ! The Fleet was in, and that was all that most of the fairies were interested in. Everyone had her own pretty sailor boy. They were all too much occupied in hearing about exploits at Gib. or at Narvic

or finding out what quarter-decks and companion-ladders were
to notice Idle Jack skulking amongst the bushes.

Jack hadn't gone to London after all. At the station he had
got cold feet. Anyway, all the trains were troop-trains, and
the sight of so many uniforms had filled him with nausea.
The nausea was almost as bad here at the prospect of so many
blue-jackets, but he hid his head under a bush and went to
sleep. He was sound asleep when the Witch passed, dragging
Tilly at the end of a rope. The Witch was so busy screaming
at Tilly that she didn't notice Jack either. She kept telling
Tilly to hurry up. 'We're on the run,' she screamed. 'But
I'm determined that I'm not going to run alone. I'm taking
you with me as a hostage. I'm going to save my own poor
old skin at any cost.'

'You're choking me!' Tilly screeched. 'You're choking
me! I'm sure it's against the Queensberry Rules and the laws
laid down by the Geneva Convention.'

'Well, hurry up then!' the Witch howled. 'It's your own
silly fault if you won't walk any quicker.'

They had just disappeared along the lane when Sinbad and
Cinderella came past the bush under which Idle Jack lay.
'Wasn't that Tilly's voice I heard?' Sinbad said. 'It sounded
like it. Or was I dreaming?'

'You must have been dreaming,' Cinderella said crossly.
'You never do anything else but dream about that stupid bird.
I wish you'd dream about me for a change. I'm tired of the
sound of Tilly's name. You talk about her and Marx and
dialectical materialism all the time. I don't see what you're
worrying about when both the Home Guard and the Navy are
looking for her. Look at that moon! Doesn't it make you
feel romantic?'

'No, it doesn't,' Sinbad said. He stopped and shouted:
'Tilly!'

'If you don't quit that,' Cinderella said, 'I've a good mind
to go and get a real sailor. He at least wouldn't bother about
a stupid old parrot.'

'One more crack like that and you and me are finished,'

Sinbad said. 'No matter what pantomime audiences may think! It's time they listened to something sensible, anyway; maybe something about the Big Bad Wolf that's waiting for them just around the corner. I'll never appear on another stage with you as long as I live. I'd rather sail away down the Clyde with Mr. Fyffe.'

'Tilly!' he shouted. 'Tilly!'

Cinderella took out her compact and began to powder her face. 'I've had enough,' she said. 'I'm going to hook a sailor.'

But Sinbad grabbed her and whispered: 'Hist! Here's the Home Guard coming! Let's hide under this bush! I should have been on parade.'

They had just crept under the bush next to the one Idle Jack was asleep under when the Home Guard marched down the lane. It was led by Long John Silver wearing a lieutenant's uniform and his famous three-cornered pirate's hat. Close behind him were the Widow Twankey, Old Mother Hubbard and the Ugly Sisters with Home Guards' caps and tunics over their own dresses. Old Mother Hubbard still retained her feather-boa.

'Left, right, left, right,' Long John was shouting. 'Company halt! Left turn! 'Shun!'

They all did as they were bid except the Widow Twankey, who turned to her right.

'Sergeant Twankey!' howled John. 'Don't you know your left from your right yet?'

'No, lieutenant,' she said coyly. 'My old Mother always us'ter tell me never to let me right 'and know what me left one was doing, and me feet never seem to have learned either!'

'Silence!' Long John shouted. 'Squad, stand at EASE. Er—um—er—Ladies of the Bickerington Ladies' Home Guard, this is an auspicious occasion. To-day our ranks are to be reviewed by the celebrated Admiral Neddy Nelson. Here he comes now. Squad, 'SHUN! Present ARMS!'

Each of them held her long 'Lord Croft' Pike in front of her as Admiral Nelson stepped out of his Jeep and began to inspect them. He stopped in front of the Widow Twankey and peered through his monocle at her buttons. 'Haven't you any Brasso, my good woman?' he roared.

'No, I needs it all for me neck,' Twankey said coyly.

The Admiral was going to say something, but he thought better of it and passed on to Old Mother Hubbard. 'Ah, you've got a lot of medals, my good woman,' he said. 'I see you're an old campaigner. What's this one for?'

'That's the medal me little dog won in the Beauty Competition at Crufts in 1905,' she said proudly. 'And this is the one I won meself in a Beauty Competition in 1885. And this one—I won this for being the Champion Pie Thrower at the local ladies W.R.I. Garden Fête last year. I fairly walked off with all the prizes, I did!'

'Well, I hope you walk off with them in the Home Guard, too,' the Admiral said, passing on to Trixie. 'Well, Corporal Ugly, you look as if you had been in a lot of engagements!'

'Ooooo, is this a proposal?' Trixie cried roguishly. 'If it is, it'll be my seventh engagement. The first six was all wash-outs—they all went away to join the Foreign Legion or emigrated to the farthest backwoods of Canada or Australia. But *you* wouldn't do that, would you?'

'I mean military engagements,' Nelson said quickly. 'Wars. How many have you been through?'

'Do you mean me own private battles or public ones?' Trixie asked suspiciously.

'I mean public ones. I expect the others would take too long to recount.'

'Well, let me see. There's this war and there was the last war and there was the war before that, and there was the Egyptian War and the Crimean War—I was with Florrie Nightingale in that one,' she said proudly. 'I was the one wot held the red lamp.'

'You don't look as if you'd need a lamp with a nose like that,' the Admiral said, stepping backward.

'Oh, wot impudence!' Bunty cried. 'You slosh him one, Trixie! See if Lord Croft's Pike will really work!'

'I'm a lidy,' Trixie said stiffly, 'even if he ain't no gentle-man.'

'You're improperly dressed, Private Ugly,' the Admiral said to Bunty.

'Whatever's the matter?' she said, looking down at herself. 'Ooooo, I thought there was something wrong when I came out of the Wagon and Horses and a young man shouted to me "They're coming down! They're coming down! You'd better hurry up!" I thought he meant flying-bombs or para-chutists, and I ran like blazes.'

The Admiral turned to Long John and said: 'Mention of the Wagon and Horses reminds me. Shall we adjourn for a short spell to discuss the plan of attack?'

'We all will,' the Widow Twankey said, and she hooked her arm into his.

But the Admiral stiffened. 'No, on second thoughts I think we'd better get started,' he said. 'Let's look at the map. Reference 1235976. That's the Witch's Web where apparently the bird, Tilly, is imprisoned. I suggest, Lieutenant Silver, that we divide in two. You take one squad and go the High Road. I'll take the other squad and go the Low Road.'

'And we'll be in the Wagon and Horses before you!' Widow Twankey said roguishly as she followed Long John and Trixie.

Then the fun started. Poor Idle Jack in his efforts to escape from both search parties crept from bush to bush, for they were always nearer to capturing him than they were to cap-turing the Witch and Tilly. The Witch's broomstick had been nationalized, so she could no longer depend upon it for support and a quick escape. She dragged Tilly behind her from cover to cover in the grim wilderness that lay beyond Lovers' Lane, but in the end she was forced to give herself and the parrot up.

Then there was universal jubilation.

But this jubilation did not last for long. No jubilation ever does. Cinderella flatly refused to have anything more to do with Sinbad the Sailor because he appeared more interested in

Tilly the Toiler than in her. She had run into a pretty young sailor in all the excitement in Lovers' Lane, so she went off with him. The Ugly Sisters began to quarrel again about Idle Jack. Widow Twankey and Old Mother Hubbard resumed their squabble about Long John Silver. The pantomime fairies remembered that they were still directed. And the Navy sailed away to wherever Navies sail.

The only ones who were happy and who could have found any moral in the tale were Sinbad, who took Tilly away back to sea, and the Witch.

The Witch really had the best end of all. Witches usually do. She was shut up in a palace and had countless servants to wait upon her and guards to keep the furious populace away. She got a ration of fifty cigarettes a day and a quarter of a pound of gum drops instead of drugs. It was decided to put her on trial, but so many witnesses were needed for the prosecution, and as none of them have been demobilized yet and are hardly ever likely to be, it looks as if her trial will never come off. But in the meantime the newspapers keep writing about what will happen at the trial and about the different punishments that can be meted out to the Witch, and so the populace are satisfied. They believe that really and truly one of these days the Witch will be put on trial. And so in the meantime they are all living happily on hope. Long may it sustain them!

Lightning Source UK Ltd.
Milton Keynes UK
UKOW04f1544111017
310802UK00001B/400/P